A GREATER MAGIC

"Don't," she whispered, trying halfheartedly to push him away. It was hard because desire was making her weak. Zayn had tried using his spells on her and it had not worked. They had both thought her immune to magical forms of ritual, sensual persuasion. Obviously that wasn't true.

Or maybe Jack wasn't using a regular spell. Maybe it was something that came from his being a death fey. That thought truly terrified her.

"I'm not a whore. Take your hands off me!" she gasped.

"Take my hands away? But why? Do you know what women say to my kind when we lay them beneath us?" he asked, his voice a soft stroke of her ear as he pulled her lower body tight against his. Heat flared where they touched and his magic washed over her, rolling up her legs and then finding its way inside.

She gripped his wrists, lean but impossibly strong, and tried to pull them away.

"They say: 'Eat my heart. Drink my soul. Love me to death.' Isn't that what you have come to say to me? 'Eat me. Drink me. Love me, Jack'?"

Other books by Melanie Jackson:

THESE BOOTS WERE MADE FOR STRUTTING (Anthology)
A CURIOUS AFFAIR
DIVINE NIGHT
WRIT ON WATER
DIVINE MADNESS
THE SAINT
THE MASTER
DIVINE FIRE
STILL LIFE
THE COURIER
OUTSIDERS
THE SELKIE
DOMINION
BELLE
AMARANTHA
NIGHT VISITOR
MANON
IONA

TRAVELER

MELANIE JACKSON

LOVE SPELL NEW YORK CITY

For Brian—
Every time I pause at a new boundary,
he smiles and says, "Push it."

LOVE SPELL®

July 2008

Published by

Dorchester Publishing Co., Inc.
200 Madison Avenue
New York, NY 10016

ISBN 10: 0-505-52533-X
ISBN 13: 978-0-505-52533-8

Printed in the United States of America.

10 9 8 7 6 5 4 3 2 1

Visit us on the web at www.dorchesterpub.com.

TRAVELER

Chapter One

Io knew something had gone horribly wrong when Xanthe called her into the inner sanctum at seven o'clock at night on the second day of her vacation.

"Io, H.U.G. took you in when no one else would have you," the woman said without preamble, looking down at her. "Now you have a chance to thank Humans Under Ground for its generosity and do the world an immeasurable service at the same time. Please sit down."

Io took a seat across from her and fixed her odd blue eyes on Xanthe, her H.U.G. mentor. Those eyes were all blue; the pupils of a dark ripe blueberry, the irises an azure that nearly glowed until the whites were also bathed in slight blue luminescence. Only those descended of certain lines of Welsh siren feys had all-blue eyes. An ancestress, not so many generations back, had been a pureblood of the Gwragedd Annwn. Outside of H.U.G., Io either wore full cosmetic contacts or wrap-around sunglasses to hide this sign of her obvious mixed heritage. It was the only physical characteristic that gave her away as being part fey.

"What do you want me to do?" she asked, expression and voice carefully blank in the face of Xanthe's sudden formality.

"I know that your training is incomplete, but we are sending you into old Motor City on a mission."

Io couldn't control her first blink of surprise.

"Motor City? Goblin Town?"

Xanthe nodded.

"We have reason to believe that the goblins are finally going after the magical generator. Obviously, we want to get the gem first."

"But—"

"I know! We are opposed to the use of magical tools of any kind." Xanthe smiled tightly. "But while we don't like them, we don't dismiss them as unimportant or impotent. If Motor City's police are too weak to keep order right now, then it behooves us to see that the generator is kept safe until they can again manage it."

"The police can't stop the goblins?"

"They are making an effort," Xanthe admitted. "They've sent in Jack Frost." Her voice was respectful as she said the name, but not happy.

She didn't need to say anything else. Free agent Jack Frost, born Jonathan Frost, had earned his name and reputation a decade ago when an artistic goblin named Jeerith had taken him prisoner and decided to do some flesh trapunto on him as a warm-up to the real torture of candle-wicking through the torso. Jeerith had gotten the cotton wicking jammed under the skin of Jack's chest and managed to stitch in the first of the runes that made up his name before he got careless: he'd leaned in a little too close and Jack had taken Jeerith's nose off with his teeth. Jack had then somehow managed to get free of the welded shackles that bound him to an iron chair, and killed the needle-wielding lutin by breaking his fat neck. Rumor in Goblin Town had it that Jack was descended of the Ankou death fey, but no one in H.U.G. seemed to know for certain if this was true or just more sensationalism. Xanthe, who might know the facts, had always been very tight-lipped about it.

Whatever the truth, it was decided then and there among the flesh-eating criminal elements of Motor City that you didn't really want Jack Frost nipping at your nose, or anything else. Everyone walked very lightly when around the mysterious Mister Frost.

He'd been banned from Goblin Town since, but Io doubted that would stop Frost from finding his way inside the city if he wanted to be there.

"But surely if Jack—"

Io's boss interrupted again.

"He's only one man, and he is going up against some big money and power. It isn't commonly known among the masses, but many of America's tycoons of industry have been replaced by modified lutins. As you have learned in your work, the process of controlling the independent blinking of goblin eyes has improved greatly in the last few years. Scent gland extraction is no longer a problem now that the perfume industry has devoted so much time and money to the cause, and almost any of a goblin's possible extra limbs can now be safely removed."

"Businessmen? Like *The Donald?*" Io asked after a moment. She fought the urge to rub her head, which was beginning to ache. She was an air element, and being underground always bothered her.

"Yes, we believe so. Other possibles are Jobs, Gates, Forbes, and Perrot. The goblins are branching out into other areas as well—sports, the arts, even religion. Who knows if they have infiltrated the FBI and CIA? If they haven't already, it's only a matter of time."

Sports were an obvious choice for infiltrations, because goblins had a bad habit of touching themselves in public, and in athletics such behavior was accepted. Likewise, being sneaky and spying on people was second nature. But religion? There hadn't been a goblin in power in the Church since the Bishop Mauger excommunicated William the Conqueror. And the arts? That was a place where beauty was highly prized. No goblin was very attractive.

Of course there were always exceptions outside

of movies and television where appearance didn't matter. Io thought about likely targets.

"Not Garrison Keillor?" she asked, appalled.

"No, but he's an obvious choice. And we fear they may have gotten Stephen King at the time of the accident. They've managed all this without having any special magical help—imagine what will happen to the human world if they get hold of true magical power and manage to tune the thing into Horroban's warped frequency."

Io shuddered. "The situation certainly sounds grim," she said. "Can't we do anything to alert people?"

"It is grim, and we need to see that human interests are protected. But you know how we are regarded: H.U.G. is a laughingstock—the lunatic fringe of conspiracy theorists." Xanthe's voice rose as she added sarcastically, "After all, who could be afraid of goblins? They're refugees. They aren't even citizens. They aren't allowed to vote; they've been moved into their goblin ghettos—really upscale refugee camps—and most people are convinced that they're happy to be there, a huddled mass that isn't yearning to breathe free because it mostly lives underground."

Xanthe paused and Io nodded in reluctant agreement. What the woman said was true. Humankind knew that goblins existed, but assumed that, since the U.S. had been generous enough to offer them shelter when they were exiled from Europe, they were and would remain grateful to and not plotting against those people who had offered them a temporary home.

Xanthe went on, "If we thought this would all stop at the borders of Motor City we wouldn't worry—but you and I both know that those boundaries won't hold Horroban forever. We have to find out who and where he is!"

This was the standard H.U.G. party line, but also fact. The unseen goblin warlord Horroban was ambitious, and Io knew firsthand about how greedy the monsters could be. Goblin greed and addiction had killed her mother.

"So you are sending me in to find the generator—the jewel?" she asked, seeking clarification.

"You and Zayn are to find Horroban. You are our only two operatives who can pass inside Motor City and not be overwhelmed by the magic. But don't worry, we aren't sending you in without some assistance." Xanthe pushed a button on her desk and a moment later her door opened to let in a small, wispy man carrying a glass dish. Io noticed his small lapel pin, which proclaimed him a priest. "This is Father Ferris. He has been working on a new toy down in the labs."

H.U.G. didn't believe in using magic in its war on goblins, but the group had embraced science and, to an extent, religion.

"This is a small sample of our new lab-grown flesh. We are going to give you a few 'birthmarks'—a heart, a star, and a crescent moon. These beauty marks all have tiny transmitters embedded in them. With these robotic ticks we can track you anywhere in the city." Xanthe looked up and added casually, "And should you find yourself in a situation where it would be advantageous, you may choose to share this flesh with some appropriate goblins. The tick will embed itself in their stomach wall and survive for forty-eight hours—if the target doesn't eat another goblin." She added matter-of-factly, "The ticks get confused when they have a choice of flesh and sometimes will pick the wrong host."

"Oh?" Io tried to sound more interested than appalled. This was beyond anything she'd heard a H.U.G. operative had ever been asked to do.

"There is also a pocketknife with two blades— one of silver and one of cold iron," Ferris explained. "If you don't cut too deeply you can remove the faux flesh without hurting yourself. The blood is minimal—each flesh attachment has just one small vein to keep it from withering."

He didn't add that most feys healed quickly and she should too.

"We've tested the flesh and it passes. No taste difference at all," Ferris assured her.

Io managed not to let her disgust show. Nor did she ask who had done the taste test.

"Of course the transmitter would not survive grinding by their giant teeth, but most goblins tend to gulp things whole, so we believe there is a good chance of this ploy working. You'll be given a hand-tracker so that you can follow anyone you 'tick.' "

Io nodded.

"We'll give you a special nose breather that fits inside the nostrils. It will filter out goblin musk, and also any chemicals in the air. There is talk that some of the Motor City nightclubs are putting hallucinogenic drugs in the ventilation systems."

"That's illegal!" Io exclaimed without thinking, then berated herself for sounding naive. She added hastily, "Is it some sort of LSD?"

"Nothing so mundane, I'm sure. But we don't really know *what* they are doing in these clubs. Maybe testing a date rape drug to find the right strength for use on humans."

Io was horrified. "But to what end? Most goblins don't like humans."

Ferris and Xanthe looked at each other and shrugged. They didn't know and didn't want to—understanding your enemy wasn't necessary if all you wanted to do was to kill them.

"We don't know," Xanthe repeated. "Nobody has died, or even got very sick, so we haven't been able to use our hospital personnel to retrieve blood samples."

"And the police?" Io asked without much hope.

"Nothing's been officially reported that's illegal enough to interest the police, and even those cops not on the goblin payroll aren't listening to our warnings about Horroban. The mayor has plugged their ears," Ferris answered. "Anyhow, it will be to your advantage to have a clear head when everyone else is incapacitated."

"Is that all?" Io asked, when Ferris fell silent. "I have some ticks and a breather?"

"No, of course that isn't all. There is also the fact that everyone entering Motor City is gifted with one magic talent. It's random and nearly always something silly and harmless so the tourists won't hurt themselves, but with your blood and background, it is possible that you and Zayn can parlay this gift into something more powerful."

Io nodded again, but she was growing warier by the minute. She would not be encouraged to use her latent magic in anything less than a crisis situation. Wasn't H.U.G. against magic?

"What else?"

Xanthe cleared her throat. "It would be ideal if you could form an alliance with Jack Frost—or at least an understanding," she added hastily. "He has been known—on occasion—to keep company with women of a certain physical type."

"Dark hair and glowing eyes?" Io suggested, trying not to feel used.

Xanthe hesitated.

"Yes." Ferris's answer was blunt. "Exactly. The rumor is that he likes those of the Gwragedd Annwn. He hasn't found a mate yet and will likely be very interested—if he's a death fey."

This explained why the arrogant and capable

Zayn wasn't going in alone. Zayn was a loner when he worked. Women were almost never sent into Motor City with him except as bait. Io's true role was potential lunch for Jack Frost, a distraction that would leave Zayn free to maneuver. After all, H.U.G. likely wanted the city jewel in their hands, not left with the people who had hired Jack Frost.

"You should begin by visiting The Madhouse. SEXXX is performing there tomorrow night and it is believed that the lead singer, Hille Bingels, answers directly to Horroban. Wear something leather—you want to make friends with the locals."

Io nodded. "All right."

"There is one last thing," Xanthe added, glancing once at Ferris. "Our chemists have been looking at Neveling Lutin's new perfume, L'air de Lutin. There is nothing wrong with the samples we've examined, if you discount the fact that they are made from goblin musk—"

"Hunc vulgus Gobelinum appelat," Ferris muttered.

Io blinked at the Latin and translated in her head. Lutin *was a common goblin name.* She supposed it was rather unsubtle of the goblins to name the scent by its main ingredient, even in French. Some Americans were bound to remember that *lutin* was the French word for goblin. But then it had been bold of the goblin perfumer Neveling to adopt the last name Lutin and pass himself off as a human being.

10

It had to be at Horroban's orders—he controlled everything in Goblin Town.

"Precisely, and it was very bold of them to call it so," Xanthe agreed hastily, which stopped Ferris from starting in a lecture. "But the base looks like the perfect carrier for some sort of biological agent. Our chemists tell me that all anyone would need to do is add a little something—perhaps powerful pheromones, perhaps something even more disturbing—before it was distributed, and give the vat a stir. Neveling's company plans on launching their campaign with a free mass mailing of the stuff. The launch date is two weeks from today. Some of the H.U.G. higher-ups are concerned."

"You want me to discover what the goblins are doing with this perfume, too? But how? Should I follow Neveling Lutin?" Io asked. She was beginning to feel overwhelmed by the size of her first real assignment.

"Tracking the perfumer isn't your main task. We already have people on the inside doing that. The boffins are probably overreacting anyway. Keeping the jewel from Horroban is the most important thing, and that is where I want you to concentrate. It shouldn't be difficult. Zayn can handle it," Xanthe assured her. "We are just being thorough in letting you know that these two events are likely not unconnected."

"Xanthe, don't forget that Horroban is a huge investor in Neveling's enterprise," Ferris added, apparently slightly more concerned than his boss.

She nodded and said to Io, "Yes, well, it may be that you and Zayn will discover something of use about this perfume while you are in Goblin Town. Just keep your eyes and ears open . . . and *get close to Frost.*" Xanthe added: "And trust Zayn. He'll keep you safe from the goblins while you find Horroban."

"Will he keep me safe from Frost? *Can* he?" Io asked, wondering if her mentor understood how much emotional danger she was in. Io came from a long line of women who not only had blue eyes, but who were very vulnerable to certain types of love. Especially in relation to creatures of magic.

"You are a pretty woman, Io, and the cause is just. God will forgive you for anything you do," Ferris answered in Xanthe's stead.

Xanthe winced at this assessment, but didn't contradict the priest.

Io nodded once more, not trusting herself to speak. She had said before that she wanted a chance to fight the goblins; she was being given one now, so she shouldn't kick at the role she had been assigned. Many women were used as bait. It was her responsibility to see that Jack didn't swallow her whole while Zayn did his job.

"Well, let's graft some flesh," Ferris said brightly, lifting a half-inch-long crescent moon out of the glass dish. "Where shall we start? Your left arm?"

Chapter Two

Jack had drawn an inside straight. His random gift this trip into Goblin Town was invisibility. In a regular person this would have meant a small parlor trick of being able to make diminutive objects like coins disappear. But in a person born with one foot in the world of the arcane, it meant a whole lot more. With a little extra will, Jack could disappear himself—not just deadening his presence by erasing people's sight of him, but muffling his scent and the sounds of his passage. Not even the goblins' infrasight would find him, because he could mask his body's heat. He was like Death moving through this evil city.

The magic felt wild, a heat on his skin, a fire in his blood that knocked on his heart and brain demanding to be let in so it could take over completely. Of course, he wouldn't let that happen, but it was pleasurable to be riding the wave of ancient power that swelled up from beneath the ground of Motor City. That made him feel almost giddy. It made him feel invincible.

The thought gave Jack one of his rare smiles. Of course, no one could see it. Especially not the confused goblin tail who had only just crawled out of his hole and started trailing Jack through the city's deserted streets when Jack vanished. He was a young goblin imp, not more than twenty years old. And chances were good he wouldn't survive to see his next birthday, let alone make it to the ripe old age of two hundred that the strongest goblins achieved. Someone was going to be very angry that Jack had managed to give him the slip, and angry goblins tended to be violent.

Jack turned about slowly. Goblin Town was just waking up. Because of the goblins' nocturnal natures, not a lot went on during the day. The place was kept up by some of the sorry humans who had become addicted to goblin fruit and stuck around so they could get a regular fix, but no activity of import happened aboveground until after the sun went down.

Of course, after dark was another matter. Goblin Town rocked when night fell. You could find a party of any perverse flavor without looking very hard.

So, what was it to be? Follow the bewildered imp back to his master and watch him get his skull caved in? Or did Jack go on to The Madhouse and catch Hille Bingel and SEXXX, and maybe pick up a little more stray magic from the drunken club-goers?

He opted for The Madhouse. He'd seen goblins get their skulls caved in before. He'd never heard the goblin diva sing.

And Hille was supposed to be making the beast with two backs with Horroban, who was purportedly Jack's main target on this mission. It made sense to stick close to Horroban's lover.

" *'Behold, as goblins dark as mien and portly tyrants dyed with crime,'* " he murmured, and then laughed. Robert Louis Stevenson had understood it all. Only Jack wasn't going to be like the wretched man in that poem. And he liked not being seen.

Zayn was descended from Gananagh, the Irish love faerie who ensnared women and kept them pining after him until they died from broken hearts. That blood had been drastically diluted over the centuries, but there was no denying that Zayn cleaned up nice when he was inclined to make the effort—which wasn't that often, and never for Io's benefit, once he'd figured out that she was determinedly immune to his particular charms.

Io and Zayn entered the city on foot just after sundown, the day after her meeting with Xanthe. The troll at the gate, assuming them to be human, collected their money with his prehensile toes and had them stick their hands in the shallow basin so they could receive their twelve-hour visitor spells.

Zayn drew an amazing voice that allowed him to

sing anything within the human range of hearing. It also allowed him to enchant weak-willed women—as if he needed any help there.

Io, her eyes temporarily hidden under masking contacts, drew a more useless spell. She was able to turn things blue. Admittedly, under less serious circumstances, she might have enjoyed this talent and had some fun with it. But in their present situation, she didn't see that this was a particularly useful ability—though she supposed that it would make a convenient explanation for her eyes, if she were questioned at the club.

Of course the spells might seem useless at first, but the good news was that she and Zayn would be able to keep them for however long they remained in Goblin Town. Because of their fey blood, the usual twelve-hour magical limit didn't apply. And all enchantment and spells were good because they could often be shaped or combined with other kinds of power. Io's mother had taught Io the art of spell recombinance when she was young.

As per Xanthe's suggestion, Io and Zayn were both wearing leather. Zayn's shirt was lower cut, but Io's heels were higher, her skirt short, and her corset more tightly laced. The fetish outfit also showed off her new birthmarks. She knew that she looked *hot* which made her feel pleased but also a bit queasy.

Though time was short, she was really hoping that they wouldn't meet up with Jack Frost right away. She needed a night to get accustomed to the idea that she was supposed to be a sexual lure for the probably fey mercenary. It was a flattering but ill deserved confidence of Xanthe's that Io could play this role without any practice.

The Madhouse, a structure that was badly bent, and designed to look like a prison ruin, certainly lived up to its name. It was a great place for those with a taste for architectural decay. Io was unfazed by the urban gothic look, but she didn't like the appearance of the iron bars that covered the building's tiny windows. They seemed entirely too functional.

Io had heard that the place went through fifty thousand a night in booze alone when Hille and SEXXX played. Probably as much money changed hands for the purchase of things less legal. She could easily believe that fortunes were traded there every Saturday night—the band wasn't even on stage yet and the crowd was already flying.

Lighting was uniformly lurid inside the gothic horror, and allowed everyone to look equally terrible; it was a great equalizer in this cross-species meat market. It was difficult to see where the auditorium actually ended because many of the walls were randomly decorated with mirrors, some warped, some fractured, others with strange writhing images embedded in them. Judging the actual size of the multitude gathered there was impossible, but it was overcrowded. Io was fairly certain that the owner didn't worry too much about what the fire marshal would have to say. Why would the marshal get any more respect than the police?

Talking to Zayn was out of the question, even had he been inclined to speak with her. They had agreed before entering the club to split up once inside. He was going to collect gossip from the ladies, and Io spells. There was a good chance that people so inebriated, would not be able to hold on to borrowed magic, and she might be able to acquire something more useful than her solo blue-crayon act.

Her contact lenses were gone, along with Zayn's. His fractal green eyes needed to be visible for him to work his charm. It wouldn't be a problem. His peculiarities were subtle and wouldn't be noticed in the strobing light.

The contacts had served their purpose in deceiving the toll-taker at the city gate, but now Io was supposed to be seen and known for being something otherworldly. She was supposed to attract Jack Frost's attention. Yet she felt very naked, being in public without her habitual disguise. Her eyes could attract more than Jack Frost, and she didn't really trust Zayn to keep her safe if it interfered with the goals of his mission.

Time to go.

Taking a deep breath, Io used her borrowed magic to make her eyes ever brighter. She knew she had reached the right level when people began to turn their heads and stare at her. The odd goblin hand even snaked out to touch her exposed arms and give her the small, sharp pinches that passed for compliments among their kind.

The crowd was multicolored, multispecied, and either ecstatic or terrified to lunacy about what was to come. Excitement ran through the room. But it wasn't natural. Nerves were being stimulated with drugs, some taken voluntarily, but many probably not. It was entirely possible that something was being pumped in through the ornamental iron grates that covered the air-conditioning outlets. Madness was drifting merrily through the hazy air, and it wasn't man-made.

In an odd way, and though she hated addicts, Io found the notion of drugs reassuring. It would have been far worse to have walked into a room humming simply with magic—big magic, not the little bits and pieces left lying about by drunken revelers. That kind of raw power was dangerous in crowds. It could cause riots and other explosions.

Io pressed between the partyers who were gearing up for their two-and-a-half-hour orgy. There were aging rockers—rail thin and almost as pasty as goblins from years of recreational drug use. There were giant-maned teenagers, too young to be there legally, but looking fresh in their muscle tees. And everywhere there was leather: braided, pierced, wrapped. Cokeheads, potheads, and poor souls addicted to worse things, they'd all come to party down in Goblin Town.

Io absorbed pieces of spells as she passed: a spell

for lighting candles, for making showers of rose petals, for being able to smell like peanut butter.

She was halfway to the raised arena, with her eye on Zayn who was rubbing up against a tall goblin female, when SEXXX finally took the stage.

Lights began to flash at a frantic number of pulses per second, and Io's optic nerves and eardrums started to vibrate under the assault of new light and sound. For a moment she felt a jolt of vertigo and realized that a wave of something unnatural had passed through the room, carried on the sound that crested through the dancing masses. If it were a drug, then it was something cooked up by a magical being. Io was profoundly grateful for the hidden nose filters and her own natural resistance to perverted forms of magic.

SEXXX wasn't into auditory discretion. They were loud, offensive in speech, and in Io's opinion, strong contenders for an award for the Worst Din Ever Created Outside of a Battlefield. Hille's voice seemed one long atonal shriek that was able to drown out the electrical guitars being plucked by long goblin teeth, fingers, and toes.

But there was a beat: the bass and drums, something primal. They pounded like a runner's heart, and as the song progressed and listeners were drawn deeper into the veins of the music, that staccato beat became a frantic tremble of a heart filled with terror, perhaps the failing organ of some titan running for his life. It plucked at the brain and tried to suck the listener in. People began to succumb, their eyes glazing over as they went into a sort of seizurelike trance.

Io stopped moving, unable to get any closer to the stage and the giant speakers that hurled dangerous sound her way. Whatever was moving through the room was coming directly from Hille and it was strong, probably too strong for Io even with her resistance to spells.

She looked hard at Hille Bingel, wondering for the first time who and what this creature really was.

Hille was tall for a goblin, very nearly human height. Her skin was pallid green, her hair and eyes goblin black. But she was something more than just goblin—perhaps reptilian fey, and maybe swamp witch. She had power, lots of it.

Io stared at the diva's chest, half amused and half appalled. Hille wore a sort of crisscross harness that left two of her four breasts bare and the others only minimally covered. She supposed that it wasn't an actual violation of the old decency code since the exposed breasts had no nipples, and that was all that was required to be covered. Yet even without nipples, the look still managed to be obscene, especially when Hille wiggled and caressed herself.

Io smiled slightly. She hadn't expected to be amused by anything she saw or heard that night, but oddly enough, she was. She was glad for many reasons to be descended from the Welsh feys, and the lack of multiple breasts was one of them. Supernumerary nonfunctional breasts were not appealing to her aesthetically, not to mention the cost of buying lingerie in multiple sets and having clothes custommade.

Hille's breasts also raised another interesting question: How many arms did Horroban have? Everyone at H.U.G had been assuming that he would have been modified to look human. But perhaps not. Maybe he still had four functional limbs.

Io began to back away from the stage and the increasingly violent gyrations of the frenzied SEXXX fans. She had only taken a few steps when she ran into something in the crowd. It wasn't anything that she could see, or smell, or hear, but she felt him. *Him!* Jack Frost. And he *was* fey, his dark magic sparked over her skin in a way immediately recognizable and alarming. It was natural magic—the kind to which she was vulnerable.

"Jack?" she called, goose bumps spilling down her arms, but he had already pulled away.

Io turned and began to follow the magic trail, pushing for the outside door, when her arms were taken in a firm two-handed grip. She spun about to look into the face of one of the club bouncers.

She didn't know the troll's name, and couldn't very well ask it with the noise whirling around them in a deafening tornado, but she managed a smile and to raise a questioning brow.

He jerked his head toward a mirrored wall, and Io saw a small door standing open with another zoot-suited bouncer with a gray fedora waiting just inside. His double-breasted coat was open and revealed double holsters. Apparently, impossibly, both sets of arms were right-handed.

Uneasy, Io nodded and allowed the troll to lead her toward the mirrored door and the tunnel beyond. Though she was not happy to be separated from Zayn, it was a relief when the door finally swung closed behind her and the sound from the stage was mostly blocked.

The passageway led downhill and there were no windows for a hundred feet. Finally there was a series of doors to break up the stony monotony, but Io and the trolls didn't stop at any of them until the tunnel reached its end.

There Troll One rapped on the thick wood panel, and hearing a rasping grunt, pushed open the door. When Io hesitated, she was gently propelled into what appeared to be the manager's office.

The room was done in early western bordello with lots of red velvet and gold gilding. There was a desk, a vast thing of gleaming mahogany, and on it was a highly polished candelabra with all twelve of its candles blazing. Someone's taste ran to the ostentatious.

The sienna leather chair behind the desk turned about slowly and a goblin Io recognized from H.U.G.'s photo gallery of rogues was sitting there, black eyes gleaming with suspicion. His name was Glashtin. He was a weather goblin and had a reputation for going berserk during storms and making them worse, but was counted as relatively sane and safe the rest of the time.

Io tried to take comfort in that fact as she embraced her first speaking part and strove for an Oscar-level performance.

"You've been a bad little girl," Glashtin said in a gruff voice, as one of his four arms pointed. "Sit down in that chair and explain yourself."

Io thought for a moment about resisting, but realized that it would be an extremely foolish thing to do. Trolls were stupid and rather slow, but very strong. Besides, it would be out of character for her assigned role to balk at seeing the manager of the club.

Io took the appointed seat making sure that a maximum of thigh showed as she allowed her leather skirt to creep up her legs.

"I don't know what you mean," she said in her breathiest voice and made herself pout. "I haven't been bad . . . yet."

Glashtin leaned back in his chair and folded one set of arms around his barreled paunch. The other set trimmed and lit a cigar, which he puffed at methodically until the end glowed red. His eyes were the coldest things Io had ever seen. He might be shaped like a bowling ball, but Io wasn't even remotely tempted to laugh.

"You know the rules: no magic for feys when they come into the city. You lied to the gatekeeper.

Someone might have to punish you." Glashtin continued to smoke as his black eyes crawled over her. Smoke dribbled out of his nostrils for a long time, suggesting that his lung capacity was enormous. Even with her nose breather, the smoke and fire made Io a little ill. "I might even do it myself. I've got a little time right now."

This was probably sexual banter, but with goblins, you just never knew.

"I'm not fey," Io answered, trying not to shudder under the goblin's scrutiny.

The two trolls snorted, and in a fit of pique she considered telling them that they looked stupid wearing hats when their noses stuck out farther than the brims.

"She's not fey!" Troll One said in the rough tongue, laughing through his long nose.

"Not fey," Two echoed.

Io pretended not to understand, preferring they go on thinking her a typical monolingual American teen with a taste for kink.

"No? Then how do you explain them bright blue peepers?"

"My eyes?" Io asked, and forced herself to giggle. "That's my magic. I can make anything blue."

Glashtin blinked, his right eyelid slightly leading his left.

"Your magic? You mean your visitor spell."

"Yes. I can make things turn blue."

"Yeah . . . well then." He thought for a moment.

25

Making threats against innocent guests wasn't good for business if word got around. Still, he clearly had doubts about her, and Io couldn't blame him—especially not if he were involved in Horroban's skulduggery. The goblin warlord was not reputed to be forgiving of those who erred in judgment. "I might believe you, little girl, if you show me that what you say is true."

"Okay," Io agreed. "What shall I turn? I think it has to be skin. I tried to make my drink blue, but it didn't work."

"Really?" Glashtin asked slowly. "Toc, come here. Let the lady turn something of yours blue."

Io felt something move up to her side, and she turned in her chair. Troll One, crouched beside her, must be Toc. His nose, a giant spade of a thing nearly a foot long, practically touched her cheek. He was grinning at her with yellowed, pointy teeth.

She was very glad that she couldn't smell anything because she bet his breath could kill a buzzard at ten paces.

Io reached out with an extended finger and tapped the nose less than gently, wondering even as she did it if she had lost her mind. Trolls were known to be sensitive about the size of their noses.

Obligingly, the giant nose went blue from tip to brow bone, a lovely shade of ultramarine that nearly matched her eyes.

Glashtin grunted, and the other troll sucked in his

foul breath and muttered something beneath it before he began to chuckle.

Toc pulled back and hurried over to the funhouse mirror mounted on the red-flocked wallpaper on the left wall.

"It's beautiful," he breathed, admiring himself.

"Can I have one too?" the other troll asked eagerly, changing his mind about the fashion when his friend decided he liked the color. Two added for good measure, "And some blue ears?"

"Sure," Io said, standing up. She moved slowly so that Glashtin would have time if he wanted to object to having his bouncers turned into clowns.

The goblin watched her, but he did nothing to interfere as she touched the other troll's nose and then each ear. She was careful to make them a little less vivid than Toc's. A human's magic would begin to wane with so much rapid use.

Immediately, both trolls were busy looking at themselves in the mirror, shoving one another out of the way and bickering about which one had the handsomer nose.

"Can you make my teeth blue?" Toc asked, baring rows of his jagged fangs.

"No. Sorry," Io said hurriedly. "It only works on skin."

"Too bad."

Seeing the trolls entertained, Io felt safe turning her back on them and facing Glashtin. She thought about chiding him for being a bad host and failing to offer her a drink, then decided not to push her luck.

A more comprehensive glance at the room's other wall showed her something alarming. There were a series of photos matted and mounted in baroque frames, all of them showing Glashtin with famous businessmen. Io made note of the faces. If these men were not modified goblins, then they were certainly goblin sympathizers. Unfortunately, there were no photos that might be Horroban.

Unless he had been altered recently and replaced one of these humans.

"So, little not-fey girl, why are you in Goblin Town?" The question was neutral, but Io suspected that the goblin was still suspicious of her. She had to admit that she had never heard of anyone receiving this sort of magical gift when entering the city. Still, that was the thing about supernatural power: it didn't always make sense or obey rules of expectation.

"I'm here to see Hille Bingels," Io said promptly, seating herself on the goblin's desk. It made her feel a little ill, but she forced herself to be flirtatious and crossed her legs to expose a lot of skin. "I was hoping to get her autograph."

"Yeah?" Glashtin's eyes seemed glued to the crescent moon on her inner thigh. "You got your souvenir book in your panties?"

"No." Io giggled again. "I thought maybe she would like to sign *me*."

"I see." Glashtin leaned back in his chair and began to relax. She gave him high marks for not touching when he clearly wanted to. Goblins rarely had that kind of discipline. "She might like to at that. But I think maybe I should warn you that Hille has—uh—other tastes. Sweet little girls sometimes get bitten when Hille starts to play."

"I'm counting on it," Io said, completely truthfully. She touched her thigh deliberately. "I've been saving myself for her."

Glashtin grunted again and he finally smiled, showing just a hint of pale green incisors. He was prepared to believe that she had caught some teen psychological leprosy that led to moral rot. That was how most young people ended up in Goblin Town.

"Then I think the two of you should meet. The band is taking a short break. Toc! Go fetch Miss Bingels. Tell her she has a special fan here to see her."

Toc reluctantly came away from the mirror. "You want I should go now?"

"Yes. Bring her here," Glashtin repeated patiently. "And Lyme, too, if he wants to come. He usually loves this sort of thing."

So, she would have an audience for her meeting with the SEXXX diva. Io's pulse leapt, running through her veins at a gallop as though seeking an escape from what awaited her. This wasn't something she wanted to do, but it was expected of her since she had the opportunity. Tracking Hille was a great way to find out where Horroban was staying.

Her instinctual repulsion would have to be subdued for a time.

If it could be.

Io swallowed and pasted on her best smile.

"Woohoo! Let's party."

Chapter Three

Io felt like an exhibit at a petting zoo, surrounded by hungry, carnivorous patrons. She knew what Hille and the others saw when they looked at her. She looked young and appealing in a healthy way, but weak, as if she never did anything more strenuous than pull on tight clothing. In a word, she was prey.

And the goblin diva had seen her unusual birthmark and was obviously intrigued by it.

"Is it real?" Hille breathed, reaching out with a thick nail, running it gently over the exposed skin of Io's thigh.

Glashtin obligingly moved the candelabra closer, and Io tried not to shudder at the inspection.

"Oh yes. It's real." Io forced herself to meet Hille's black insectlike eyes. It took an act of will to make herself speak the next words, but she managed to add, "Would you like to taste?"

Greed flared red in the diva's eyes. The others also sucked in their breaths. The trolls seemed especially excited by this idea, and Io wished that Glashtin would send them out of the room. Trolls didn't just eat a little flesh, they crunched bones. And they had notoriously poor self-control.

"What do you mean?" Hille asked cautiously, a dark tongue snaking over her wide mouth. There was definitely reptile somewhere in her family tree.

There were laws on the books that the police were still willing to enforce in Goblin Town, only a very few, but they were firm about goblins taking flesh from unwilling victims. Or even willing ones who were drunk, drugged, or underage. Io knew that she looked to be all three.

"I could . . ." Io reached inside her boot and pulled out her tiny knife and a white handkerchief. Black linen would have made more sense, but she knew that the goblin would like seeing her blood on the pristine cloth.

Everyone in the room leaned a little closer as Io braced her booted foot against the desk and pulled back her skirt. She unfolded the knife in a perverse form of striptease, and laid the small silver blade against her skin. She said a brief prayer that Ferris was not lying about the amount of pain and blood that would be involved with removing the ticked birthmark. Too much blood in the air could be a very bad thing. For her. Trolls sometimes frenzied.

She cut quickly, keeping the blade's penetration

shallow. As promised, there was only a small sting as she cut the graft's thin blood supply. She quickly laid her hankie over the wound, hiding its unnaturally small size from her audience, and then extended the bit of brown flesh toward the diva. The dark crescent dangled from her knife's silver tip as a small bead of blood rolled down its blade.

"Take it. It's for you." Io's voice was husky.

The room filled with heavy breathing as the creatures began to pant.

With a small moan, Hille snatched at the tidbit and popped it in her mouth. Her black eyes rolled back in her head, reminding Io of a shark as it attacked.

As Ferris had predicted, the diva didn't chew, but rather sucked on the skin for a moment and then swallowed it whole.

Apparently the priest was also correct that it tasted right, because the diva made another humming noise that could only be a sign of pleasure.

Io looked away and tried not to think about what she had just done. The only positive thing that she could say was that the act had failed completely to arouse her, so there was no danger of her actually falling for Hille's intense sexual vibes. Apparently her vulnerability to sexual magic was purely heterosexual in orientation.

After Hille had returned to herself and stopped moaning, Io opened the desk's center drawer and plucked out a pen. Glashtin made an abortive move to stop her as she reached inside, but paused when he saw that all she wanted was a writing implement.

"Could I have your autograph, please?" Io asked, doing her best to sound about twelve.

The still-dreamy-eyed diva took the pen in her lower right hand and scrawled a signature across Io's leg, considerately avoiding the bloodied hankie.

"Thank you," Io said brightly.

"No. Thank you," the diva replied. Her tongue flicked out and then she swallowed twice. "I have to go now but maybe later—"

"You have plans," Glashtin reminded her. His voice was also thick and he seemed unable to pull his eyes away from Io's thigh.

Carefully, Io lowered her leg and pulled down her skirt as far as it would go.

"Yes, I do," the diva admitted reluctantly. She looked at Io hungrily, making Io feel ill. "But you'll come to the club again, won't you, pretty?"

"Oh yes!" Io answered. She would probably have to. With her luck the diva would stop for a snack and mess up the tick before she led them to Hor-roban.

A shaken Io returned to the auditorium long enough to give Zayn a signal that a tick was in place, and then she fought her way through the crowd to the door that led outside. She was praying that she wouldn't be sick.

She made it into the street and leaned up against

the rough wall, gulping down lungfuls of the hazy air. After a time her roiling stomach settled and she was able to straighten.

She sensed Jack only the moment before he took her arm and drew her away onto the sidewalk. He didn't speak and neither did she in case anyone was watching. They walked along briskly, she appearing to be alone but with one arm held out awkwardly. It wouldn't fool anyone near enough to hear her breathing. Her invisible pulse thrummed beneath Jack's hand and her respiration was ragged.

They continued in this odd fashion down the nearly deserted block until Jack found an unlit alcove of an abandoned store, and then he drew her inside the brick shelter.

As soon as they were away from prying eyes, he dropped his magic, allowing her to see him.

They stood chest to chest in the small space, staring into each other's eyes. Io was tall, but Jack was still taller. Many death feys were.

Jack's Ankou ancestor had also left visible reminders of his presence in his descendant's face. The eyes were gray, a flat impenetrable shade of pewter that gave lie to the notion that eyes were windows into the soul. His skin was slightly darker than that of most feys, so he could pass for human unless you got close enough to touch.

His features were harsh but still beautiful, even under the green lights.

Io willed her heart to stop its betraying pounding,

but it was not feeling obedient. It had already been asked to suppress too much emotion for one night— disgust, terror, rage. It could not, or would not, again deny what it was feeling.

"You came into the city with the oh-so-arrogant Zayn," Jack murmured. His voice was a rough caress. "Does that mean that you are also with Humans Under Ground? Were you perhaps sent to distract me from finding the jewel? It is the sort of tricky thing Xanthe would do."

Io didn't answer and tried to blank her mind in case he was somehow reading her thoughts. She knew that she should force herself to relax against Jack, to flirt and charm, but she couldn't do it. Something about him was frightening, more frightening than Hille Bingel had been, and his voice disturbed her at a visceral level. She had to remain on guard.

Or maybe she had just played the flirt too many times that night and her mind was rebelling at doing it again. She decided that she liked that explanation better. It was less frightening.

"You aren't going to deny it?" he asked, running a finger down her cheek. Magic leaped from his flesh to hers, making her catch her breath. Something inside of her clenched tight and she felt a wave of heat wash over her face and chest. Her impulse was to touch him back, but she clenched hands against the urge, squeezing so tight the muscles ached. He was manipulating her. The impulse wasn't likely to be her own.

"I can't reasonably deny that Zayn is arrogant," she whispered, twisting her face away from his touch as shivers of desire marched up and down her nape. "We all know it's true. Why lie?"

Jack laughed softly, and Io realized that he was feeling a little high, riding the euphoria of the influx of new magic. No wonder she hadn't been able to gather up much in the way of stray spells in the club. Obviously Jack had been there before her, picking magical pockets and socking the power away.

"So you don't deny being Xanthe's sacrificial offering. How conveniently refreshing."

Jack set hands to her waist and pulled her close. He wasn't rough, but there was no way that she could fight him in such close quarters even if she weren't feeling suddenly weak, and able to count pulses in her abdomen where his groin pressed against her.

"But are you intended for me, or for Hille? Or both? She seems to have written her name on you, but I still think that you are here mainly for me. What's your name, little lure?"

"Don't," she whispered, trying half-heartedly to push him away. It was hard because desire was making her weak. Zayn had tried using his spells on her and it had not worked. They had both thought her immune to such magical forms of ritual, sensual persuasion. Obviously that wasn't true.

Or maybe Jack wasn't using a regular spell. Maybe

it was something that came from his being a death fey. That thought truly terrified her.

"I'm not a whore. Take your hands off of me!" she gasped.

"Take my hands away? But why? Do you know what women say to my kind when we lay them beneath us?" he asked, his voice a soft stroke of her ear as he pulled her lower body tight against his. Heat flared where they touched and his magic washed over her, rolling up her legs and then finding its way inside.

She gripped his wrists, lean but impossibly strong, and tried to pull them away.

"They say, 'Eat my heart. Drink my soul. Love me to death.' Isn't that what you have come to say to me? 'Eat me? Drink me? Love me, Jack?' "

"No! I'd never say that." She denied both his words and the ritualistic syntax, which called more seductive magic to his aid. She knew all about crafting spells. She had to stop him, had to escape before he wove the net of desire tight about her.

"But you want to. We both know that you do."

Her body answered. She only had two breasts, but they were both functional and the nipples were hard and pushing against her leather corset. Her breath broke in frustration. She wanted, and she hated wanting, and thought she probably hated Jack Frost too.

"No? Are you certain that you are not one of those poor creatures who is afraid of the responsibility of owning a body, of keeping a soul? Wouldn't you feel better giving it away to a caretaker?" he asked, his tone seductive and at complete odds with his words. "Give it to me. I'll take you, if you ask. I'll do it now. You needn't ever feel confused and unloved again."

Io froze for an instant. *He couldn't know! He couldn't!*

"No!" And this time she said it with more force. Anger was moving through her, momentary lust turning into rage at this insult to her spirit and mind. She shoved his magic back at him with all her will. "How dare you touch me? Get your magic off of my body!"

Jack sucked in his breath and his eyes widened as her power punched through him, driven by fear and rage.

"I smell your anger," he said.

His body was hard as he leaned into her. His magic was back, harsher than before, racing through her, making her hot, making her weak, making her *want*. Before he had been teasing; now he was serious. If he asked for heart or body she would probably give it. He could break her. He could kill her.

"Will I taste rage in your mouth, on your tongue, in your tears?" Jack asked.

"The only thing you'll taste is blood—and it will be your own," Io spat at him, even as another nearly climactic shiver seized the muscles in her belly and groin.

39

She could have wept with embarrassment at her body's betrayal, but refused to let any tears cloud her eyes, lest he take it as invitation to dine. Stealing someone's tears gave the thief immense control of the victim's dreams. She could *not* allow him to wander at will through her subconscious.

"Maybe. And maybe I'll enjoy the blood too," he said, and then he took her with a poisoned kiss that seared her lips and enflamed the rest of her body.

Io had no choice but to ride the forced desire he poured into her all the way to climax, but even as her knees buckled and her back arched in surrender to his greater magic, she reached out with her own inner power, punching into him again and leaving him with a souvenir of his assault.

Surprisingly, Jack wasn't a total bastard. He could have dropped her onto the filthy ground, but instead he held her up with his hard arms until she was able to regain her footing, and even then he was gentle as he smoothed her ruched skirt back into place. He was careful not to touch the small wound on her leg.

"You're a nice girl, Annwn. But too tasty for Goblin Town. Hille's had a piece of you, and she'll want more." Jack stepped back, his face serious. "Leave, and don't come back, no matter what Xanthe says about duty and jewels. After all, now Hille isn't the only one who has had a taste, and I might decide that I really do want you."

Io stared at him, trembling with fury and maybe

something else. She knew her eyes were still blazing with unnatural fire because it cast a blue pall over Jack's harsh features.

"I can read your face, little fey. Consider carefully what might happen if you made love to a death fey. Gives new meaning to la petite mort, doesn't it?"

And with that, Jack drew his invisibility back over himself and disappeared into the night.

"You rotten son of an Ankou," Io whispered after him.

She slumped against the wall as tremors took her. Jack had no idea how badly he had frightened her. At least she sincerely hoped not.

Jack returned to his room in the house on Winder Street in Little Paris and stripped off his shirt. He was in no hurry to wash off the smell of the pretty Gwragedd Annwn, but the goblin sweat that he had picked up in the club was beginning to itch. He needed a shower.

He cranked on the rusty taps in the Goblin Town hovel and then set about removing his leather pants. The costume had been wasted since he had remained invisible much of the night, but leather was a better barrier at keeping bodily fluids off of the skin, and the Annwn had seemed fond of fetish clothing.

What an angry thing she was! Maybe the high of so much magic had led him to a minor miscalculation. Perhaps it had been overkill to warn her off the way he had—not that he hadn't enjoyed parts of discouraging her. The trouble was that after something like that, it was often hard for a woman to just forgive and forget. Especially if the girl had been truly frightened, which he had finally noticed that she seemed to be. The fear was bound to make it all very personal.

Too bad he couldn't send her flowers, but apologizing was out of the question. For her own good, she had to remain well and truly frightened of him.

Jack slipped off his shoes and unlaced the grommeted fly of his pants, and then he stopped, stunned at the sight that met his eyes. His angry little fey had turned his balls bright blue!

He began laughing. He'd felt her magic entering his body and wondered at the time what it would do. Now Jack wondered, as he stepped into the shower, how long it would last.

Chapter Four

That night, outside of Goblin Town in her very own tree house, Io dreamed of Jack. It didn't take a psychologist to understand what was going on. Her vision of lying naked under Jack was just his leftover magic slinking through her body on little velvet paws while it toyed with her brain.

But as much as she would have liked to dismiss the dream as a one-time aberration, there was no denying the effect his presence had on her; and her uncontrolled reaction made her both angry and fearful. Even in thought, his hands, mouth, and body seduced her. He'd whispered softly to her in dreams, and her body remembered the heat he'd drawn when they were pressed together. The passion the memory summoned was all at once too familiar for comfort, and altogether too rare to be dismissed.

"Say it," he had urged her, lapping at the center-line between her breasts and stopping as he reached her heart. "Eat my heart, drink my soul, love me to death, Jack."

But her dream self answered as she had done earlier.

"No."

Whatever her words, the dreaming Io had been unable to keep her fear and longing for Jack's touch from leaking out of her eyes in long silver streams, and the pewter-eyed death fey had seen and happily dined on her tears.

She woke up crying, something she hadn't done since her mother died ten years before.

"I am not my mother! I cannot be seduced by magic!"

Infuriated at her lack of control, Io hurled her damp pillow at the closet door and dropped her head onto her drawn-up knees where she blotted her eyes with a rumpled sheet. Then, quickly, she checked the sheet for color. No damp silver streaks marred the linen. There were no patches of red tears. She was only crying tears—not magic, not blood. It was just a dream. Jack hadn't really been there.

"Damn it," Io sighed. She didn't want to revisit this old fear that she was her mother's daughter, that if she strayed away from relations with human men who were the natural prey of sirens, that she could herself become prey to some other magical being.

Well, life could be harder. So her mother hadn't loved her and she didn't know her human father—

at least Io wasn't some goblin's bastard. And the world was full of orphans who didn't know their parents! Some of them were even fey, though that was rare. Anyhow, the human and feys—they all got on just fine. Not every sin was visited on the children. Io wasn't the first child neglected because her drug-addicted mother wouldn't allow anything to intrude on the illusion that her supplier actually loved her. Io had already cried for those things—cried and cried until they were tears of blood instead of salt. It hadn't solved anything then. It wouldn't solve anything now.

Her mother was dead and buried, her sins and weakness buried with her. Io could choose any destiny she wanted. *I have free will. I have a choice,* Io assured herself fiercely, even though a part of her disbelieved this vow.

The wind outside whistled a tuneless threnody, announcing that autumn had truly arrived. Io braced her foot against the wall and gave a tiny shove, setting her bed to rocking. She huddled under the covers and let the swaying of the hammock soothe her. When she felt more collected and able to balance her thoughts with reason, she opened her eyes and looked out the multipaned window set afire with diamondlike brilliance by the rising sun.

Her night in Goblin Town had convinced Io of two things. The first was that she should probably avoid Jack Frost forevermore. It was hard to admit, since she had made it to adulthood unscathed by any weakness of the heart, but she wasn't immune to such folly after all—and Jack had somehow managed to get his mental bristles in her brain even without drinking her tears. The tiny barbs had sunk deep in Io's psyche, giving him a limited power over her. Distance was probably the only thing that could diminish his hold.

Unfortunately, Io had a feeling that Fate and Xanthe had arranged for her path to cross and recross the death fey's trail.

The second thing she had come away with was an unsupportable conviction that whatever drugs they were experimenting with at The Madhouse were of a truly dangerous kind. She had seen what addiction to goblin fruit did, and the goblins knew what it did too. It was one of their favorite tools for manipulating people.

Fortunately, the goblins of Goblin Town couldn't grow enough of the fruit to support a whole city of addicts—but Io wouldn't put it past Glashtin to contaminate everyone who entered his nightclub with something just as nasty to ensure a steady business for his wares.

He had to be stopped! He *had* to be.

Xanthe wouldn't like the suggestion, because it meant treading on sensitive toes in both business and law enforcement, but the best place to look for stores of magical drug concoctions was with Goblin Town's only commercial chemist: Neveling Lutin—an exception among goblins, a magical creature not afraid of high-tech. If someone in Motor City were making poison aerosols, it would be Neveling Lutin. The possibility had to be investigated, and if such a poison were found, it had to be neutralized.

Feeling tired but resolved, Io rolled out of her hammock and, not bothering with its cloth ladder, dropped lightly to the floor. She padded to the shower on swift feet, feeling the cold of the wood flooring even through the needlepoint rug. Clearly it was time to start wearing nightgowns and socks to bed. It got wintry early up in her tree house.

As expected, Xanthe was not convinced that a change of plan was in order, even after hearing Io's report of the strange trance of the crowds at The Madhouse. Zayn had felt something too, but apparently he wasn't concerned by it, so Xanthe was choosing not to make waves and possibly endanger her mole in Lutin's factory.

Io could understand her boss's decision, but she didn't agree with it: something that was happening more and more frequently. Io was grateful to the woman for offering her important work after her mother's murder, but she didn't care for the assumption on Xanthe's part of a controlling interest in Io's life stock. Xanthe wasn't chairman of the board in Io's life. Nor had she the right to ask Io to suspend thinking. They hadn't made any such bargains when Io came to H.U.G.

"We want you to go back in tonight and make contact with Jack again."

Io's heart rolled over, but she didn't allow herself to panic. "That is not wise. I told you what happened."

"He took you by surprise at your first meeting. It won't happen now that you know to be on guard," her mentor insisted. "Io, you must do this. We need to know what Jack Frost is up to. I don't trust him. He's a loose cannon and could ruin everything!"

Io looked at Xanthe's determined face and suddenly wondered if this were something personal. Jack had certainly seemed to know Xanthe well enough to guess at her actions. The possibility of the two of them having a relationship, either past or present, raised a lot of uncomfortable questions about conflicts of interest on Xanthe's part, questions about the woman's motivation.

Io wanted some answers, but chose not to press for them at that moment. Xanthe wasn't ready to admit to any rivalry, and arguing about Neveling was futile when she was in this mood. Io rose without further dispute.

"You'll go back tonight?" Xanthe asked sharply. Worry pulled at the woman's eyes and stitched itself between her brows.

"Yes. I'll go back." Io buttoned up her sweater. She was going above ground to do some shopping for appropriate clothing, and it was cold outside. "Was Zayn able to track Hille?"

"Yes. The tick worked like a charm." Xanthe answered with satisfaction, smoothing down her blond hair. "She went into the old art museum and then down into the Labyrinth. Zayn wasn't able to follow there, but the tick showed Hille heading toward the lake where Horroban's villa is thought to be. We need to find it as quickly as possible."

"Why?" Io asked. She got a swift worried look for her question.

"Because that is also where they have been doing a lot of excavation, of course." Xanthe's answer was slow in coming, as though she had to dredge it from some uninhabited part of her brain. "It seems likely that this is where they expect the jewel to be found."

Io nodded once. She knew that she should be concerned about Horroban finding the jewel that powered the magic of Goblin Town, but somehow it didn't seem worth the effort. None of the magical cities' jewels had ever been found—even by the wizard's guild that had been searching in New Orleans for over three hundred years. Io was convinced that Horroban was being clever and using a quest for the jewel as a red herring to distract his enemies while he got on with whatever piece of villainy he'd really been dreaming up in his twisted green mind.

Moreover, now that she had cleared out the distracting emotions from the night before, Io was thinking that Jack Frost had probably guessed this too. He'd been at the club last night; he had to have felt whatever was riding the air. *He* wouldn't be wasting his time looking for the Motor City's impossible-to-find magic generator.

Chapter Five

The hour before dawn found Io back in Goblin Town, leaning against the flying buttress that propped up the north side of the old Trinity Lutheran Church tower. The granite and limestone building was wonderfully deserted, and inspirationally tall, which suited her purposes, so in that respect it was an ideal place to be.

In terms of comfort, it left a lot to be desired. Io turned her head out of the wind. From up there on the slate tiles and tasteless sixteenth-century gothic-style tower, the city had a certain Victorian dignity. Even ruined Brush Park still had a stateliness about it.

But it was cold! Abnormally, bitterly cold. Nor did it relieve Io's chill to look at the unhappy figures who waited with her: martyrs, confessors, saints, and judges, all frozen in stone. She was especially careful not to stare at the crucified Jesus who asked

51

plaintively: *Is it nothing to you, all ye who pass by?*

Instead she alternately looked at her target and at the old Fox Theater, whose exterior was lit up like the Las Vegas strip. It was gaudy but beautiful. She had heard that they still showed movies there. Perhaps one night . . .

A sharp wind came around the side of the buttress and buffeted her, slapping at her face with damp hands.

"Damn it."

She was hoping that her luck held and that it didn't rain. Spying on Neveling Lutin's perfume factory was difficult enough without adding obscuring weather. Rain would also make the stone parapets slippery, something she didn't need.

Io shivered. She had skipped wearing leather clothes and opted for dark jeans and a black pullover sweater. The garb was practical and flexible for what she had in mind, but not nearly enough protection from the wind, which had a bad habit of sending sudden gusts to creep down her nape with ruffling fingers.

Io wished, not for the first time, that she could smoke. A burning cigarette would keep her hands warm and help her kill off the hours before she could go inside. But that wasn't something feys did, fire in nearly all forms being anathema to her kind. Only certain fire elementals and death feys—

Io slammed the door on that thought.

She flexed her freezing fingers inside her new

leather gloves and looked about for the hundredth time, assessing her chances of making the leap to factory ledge and the French doors beyond. The narrow outcropping was flanked on either side by a pair of stupid but friendly looking stone gargoyles, which were bolted into the sidewall. There were also power lines running everywhere in lethal nets. Most were dead, but a few connected to the factory were still humming with power, their electrical hissing charging the dampening atmosphere with static. The smoking remains of a dead squirrel hung between two lines, testimony to their power. Io would have to avoid those or she'd end up crispier than that fried critter.

The image was not a felicitous one, and Io closed her eyes and began controlled breathing to counteract the nausea. She tried not to think about either Jack or Xanthe, who were both probably wondering what she was up to.

Io opened her eyes when she felt the night sky shift over to morning. The Fox Theater went dark. Next to it, the last of the dim green lights in Neveling's factory finally shut down and the street below quieted, though the strange light that lurked beneath the manhole covers didn't fade for a few minutes more. The goblins were going underground and the few humans left in town would be heading for their beds.

It was time to go . . . if she was going to do it.

"Yes, time to go," she whispered to herself.

Io caught the edge of the parapet while she found her balance and then began her run down the narrow abutment toward the nearby factory. Her soft-soled climbing shoes ran out of slate after a half dozen steps and Io launched her body into the air, arms reaching before her as she fell toward Lutin's building.

Startled pigeons flapped off in alarm as she hurtled at them out of the dimness, but Io didn't look at them or the street beneath her. Her eyes were fixed on the ledge-sized balcony sandwiched between Lutin's twin iconic monsters. She might be part fey and therefore have an edge over her human neighbors when it came to healing, but if she fell from this height, she was as dead as anyone would be.

Impact with the factory was hard enough to knock the air from her lungs, but she stayed on the ledge. Her fingers were wrapped around a gargoyle's stony face, her feet safely in the middle of the unrailed balcony as she gasped for suddenly missing breath and fought the urge to look down.

"Thank you, goddess," she wheezed, grateful that goblins didn't use railings on their skyscrapers. She would not have been able to make the jump if the usually spiked fence they often favored on shorter buildings was in place.

She barely had her breathing under control when she heard the latch on the French doors turn. Startled, she twisted about. Flight was impossible. Her muscles tightened in preparation to fight whoever stepped over the threshold.

"Calm down, little fey," Jack said quietly. "And get inside before you fall off that ledge. You aren't a gargoyle, you know."

Cursing inwardly, Io loosed her hold on the stone monster and stepped through into a darkened conference room. She kept a good arm's length between her body and Jack's, but even with that space she could feel the hum of his magic. It danced wildly on her skin.

She didn't want to notice, but it was impossible to escape the fact that while moonlight loved him, so did the dawn. His skin drank in the new gold light. His silvered eyes refracted the fresh radiance and returned it to the sky. He didn't look human, but he was beautiful.

"I had a feeling that we'd be seeing each other again," Jack said, closing the doors behind her. He sounded more amused than disapproving.

"Unfortunately, so did I," Io muttered truthfully. "Could you turn down the juju wattage a bit? I feel like I have ants crawling all over me."

Jack stared at her as though puzzled by her request, but obligingly throttled back on his power.

"Your stunt just now really has me wondering about you. You aren't Xanthe's usual style of female operative. Considering her standard tunnel vision, I had the feeling that she and Zayn were worried exclusively about Horroban's scavenger hunt out at the lake." The words were casual, but Jack's eyes were measuring.

"They *are* worried about it," Io answered without thinking. For some reason, it didn't occur to her to lie. "This is just some extracurricular snooping I am doing on my own. The jewel really isn't important. Not to me."

Jack looked into her eyes as though weighing her sincerity. Io let him look his fill. She had her contacts in and felt protected.

"I've checked all the offices. All that's left aboveground is the lab," he informed her at last. "Let's go see what they are brewing up in the bathtubs. My bet is that it ain't gin."

Io shook her head. "I wouldn't take that bet because I think you're right."

"Lady feys first?"

"No thanks. Lead on."

"As you like." He moved toward the hallway and out into it.

"So, what spell did you draw tonight?" he inquired conversationally, taking her off guard.

"I can make things smell like apples," Io answered in disgust.

Jack chuckled. The sound was low and made Io shiver.

"For a magical being, you have rotten luck. . . . By the way, I knew the moment you left the city last night," he added, as he led the way down a white-tiled corridor that shone painfully with the rising sun's probing rays.

"You did?"

"Yes." He turned and grinned at her. "I lost my blue balls. It was such a relief. Good trick though."

Io felt herself color. She cursed her fair skin that raised notice of her embarrassment like red banners in a pale sky.

"Serves you right for being a pig."

"I quite agree. I'll try not to let my porcine tendencies overwhelm me again."

"That isn't a very good apology," Io commented.

"It isn't one at all, just a statement of intent. So, take a guess at what spell *I* drew tonight," he urged her, grinning.

"I haven't a clue." She was attracted to, but didn't trust, his new playfulness.

Jack stopped outside a brown wood door with a half window of frosted glass and took a lock pick from his pocket.

"Not a magic key, obviously," she added.

"Nope. Something even better," he answered, turning the knob and swinging the old door open. The hinges creaked and made Io wince.

"So . . . what?"

"A truth spell. You have to answer truthfully anything I ask you." Jack stepped inside. "Won't that be fun?"

Io thought about her already unguarded responses and groaned. She should have guessed that something like that was in the air.

"Fun for whom?" she grumbled.

"Hey, it's all about me, babe."

"*Hmph!* I don't have to tell you the truth, you know," she warned. "I can just tell you to go to Hell."

"Yeah—but only if you mean it."

"Well damn. I don't actually believe in Hell."

Jack's voice was amused. "Works for me. I can't wait to start the interrogation."

But in spite of Jack's teasing, he was very businesslike while they searched the room, and he confined himself to impersonal questions and remarks related to their explorations.

The lab was an eerie place, even with dawn light spilling through the louvered blinds. Lab coats, stained with green oil, were suspended like headless corpses in a neat line by the door.

There were a number of plastic tubes hanging down from the ceiling, looking a bit like some giant jellyfish tentacles. Io made herself touch one. The shutoff valve was cranked tight, even though the tube was obviously empty and showed no sign of use.

On the back wall were a number of plastic containers that looked like cooking oil but were labeled 110 % DISTILLED NEUTRAL GRAPE SPIRITS. Outwardly, the place appeared to be a perfume factory, not a biological warfare lab. This only made Io more nervous.

She gave wide berth to a device Jack was tinkering with. It looked for all the world like a giant espresso machine, except it had way too much tubing snaking into the wall. Io was okay with most tech, but some devices made her uneasy and this was one of them.

"You don't like this thing?" Jack asked, noticing her reaction.

"No."

He waited for her to explain, but she couldn't. Some machines would work for her; others wouldn't.

Uncertain of where to start her search for clues, Io concentrated on looking through the shelves and drawers for perfume samples to steal.

She found a number of empty toothpaste tubes, which she tried not to consider. She had never wondered about what goblins brushed their teeth with, and wasn't about to start. It couldn't be anything nice; that was for sure.

Io found some jars of *Nuit Crème* with the trademark gargoyle on the lid.

"Do you think this stuff is supposed to make goblins uglier?" She uncapped the lid. The green cream was luminescent, the shade of bread mold.

"Ugliness, like beauty," Jack answered, "is in the eye of the beholder. Of course, they also say that while beauty is only skin deep, ugly is to the bone— so I wouldn't put any on, if I were you. Just in case. You wouldn't want an ugly femur."

He abandoned his empty machine and helped

her ransack desk drawers. They found a number of little green vials, some filled, some not, but there was no sign of standard-sized perfume flacons.

Io commented on it. "Could there be another lab underground? Or a storeroom you missed?"

"Possibly. I had to be a little discreet while ghosting around during working hours. It could also be that supplies just haven't arrived yet. They certainly seem set up for bottling here."

"Yes, they do."

"Well, this haul will do as a starter. It's time to leave. Whose lab shall it be? Yours or mine?" Jack asked, holding a vial up to the window. It didn't have a skull and crossbones on it, but that didn't mean anything. Goblins didn't believe in truth in labeling any more than they believed in public safety or the sanctity of life.

"It had better be yours. Though she told me to be alert to them, Xanthe doesn't believe the importance of the drugs in the ventilation system, and she isn't real interested in Neveling's perfume endeavors." Io bit her lip and cursed inwardly for forgetting about the truth spell. She couldn't lie to Jack, but that didn't mean that she *had* to answer him and spill her guts. Silence was an option she needed to use.

"Suits me. But you hold on to this for now," Jack said, handing her his vial and then pulling open the file cabinet. "There is one last thing I want to do. Keep an eye out, especially on the street, on the manhole covers. We've been in here too long. Some goblin is going to come by eventually."

Io turned toward the window and cracked open the louvers. "No guards yet. All I see are a pair of addicts."

"Watch them. We don't want them deciding to break into the building and setting off the alarm. What kind are they?"

"The worst. They've sold everything but their souls for 'the bitterness without name,' " Io murmured, looking out the window at the pathetic scene unfolding below. Two addicts were kneeling in the street, scooping up bits of dry goblin-fruit pulp left from the previous night's street faire and stuffing it in their mouths with filthy hands. When the larger pieces were gone, they leaned down and licked the pavement. Io added to herself, "Except it has a name and we all know it: goblin fruit. Why haven't the police outlawed it?"

Jack answered. "The police don't make the laws. The politicians do. And you know why *they* don't outlaw it," he said impatiently.

"Money."

"Yes."

"It's so wrong though," Io whispered. "Look at them. This should never happen."

"They are truly imp-ridden," Jack agreed, glancing outside. Then, turning back to the file cabinet he added, "Stay back from the glass. You don't want to be seen."

The bigger addict—a girl with matted hair as

white as moonlight and a face that was skeletally thin—ran out of crushed fruit leavings. Seeing the smears on the other girl's dress, she fell on her. Mewling, she squeezed the smaller addict's juice-stained garment. She seemed to be trying to wring fluid from the fabric and didn't care if she got a bit of the girl inside.

The smaller addict laughed in a drugged voice—until she felt her assailant's teeth on her belly. Then, howling, she shoved the other girl away. Rolling to her feet she stood panting for a moment, and then distracted by the juice stains on her hand, she stuck her fingers in her mouth and started suckling. Her eyes went blank.

The first girl huddled on the ground shaking, and then gave in to cries of despair as the other ran away. She didn't seem to notice that she was drooling as she cried.

Io made a small noise.

"What is it?" Jack asked, moving swiftly to the window.

"Jack," Io whispered, moved to compassion for the wretched creature below that was barely still human. "I know it's stupid, but couldn't you . . . ?"

"No. Don't even think it."

"Please. I . . . I can't stand her keening. I just can't," she said honestly. "And she'll attract attention if we don't shut her up."

Jack considered this point. "It's only temporary, and you know it," he said. "She's going to die soon if she doesn't get some goblin fruit. She'll probably die even if she does get it. She's too far gone."

"But we can help her now."

Jack looked at Io, his face unreadable. She felt naive for suggesting that they stop their own task to help an addict who would certainly turn them in for a piece of blood-fruit. But she truly could not bear looking at the poor, mad creature. There but for the grace of the goddess might have gone her mother.

"We can't *help* her," Jack said more kindly, speaking to Io as if she were a child. "The addiction is rarely reversible. And you know that there are other dangers in dealing with a weak mind."

Io knew this better than anyone, having grown up with it, but she couldn't let it go.

They could get caught out in the street. The girl could turn them in. And Jack was a death fey. If the girl was wretched enough, given the choice, she might decide to give herself over to permanent oblivion and die in his arms. Hadn't Io been tempted herself? And she wasn't a junkie in withdrawal. Could she do that to Jack—make him responsible for someone's death? It wasn't fair—wasn't right.

Yet none of that mattered very much in the face of such complete suffering.

"Please do what you can." For the first time, Io touched Jack voluntarily. She added obliquely, "If you have to . . . Well, it would be a kindness. And it wouldn't be your fault. It would be mine."

Jack exhaled and a small current passed from his skin to hers as he roused his magic. Io dropped her hand and stepped away before anything substantial could leak over onto her.

"We are done here anyway. There's nothing else to look at," she pointed out. "Either we have the goods, or we'll have to go into the Labyrinth to find them."

"*I'll* have to go into the Labyrinth," he corrected, watching her retreat from him. His expression was annoyed. Apparently he didn't like having his magic treated like a case of cooties. But that was just too bad for him! Io only had so much strength.

"Just remember that nothing comes for free," he warned her. "I work for wages, not charity. This girl is going to cost you."

Io answered sharply, trying to ignore the way her stomach rolled over at the implied sensual threat. "Don't be such a bastard. You know this is the right thing to do."

Probably he was just teasing her. They were sort of partners now, weren't they? He couldn't wish to harm her.

Of course, it was a little early in the relationship to be guessing about what he might consider harmful.

"Nevertheless, there is a price. I doubt it'll be high enough, though, since I'm not the total bastard you think me. I knew that I was going to regret getting involved with you," he added, sotto voce, pulling on his invisibility and opening the door. Then, louder, "The coast is clear. You coming, softheart? May as well see what you'll be paying for."

"I'm coming."

Io slipped out of the lab and closed the door behind her. The sample vials of perfume and cream she had taken clinked softly in her pockets as she walked. She had removed one of everything they'd found. Not being able to smell with her breather in place, short of rubbing each item on her skin she had no way of knowing which samples might contain the magic-charged elixir that had been aerosolized into the ventilation system of The Madhouse.

She stopped at the top of the staircase and peered after Jack. The stairwell was tight, twisted, and very dark.

"This has to violate fire code," she muttered, starting after him.

"Write your congressman." The floating voice was growing faint, so Io hurried after it.

Chapter Six

Jack knew a whole lot more about Io Cyphre than he had the day before, and it had changed his view of her. A few brief words with his contacts on the force and, mere hours after meeting her, he had received and read her entire file.

There wasn't much about the fey herself in the papers—she lived a very low-profile sort of life—but there was rather a lot in the archive on the girl's mother. Everything was very circumspect, since Tigre Cyphre had worked for the State Department, but the French police's attitude about her killing had been summed up by the penciled-in comment: *Ne sei s'esteit lutin ou non.*

We cannot say if he was a goblin . . .

Jack shook his head. Leave it to the French to deny all knowledge that Drakkar was a goblin.

But even with the official obfuscation, reading between the lines it was easy enough to see that Tigre

Cyphre had been in love with—or at least en-chanted by—the French goblin warlord. And she'd been willing to do anything to please him, including using her political contacts to further his business interests.

Unfortunately, European gangland wars had been especially messy that year because of turf battles over the fruit farms in Grasse, and there had been a lot of collateral damage when Drakkar's empire went down. Tigre Cyphre; the H.U.G. agent Zayn's twin brother, Syrin; and several other H.U.G. activists had been among the roadkill left by Harkel-Barend's thugs.

Harkel himself had died two weeks after taking out Drakkar. The files said it was an accident—a freak explosion caused by a faulty water-heater had boiled him in his bath—but the suggestion lurking between the lines of Io's file was that it was a retal-iation slaying, by either Drakkar's goblins or H.U.G..

The slaying was a nasty bit of work, Jack admitted, but not beyond H.U.G., who were growing increas-ingly more militant and creative in their fight against goblins. And the story explained Io's involvement in an organization not usually tolerant of magical be-ings because of their official stance on the super-natural.

The circumstances surrounding her mother's life and death also explained Io's revulsion for drugs and her fear of Jack's magic: It had probably been some combination of deadly goblin fruit and magical coercion that enslaved Tigre.

What remained unknown was whether Io herself had had any hand in the dirty business of offing Harkel. She had been in France at the time, arranging to have her mother's body transported back to the States, so it was possible.

Jack paused at the factory's side door and waited for Io to catch up.

Should he ask her about this? If she answered tonight, it would be the truth.

He was still wondering about how to phrase his question when Io arrived. He looked down into her concerned face, added to it her compassion for the unknown addict in the street, and decided he didn't need to upset the applecart by asking.

Io Cyphre was brave and resourceful—and reckless—but she didn't have a natural killer's instincts. It was perhaps regrettable, given their present circumstances, but it made her more likable as a person.

Also, fortunately, he had enough killer instinct for both of them.

They stepped outside, Jack being careful to go first in case there were any magic trip lines waiting to snare them. Even with the sun up it was cold. Soot blew along the deserted street, making everything at ground level appear shadowed and adding to the perceived chill of the autumn morning. The whorls of grime also had the disconcerting effect of making the imagination see things at the periphery of one's vision. Shade became something warped and sly. It could turn your own shadow into a sinister stalker, and sometimes nervous people ended up with gooseflesh of the brain. Jack had learned to ignore the optical weirdness of Goblin Town, but he could see that Io was bothered. He didn't say anything. The little fey seemed touchy about admitting to nerves.

At street level, Neveling's factory looked like an old-style movie theater. This was partly due to the idiot gargoyles etched in the glass of the front doors, and the marquees advertising cosmetics. The rest was the geometry of the architecture. It was as close to a grand public building as the goblins had yet built.

Jack looked quickly up and down the street. There were some parked cars—mostly Hondas and Toyotas. Goblins didn't buy American because they had trouble reaching the pedals of most models. There was talk among the young and ambitious goblins of reopening the old GM plant and producing custom autos. However, ambition didn't have them out that morning. Other than the dirty wind and the swaying junkie, nothing else moved.

"Time to go," Jack thought he heard Io whisper.

"Yeah."

He walked boldly toward the ravaged girl, who stopped wailing long enough to ask in a slurred voice, "Do you have any?"

"Yes, I have something for you," he answered,

69

kneeling down. He took her chin in a hard grip and looked into her mindless eyes. "Who called you to the feast, girl?"

"Odyr and Binns," she answered. Her mouth slackened even as she spoke the names of her seducers.

Standing in the cold gray shadow of the old church, Io felt rather like the morning after the night before. Only she hadn't had anything to drink, so the hangover dawn seemed unfair.

She watched Jack go to the addict and take the demented creature's chin in his hand. Immediately the girl stilled, her face drooping.

Curious, Io ventured closer. She stopped before actually touching either Jack or his patient. She didn't need to get any closer; she could feel them both, even over the magic pulsing along just below the pavement. Jack gave off an aroma of earth and enchantment that somehow managed to evade her nose filter. It upset her breathing and hurried her pulse. Her attempt to steady her heart was for naught.

She stiffened at the names of Odyr and Binns. They were known to H.U.G. as pushers of goblin fruit. Neither was on the most-wanted list since they didn't recruit outside of Goblin Town, but they weren't on anyone's step-on-the-brakes-if-they-got-in-front-of-your-car list either.

Jack murmured something to the junkie Io

70

couldn't hear, and the last little bit of consciousness slipped away from her. He eased the girl's body onto the ground and she lay there like dropped laundry.

"Is she . . . ?"

"No." Jack stood. "But she will be before sundown. At least she isn't in pain."

Anger licked at Io. "We should just burn this whole place down. It would be a public service. We could have a giant weenie roast. We could toast marshmallows in Neveling Lutin's building. That alone would be a cause for celebration."

Jack laughed at her. "A girl after my own heart—how my father would have loved you!" His face stilled as suddenly as it had animated. "But you know we can't do it. We'd only be killing people. Addicts are all that are left up here above ground. The real goblin infrastructure is below. Horroban has seen to that. We wouldn't do anything more than annoy him."

"Horroban! How I'd like to see this creature."

Jack shrugged. "Wouldn't we all. But here in Goblin Town, trouble travels in pairs and even packs. And our goblin warlord has the biggest and baddest pack of trouble around. No one has ever gotten close. We don't even know what he looks like."

And *that* was the problem. Goblins were flesh-and-blood creatures—but whose flesh and blood was always a question. The monsters swapped tissue and fluids and magic with several species—often on

71

a whim—changing their appearance more often than Paris changed hemlines.

Which made finding Horroban near impossible. Word from one of his rare surviving victims was that looking at the goblin warlord was like staring at a colorless mask with empty holes for eyes. Everything about him was bleached and ghostly—as if he suffered from a sort of goblin albinism. But that report had come last week. There'd been plenty of time for him to change faces, assuming that he even needed to. It was just as possible that he had clouded Jilly's mind before letting her go report back to H.U.G.— he was strong enough magically to do that.

"Horro . . ." Io muttered, and then stopped herself. She had already invoked the name twice. Three times would be an invitation. There was too much stray magic floating around to risk it. She wanted to know the goblin's identity, but not have him visit her in her bedroom some dark night while she was sleeping.

"We really do have a problem," Io said, looking down at the unconscious addict Jack had just helped. The girl lay toppled as if already lifeless.

"Do *we?*" Jack's emphasis was subtle.

"You know we do. And I don't think that H.U.G. will be any help in this situation. Xanthe is taking halfhearted swipes at this problem—and missing the target because she is more worried about you than what is really going on." Io looked up, digging for information. "Why *is* that, Jack? What is there

72

between you two that has her panties in a twist?"

"Professional rivalry?" he suggested, tactfully not commenting on Xanthe's underwear. Again, the words were playful but the expression was not.

"Try again please. It has to be something more than that."

Jack reached out and combed her hair back with gentle fingers. Because she was cold and a little frightened, Io let him make the comforting gesture.

"Jealous?" he asked.

"Please! Even *your* ego isn't that big."

Jack smiled briefly. "It's just the usual old story really. Boy meets girl. Boy gets girl . . ."

"Boy screws girl and then leaves?"

"Not without a strongly worded suggestion from her." He shrugged. "Let's just say that the girl got the magical night she always wanted, but then couldn't handle the *real* magic when it started to happen. She thought she could, but her training went too deep. She freaked."

"Your magic frightened her?" Io asked. She noted that if Jack was telling the truth, then Xanthe had known about Jack's powers and hadn't warned her about them. "What parts specifically?"

Jack smoothed her hair back again. "If you ever draw a strong-enough truth spell you'll find out. Or if you come to me and ask to see *those parts,* of course. But those are the only ways, little fey. I don't kiss and tell. Anyway, I doubt those things that terrified Xanthe would scare you much."

"Well, I don't think that kissing would be the problem," she muttered, forgetting about the spell and again saying what was on her mind.

"No?" Jack cocked an eyebrow. That was all that moved. He didn't shift position or draw in a breath, but suddenly his posture became explicit of intent. He went from sexless companion to prowling predator. Mind and body were both looking out of his eyes, and they wanted the same thing. "Let's just test this theory of yours."

"Payback already? But, Jack, I don't think—"

"Good. Don't think. *Feel.*"

Her magical instincts were begging her to flee Jack. Her primitive brain said the same. But her body didn't agree. Her libido awoke and started to struggle against common sense. She knew it had to be subdued and quickly, but the battle was an even one: long-held mental fear versus a lifetime of physical longing for this very thing.

Jack was smart, too, knocking her off-balance with a change in tactics. His kiss was gentle, not at all the assault he had made the night before. No rough magic coerced her. Instead Jack's kiss teased. It seduced. And in its own way, it was even more relentless about pulling a response from her.

She had expected him to feel cold like the rest of the world, but he wasn't. He was all heat, banked-down fires that warmed the soul, the heart, the body. Walls of resistance constructed with so much care began to crack. Io knew that if he pushed, her whole defensive structure would come tumbling down, leaving nothing but rubble about her tender emotions—which hadn't been out of their shell since the day her mother was seduced by a French goblin and stopped loving her daughter.

"I don't want to feel," she whispered against his lips. But even the gentle movements of speech caused further sparks between them.

"I know." Jack slowly lifted his head. His expression was more sober than languorous. "But if you stay with me, you will feel. Lots of things, many of them horrible. So think carefully, little fey, before you commit. I know you're out for revenge, and I know why. Can't blame you a bit for wanting it either. But you have forgotten that revenge is a thing of the heart and soul rather than the mind. It is the hate in the heart that gives us the strength to do what we must. Ideology alone isn't enough to carry the day. All dogma will do is blind you. Especially here. This is the magical world and you have to use gut-think. You have to *feel*."

His hands were soothing as he smoothed them down her arms. He cupped her cold hands with his larger, warmer ones. She appreciated the gesture of consolation, even as she hated his words.

"If you can't face your emotions, then now is the time for you to get out of the game." Jack's voice was dispassionate, giving no hint of his own feelings. "Go home and think about it for a bit. If you're still in, then meet me outside The Madhouse at midnight tonight."

"I'm in!" Io answered immediately.

Jack shook his head.

"*Think* about it, Io. *Feel* about it. Aren't you nervous? I sure as hell am. I don't trust it when things are going so smooth and sweet that you can spread it on toast and have it with tea. Experience says the pendulum is due to swing the other way and things are gonna get ugly. I don't want you getting killed because you flinched at the wrong moment, or walked into a situation with blinders on."

"I'm not a coward," she said hotly. *Not about facing goblins.* "And I'm not stupid."

"I never said you were." Jack dropped his hands and stepped back. Io once again felt cold and bereft. "By the way, if you come tonight, try to draw a better spell. Cheat a little—have a stir around in the bowl and look for something with a bit of kick. I don't think apple perfume is going to help you much if you get cornered by bad guys with big teeth. And speaking of things that smell bad, you'd better give me those samples."

Io reached into her pocket with trembling hands. She handed the vials of Neveling's perfume over quickly.

"Where can I find you?" She asked as he turned to leave. "If I need you."

"Just follow the magic, little fey. It knows where

to find me." Jack's voice floated back as he vanished into the black fog that was rolling up the street. "And I wouldn't tell Xanthe about our next little outing. Odds are good she won't like it."

Chapter Seven

Moonlight was beginning to trickle out of the sky and into the dirty streets of Goblin Town when Jack arrived at The Madhouse.

Io watched him come striding up the street, his black duster flowing open like a cape, and the spurs of his black boots jingling musically. Not that the sound called up the same merry thoughts as sleigh bells. It was more the sound of Death moving toward a shootout at a saloon.

And how the night loved him as he stalked along under it: his eyes, his hair, his very flesh!

He didn't smile when he saw her, but she was coming to know him and recognized that there was satisfaction in his gaze when he looked down at her.

"So, guess what spell I drew?" she greeted him.

Jack sniffed the air. "Something violent."

Io lowered her voice. "Yep. It started out as a stupid spell to open cans with my finger. But I've been working on it and now I can stuff my right fist through concrete. Or wood, or metal. It probably works pretty well on goblins, too, but I haven't tried it yet."

Jack finally smiled. His teeth were very white and strong. "I guess we're ready then."

"As ready as we can be."

And she *was* ready. An afternoon up in the solitude of the treehouse had helped her clarify her feelings and sort them out from facts. Fact one: Goblins were pushing their addictive fruit and killing people. So far, their victims had been willing, but that could change.

Fact two: Horroban was working on something new and nasty on the drug front, and in all likelihood Neveling Lutin was involved.

Another fact: H.U.G. wasn't going to be any help because bitterness over an old love affair had Xanthe looking the wrong way, and however much she wanted to, Io couldn't stop the goblins on her own.

Talk about a one-two punch.

Last fact: The police couldn't or wouldn't do anything this time about what was going on inside Goblin Town.

That left Io's feelings. Those were trickier bits to catalog and deal with. They were as basic as breathing and just as hard to resist. She wanted Jack—badly. But she also wanted emotional safety. Chances were she couldn't have both, not indefinitely. Maybe not at all.

Yet perhaps she could juggle her emotions long enough to stop Horroban. Surely she could say no to Jack and make it stick for the next two weeks. Lust was *not* that overwhelming. It just couldn't be.

"You're thinking again," Jack accused as they set off down the street, forcing a path through the throngs of tipsy tourists. The crowds were getting thicker now that the witching hour—and the traditional free drinks at midnight—were near. Fortunately, with Jack along, people tended to get out of the way.

"Someone's gotta do it," Io answered, matching her stride to his. She was glad she had worn boots with moderate heels. "So, do you have a plan?"

"The general outlines of one."

"Oh good. I'd hate to think we were just making this up as we went along."

"Not spontaneous, are we?"

"Not in situations where I can die."

Jack let his eyes travel up and down her once and then grinned. "That's a real shame, 'cause I can think of one situation—"

"Let's leave the thinking to me," Io interrupted. She was *not* going to flirt with Jack. "I'll be the brain and you be the brawn."

"But you have the fist of steel. Why should I play the troll?"

"Because you look more like one," she answered untruthfully. The wrench the words caused told her that Jack still had his truth spell even if he wasn't using it on her at the moment.

"How do you do it?" she demanded after a moment.

"What? Look like a troll? You know what they say about the correlation between the size of a man's nose and the size of his—"

"Jack!" Io kept her voice low. They were entering a less crowded part of town, but Io hadn't explored the business district before.

"What I meant was, how do you keep your spells? You still have your invisibility too. I can feel it."

"I didn't leave town," Jack answered. "I found a place to crash down at Brush Park."

"Oh. That makes sense." Io nodded, though she didn't care for the idea of sleeping in the ruins of Brush Park. She would never feel safe enough to sleep out there.

"I buy extra spells off of junkies who need money for a fix. Sometimes people drop spells . . . A little tweaking, a little power and—voilà—a customized spell."

Io didn't approve of giving money to the junkies, but she supposed it was more ethical than simply stealing their magic. It also kept them from mugging tourists for the cash to get their fixes.

"It might be a good idea if you did the same thing," Jack suggested, lowering his voice. "One of these days, Xanthe is going to figure out what you're really doing, and she is going to try to pull you out of the game."

Xanthe! Io swore.

"What?" Jack looked down at her, his brows drawing together. "And where did you learn gutter troll?"

"We need to find a safe place," Io told him. "Somewhere that I can undress out of the public eye."

Jack raised a brow but didn't make any suggestive comments. He really was trying.

"I'm 'ticked,' " Io said. "I can get the ones on my arms and legs, but I have a feeling that Ferris may have slipped one onto my back. He isn't usually a *pat-them-on-the-back* sort of guy, but he glad-handed me a few times the day he grafted on these birthmarks."

Jack considered for a moment. "We'll go to my place. I have some equipment."

"We don't need much. I have a knife."

"Yeah, but we don't want to kill the ticks. They may be useful to us later. We'll put them in some gelatin with a little blood and then hide them somewhere innocuous."

Io nodded. He wouldn't want them at his crash pad. The place was probably warded, but Xanthe could possibly find him anyway, and clearly he didn't want to be found.

Io, on the other hand, still felt that she might like to have someone on the outside know where she was. Eventually, just not right now. Another Gordian knot. Damn! She felt as if she was in constant bondage.

Jack's room was in a dilapidated building of brick where junkies had stayed during the daylight hours. As their addictions grew, so did their sensitivity to sunlight. This building would have been ideal because it had very few unshuttered windows. However, the junkies were all gone now. Jack had scared them away.

He opened the wards on his door, and then using a bit of fire magic he set the kerosene lamp alight. As Io had suspected, fire didn't bother him.

The room was empty except for a duffle bag that sat on top of an old claw-footed table. There was a hammock in the corner, suspended from two sturdy bolts that had made new wounds in the walls. Most earth feys preferred to sleep grounded, but given the filth accumulated on the water-damaged floor, Io couldn't blame Jack for choosing to sleep up off of it.

"Okay, let's see these ticks."

"I can manage the arm and leg," Io said, realizing that she was going to have to undress in order to get the trackers off of her. She was wearing another leather outfit that passed for goblin couture, and this one was skintight. "It's just my back that's the problem."

"It's not a problem. Your knife or mine?"

"Mine. It has a silver blade. It also has one of cold

iron, so be careful. You don't want burned fingers."

"And you don't need a burn on your back."

"Not if I can avoid it." She pulled her small pocketknife from her boot and handed it to him. "It's the top blade."

"I feel it."

Io took a deep breath and then turned away from Jack. She undid the corset belt and quickly pulled her sweater up over her head. She didn't wear a bra, so there was no need to do more.

"Look for moles or any raised skin. It might not be dark. Ferris is sneaky." Her voice was a little shaky. She hoped Jack thought it was fear and not arousal that made it tremble.

Jack got something out of his duffle bag and then stepped over to her. He ran a slow hand over her bare flesh. He wasn't using his magic, but his hands were still hot, and they disturbed her pulse and breathing. Io bit her tongue so she wouldn't tell him to hurry. Or to slow down and take his time.

"Got it. Looks like I spoke too soon. Grit your teeth, little fey. This will hurt."

"Keep it shallow and it won't hurt a lot. It should be connected by a single vein."

"Sorry. Not this time. Your Ferris stuck it on good. It has grafted itself smooth and sent down roots. This sucker is grafted on as tight as your own skin—maybe tighter."

Io said another bad troll word.

"You want to go on with it?" Jack asked.

"Just do it. I'll heal."

"Okay."

Jack was fast and kept the cut shallow, but Io couldn't help flinching as the tick was pulled loose. Pure silver was better than any other metal for surgical use on magical beings, but they all hurt. Of course, that was the point of the silver and iron blades—she was supposed to hurt goblins if she got in a jam.

As she felt the blood roll down her back, she made a note to bring a bone knife next time she came to town. She wanted something she could use on herself that wouldn't hurt like metal.

Jack pressed his hand over her shoulder blade and muttered something. There was a flash of intense heat as he used his fire spell on her.

"Ow!" Her knees almost buckled as the flame shot through her.

Jack quickly steadied her, bracing her against his body with his free hand.

"Sorry, but it needed to be cauterized. It was that or stitches." He sounded genuinely regretful at causing her pain, but Io didn't turn around and seek visual confirmation of his feeling.

"So much for no burns on my back," she groused.

There was a sound of paper tearing and then Jack wiped her lower spine with some sort of alcohol swab. The cold, or something, raised gooseflesh on her back and arms.

"You need some help getting that sweater back on?" he asked casually.

"No." It hurt to lift her arm, but she managed to pull the turtleneck back on. Only then did she turn around.

Quickly, she pushed up her sleeve and held out her hand.

"Give me the knife."

Jack hesitated a moment and then handed her the blade. A few drops of blood had run down the handle.

Io ignored them as best she could, but her hands were still shaking and the blade was slippery.

"Let me," Jack began, but she made the cut fast.

Jack handed her the stained disposable wipe and took the blade from her. He quickly added the small brown tick from her arm to the larger flesh-colored blob in his lab dish. He also shook off the few drops of blood onto the ticks.

"Where's the last one?" he asked.

"Outer right thigh," Io answered, grateful for his matter-of-fact tone. She was also grateful that she'd worn panties under her leather pants—she wouldn't have bothered wearing them with jeans.

Taking another deep breath, she tugged down the double zippers past her hip bones and shoved her pants down to just below the tick. Her hands were a lot steadier this time, so Jack didn't offer again to do the cut.

Io worked quickly, and after a fast swipe with the

now very stained wipe, she hurriedly rezipped her clothing into place.

"You're sure that's all of them?"

Io did a quick mental search of her body. She was finding it easier to use her magic now. It was like riding a bike. The parts of her that were fey could never really forget what it was.

"Yes, that's all of them." She refastened her corset.

"All set then?" Jack asked, taking the wipe and dropping it into the dish with the ticks. "That should keep them happy for a while."

"Good—blood-sucking leeches."

"No, blood-sucking ticks." He fitted a lid onto the dish and wrapped it in a bandanna before slipping the thing into his coat pocket. He then reached into his duffle and pulled out a roll of duct tape.

"Where are we going to take them?" Io asked, watching him add the tape to his coat pocket.

"Back into the nightclub district. I think we'll leave them in a public restroom taped under a tank while we tour the hive. Goblins almost never clean the bathrooms, so the ticks would be safe enough there until we need them again."

"Sounds good."

"I think we may also stop for some dinner."

Io grimaced. "You'd eat here?"

"We have to kill some time while the crowds thin," Jack reminded her. "And I know some places that are reasonably safe. No nasty bloodroot vegetables or truly questionable meat."

"If you say so," Io replied, knowing she sounded dubious.

"You know, I'm glad we had this moment together," Jack said, his voice again turning light and teasing.

"I really can't say the same," she answered, moving her shoulders gingerly.

"No? But just think what we've learned about each other."

"Such as?"

"I know that you don't faint at the sight of blood."

"You don't either—at least not at the sight of mine. That's always useful," Io agreed.

"Very. I also know that you like black lace panties—and that you'll ask for help if you need it." He grinned his cold smile. "I like it when girls ask me for things."

Io refrained from comment on his last point. Sexual recidivism was not to be encouraged, even it was only verbal.

"And what have I learned?" she asked.

"You now know that while I may stick a knife in your back, I probably won't stick it very far."

Io laughed. "This little fact is supposed to comfort me?"

Jack opened his door and looked out into the hall. Even when he was reasonably sure that they were alone, he was still cautious. "Hey, you gotta take your comforts any way you can," he answered, resetting the wards with a wave of his hand.

"Well, that's the truth," Io muttered.

Chapter Eight

"Looking forward to trying out your spell?" Jack asked as he seated Io in the booth at the back of the diner where they could not be seen from the windows. The place was a little dingy and frayed around the edges, but mostly clean. And it didn't reek of goblin.

"I guess so. There are spells I would have liked more."

"Such as?"

"Precognition would have been good. Or one of those truth spells."

"I could give it to you," Jack volunteered, deliberately trying to surprise her. He wanted to put her at ease. She had been very careful not to touch him since they left his crash pad, even though he had been vigilant about not using any magic on her. "It would be a loaner, of course. Just for the night."

"You could lend it, but why would you?" she asked suspiciously.

"Well, it doesn't matter which of us has it," he answered virtuously. "We're partners, aren't we? And I don't need it with you. You have very speaking eyes. That's almost as good as a very speaking mouth."

"Uh-huh." Io's expressive eyes narrowed in a gratifying manner as she scanned Jack from loose hair to folded arms. She took a guess. "Also, it doesn't matter what I ask you because you picked up a truth-resistance spell as well."

Jack smiled. "You're good, little fey. Just keep looking with your gut as well as those superior eyes and we'll be fine."

"So, where are we looking with our guts and eyes tonight?"

"We are heading out toward Neveling Lutin's end of the hive."

"Hive?" She cocked her head.

"I think of the Labyrinth that way. Have you ever been down there?"

"No."

"It isn't like up top—there's no paving or street signs to guide you. They aren't real big on clean angles in their architecture either. It takes some getting used to. We'll go slow tonight, just a reconnaissance pass to get you oriented. And perhaps a small bit of looting and sabotage if the situation presents itself."

"Knowing you, it probably will."

"Probably," he agreed. "But we need to be a little cautious. No need to tip our hand. And as you probably know, Neveling is rumored to have two pet gargoyles about the house."

"Of course he does. For cachet. After all, they're rare in the States outside of zoos. And that's because it's *illegal* to import them."

"Uh-huh," Jack agreed blandly.

She glared at him. "And just because they eat everything—alive and screaming—and have put several of the native birds and mammals on the endangered species list, not to mention how they annoy the neighbors by gobbling up small pets and children, that is no reason to obey the importation laws or even common sense."

"Exactly." Jack handed her a laminated menu, amused by her indignation. He found her lingering loyalty to law and order to be endearing. It also made him wonder how she functioned in a rogue organization like H.U.G. He added as the devil's advocate, "It's likely that Neveling would say in his defense that laws and common sense around here are very different things than on the outside. Goblin Town is a world unto itself."

"I'm sure he *would* say that. And he'd mean every word of it, too. Hell! What could immigration have been thinking letting so many goblins into the U.S.?" Io looked at Jack over the top of the diner's limited dessert selections.

91

He shrugged. "They didn't ask my opinion. At least we haven't given them the vote. Yet."

Io snorted. "As if that has ever stopped them from getting what they want. And while we are talking about imponderables, I wish someone could explain to me how it is that when magical entropy happened all over the world, goblins and gargoyles weren't wiped out too."

Io sounded both angry and bitter. She lowered her head to study the menu and seemed to be collecting herself.

"We survived. I'm not complaining."

"Yeah, but we only made it because we aren't pure fey. A lot of my family didn't make it. I bet a lot of yours didn't either." She stared hard at the menu's entrées.

"A lot of people would argue that fewer death feys are probably a good thing." Jack's tone was neutral.

Io raised the menu higher and murmured something unintelligible.

"Some of the selkies made it," Jack pointed out when she didn't reappear.

"But why?" she asked from behind her menu. "Why did they survive when the pixies and elves didn't?"

"Truthfully? I think they may still be here because they weren't above the ground when the last solar flare happened."

Io lowered her menu and looked at him, clearly

surprised at a serious answer when she hadn't expected there to be one.

Sometimes Jack surprised himself.

"What do you mean?"

"This is just a theory," he warned, "but I've been doing some reading on the research boffins' latest black-box theories. The guys in the skunk works think that the wipeout began right after the solar flares that caused the big drought. They believe that it was the earth and air fey at higher elevations that took the most hits from the radiation—they couldn't stand the solar pollution. It killed their magic, and then it killed them."

"And the selkies?"

"I think selkies were spared because they are water spirits and went deep to escape."

Io nodded encouragingly, so Jack went on. "I think the goblins and gargoyles survived because they live underground. Anyway, these goblins are as much insect as magical being. You know how hard it is to kill cockroaches or ants."

"You're right," Io said slowly. "They are a lot like insects, aren't they? They even have six limbs. And their hair is like wire. I was looking closely at Hille and Glashtin. Theirs isn't anything like animal hair. And it sticks in your clothes like it has barbs."

Jack nodded. "The ones who survived have six limbs—four arms and two legs. Remember, not all goblins were like this. Many European ones had only two arms and two legs. They died out, too, with

93

the rest of the earth and air feys. These things down here are mutants. Hell! I'm not sure we should even be calling them goblins. The old goblins were so neat they were prissy. These creatures are pigs. And they live like ants—swarms of them. The old goblins never did that."

"These goblins also have a magical generator nearby. Maybe the power spilling off that is what draws them," Io said, thinking aloud. "And they seem to be able to produce their horrible fruit at an incredible pace, given how cold the climate is here in their city. That has bothered me since coming into town: There are too many junkies around. Could magic be keeping the Labyrinth unseasonably warm? Is that why they are able to support more addicts?"

Jack gave the question a ponder.

"And what are they feeding the plants to make them produce so fast? It has to be blood, right?" Io went on. "Are they growing crops with hydroponics underground—maybe with blood meal? They could have found some way to make plants that don't need human blood, I suppose. Genetic engineering or something."

Jack nodded slowly. "Possibly. But what would it addict then? Cows? Chickens? The power of goblin fruit to addict humans comes from it being nurtured with human blood and bone." He paused. "The goblins do live on a natural power point, though. That

94

we know for certain. This magical power source has to play a part somehow."

Io shook her head. "It isn't right. I was taught that magic is supposed to be neutral, unownable. Could these goblins truly have perverted it?"

"They don't own the magic here, but they do seem to have sole usage rights. You know what magic is like—it hates to be neglected. The Motor City jewel may have some protective properties that are being used to shield the goblins, and maybe such jewel usage is part of what saved them here and in New Orleans during the drought. It sure wasn't their looks or winning personalities."

Io guessed, "So the jewel could be helping them produce more crops, couldn't it?"

"Yes, but not without blood. And I have a sudden nasty suspicion about where they are getting their blood. As you said, the number of junkies—"

Jack stopped speaking as a blond waitress pushed through the swinging doors that led from the diner's kitchen, and waddled up to their table. She was a goblin-fruit junkie, but not too far gone. Her hair hadn't started to turn yet.

Io looked from Jack to the waitress and back again. Her expression was troubled.

"What'll it be?" the waitress asked, pulling a pad and pencil out of her pocket.

"Have the turkey cutlets," Jack suggested. He added deadpan, "They taste just like chicken."

Io exhaled slowly and began to smile. She didn't

do it very often and it pleased Jack to see.

"Why shouldn't I just have the chicken?" she asked.

"Because I can't swear that it *is* chicken. It doesn't *taste* like chicken."

"And the meatloaf?"

"Well, I wouldn't eat it. But I tend to be fussy about what I dine on. Grind it up and how can you tell what it really is?"

"Then I guess I'll be having the turkey cutlets," Io decided, smiling up at the waitress, who simply stared back blankly. "Do you have fruit juice?" she asked.

"Something in a sealed bottle or can," Jack stipulated.

"Apple," the waitress said, scribbling the order in a laborious scrawl. Her hands, like all junkies', were tremored.

"I'll have the same," Jack said when she was done, dropping both his and Io's menus back in the slot behind the napkin dispenser. He added, "That's all for now."

"Okay." The waitress was still writing as she waddled obediently back toward the kitchen.

"Don't those contacts bother you?" Jack asked, changing the subject completely. He'd decided that Io didn't need to hear his theory about where the goblins here were getting human fertilizer for their crops. Ghouls weren't the only ones to make use of the dead, but there was no need to point it out before dinner.

"Not as much as having people look at my eyes."

"I like your eyes. I don't like the contacts. You'll have to take them out when we make love."

Io exhaled in a whoosh, and colored. "No teasing!" she warned him. "I can't afford the distraction, Jack. Really. And neither can you."

"Who said I'm teasing?" He made sure that his eyes and smile were lazy as he looked her over. He kept his magic tamped down, since that seemed to be what made her nervous.

"No flirting either, then. I mean it, Jack." She pointed a finger at him.

"I never flirt," Jack assured her. He waited until she had put her finger away to add, "The word implies a lack of solemn intent. I take my seductions very seriously."

"I wish I thought you were kidding," she muttered.

"I'm sure you do," he answered sympathetically.

"Why _do_ you tease me?" she demanded. She obviously labored against the latent truth spell as she added, "You know I don't like it."

Jack opened his mouth to tell her again that he wasn't teasing—and that she was lying, but decided he'd rattled her cage enough for the moment.

"Anger is as blinding as lust," he said instead. "You needed to chill a bit before we go down. Think of what we are doing as a sort of a game of chess."

He pulled out some napkins and shoved one her way. "So, do you want to trade spells?"

"What for what?" she asked.

"Your fist of steel for my invisibility."

Io considered it. "It's a pity we can't share."

"Well"—Jack waved a hand—"actually, we can."

Io blinked and asked warily, "How?"

"It involves us getting very, very close."

"How close?"

"As close as two people can get."

"That's too close," she said firmly.

Jack looked at his comrade-in-arms and had to grin. He'd been doing that a lot lately. Something about this wary little fey attracted him like no one had in the last twenty years. And all he had to do was touch her and the sparks literally flew. Hell, they flew even when he didn't touch her.

She was right though about the flirting. It was a fun way to kill some time, but it would have to end when they went into the Labyrinth. Neither of them could afford to be distracted.

Still . . .

Jack glanced at his watch.

"So, are we agreed that the real danger isn't Horroban finding the generator, but whatever he has Neveling Lutin cooking up?" Io asked practically.

Jack shrugged. "As I don't think Horroban *can* find the generator, yes, the greater danger is Neveling Lutin's hellbroth. And by the way, the lab didn't turn up anything on those samples. They are just

98

your same old basic goblin cosmetics: eye of newt, tongue of frog stuff. If he's making poison, it isn't in his factory. Yet."

"Damn."

"Well, if nothing else, we should be able to get a sample of the recent crop of goblin fruit tonight. Our labs can do a DNA breakdown on it and see if and how it is different from the old fruit." Jack hadn't intended to offer to do this, but knew it would please Io.

It was also a sound idea. He hadn't been paying any particular attention to the junkie problems, but looking back on it, it seemed like there were more of them in Goblin Town than ever before, and they were deteriorating faster than they used to. The city's cops hadn't noticed because there weren't any bodies turning up at the morgue. Now Jack suspected why.

The blond waitress reappeared with two plates, which she set carefully on the table. Jack and Io didn't speak until she returned with their bottles of apple juice and some silverware.

"How long has she got?" Io asked, her voice hushed as the girl waddled back to the kitchen.

"I'd have said six or seven months based on her hair and skin. But . . ."

"But?"

"My nose doesn't agree. She *smells* sicker than that. I'd say she has no more than four months left."

"We've got to stop them. Somehow. They'll kill us

all eventually if we don't," Io said. Her voice was level and calm, but Jack knew that she meant every word. He was coming to know her. She was terrified of failing at this—thankfully more frightened of the situation than she was of him now, or than she had been after his harsh first-night warning. He realized that if that fear had lived, it would have grown and consumed her. Jack was certain that she would have left Goblin Town and never come back rather than allow herself to be taken over as her mother had been. Being addicted, especially being addicted to a man, was Io's version of *worse-than-death*.

"We will stop them," he heard himself promise. "Now eat your dinner. We'll swap spells in the restroom after. I need to put in a nose breather anyway."

"Swap spells? You were serious then?"

"Yes, I've decided that I want to punch some things really, really hard." He grinned at her. "And frankly, you should be neither seen nor heard if I am to keep my mind on being a spy."

"Hmph!" Io picked up her fork and stabbed her cutlets. The plate shrieked as the tines raked over it.

"Careful, that's your enchanted hand," Jack warned. "You don't want to stick that fork clean through the table."

"No, but I wouldn't mind sticking it through you." She added, "You know, you smile way too much. You're a death fey. You are supposed to be grim."

"What can I say? Sometimes I just love my work."

Io sighed. Lifting her cutlet out of its sauce, she stared at it intently. "It looks like turkey. Are you sure it's safe?"

"Safe, yes. Turkey, no."

Io shook her head at him, sending her dark hair sliding over her shoulders. "I can see why you aren't married. No woman would ever be brave enough to date you twice. One dinner with you and they would all run away." She paused, then complained in an amused voice, "You said no dubious meats."

"Dubious meat wasn't the problem. They were all terrified by my giant . . . uh . . ."

"Feet?" she asked sweetly; adding to the retort, "Which you like to keep in your mouth, right?" She colored again as she spoke, but refused to be drawn into his offered exchange of innuendo.

"Not *feet*. Don't be ridiculous. And it's just ten inches. And no, I don't like to put it in *my* mouth," he answered, enjoying her blush.

Io shook her head again and gingerly began eating. Her nose wrinkled as she chewed.

"I bet you spent a lot of time in the principal's office when you were a kid," she offered at last, after swallowing her first bite.

"Yeah." He sighed reminiscently. "She loved me too."

Io gave him a withering look and Jack promised himself that he would stop teasing her.

Soon.

Chapter Nine

They found a manhole cover in a deserted part of town and, after having a long listen for any suggestive noise from the underground, they climbed down the rusting iron ladder into the Labyrinth.

Io was without her protective contacts because Jack had insisted that they would impede her vision down in the dark tunnels. She also had the temporary charge of Jack's invisibility spell. He had been adamant that they swap powers, and she had been so unnerved by the feel of his hands on her face and his unblinking gaze that she had quickly agreed to the switch.

It might have been a mistake, because she now had a vague feeling that Jack was all over her, like sweat on her skin. The constant vague tingling of his magic made it hard to ignore him.

They entered the first subterranean layer of Goblin Town to find a garbage dump that consisted mainly of dried fruit pulp. Io had a suspicion that it probably stank of vinegar and worse, and was grateful for her nose breather.

"This whole labyrinth's a formicary," Jack said softly. "And this is a goblin fruit compost heap. When the fruit rots enough, it'll be recycled to feed the new plants."

Io nodded, preferring not to open her mouth lest some of the air get in and coat her tongue. She thought she would likely gag if that happened. The "turkey" cutlets were not sitting all that well with her anyway.

The low spots in the tunnel they traveled had small puddles of dirty water that seemed to have seeped in through the tacky, glowing plaster that lined the uneven walls. Those tiny pools vibrated constantly, and Io made a point of avoiding them. It was a silly idea, but she had formed the notion that some of the puddles might be bottomless.

The level was laid out in a very gridlike manner, large open spaces lined with windowless buildings connected to other areas by more of the uneven tunnels. It was also largely deserted. Jack and Io only had to hang back twice while a scurrying goblin hurried from building to building with large parcels and baskets.

It was hot, humid, and as desolate as the moon, all under the pall of green light given off by the sticky plaster.

A constant clicking noise followed them, heard

even over the growing hum of magic and machinery. Io found that the constant aural stimulation was making her teeth ache, and it scratched her nerves until they were raw.

They passed a water reservoir, its walls spackled with the same glowing plaster as the tunnels. The coating had an annoying habit of sticking to the soles of her shoes, and Io wondered if the goblins found it irritating to have on their feet. It certainly made moving about with stealth difficult since every step was accompanied by the sound of bubblegum peeling off linoleum.

Jack didn't touch her once they were inside, but he stayed close. He was looking after her like Little Bo Peep, shepherding Io away from any bad wolves while she looked for her lost lambs. Only she wasn't looking for innocent sheep. She was looking for a chemistry lab and the unseasonal fields of goblin fruit she suspected were growing there. And all the while she and Jack were playing hide-and-seek with subterranean nasties that worked for Horroban.

Goblin king, goblin king, where was the goblin king?

"It's vast, isn't it?" she whispered, trying to dispel the singsong voice in her head. She didn't need auditory hallucinations to make the situation worse. "I had no idea it was this big."

"I've never found the end of it," Jack answered, his voice barely louder than the mechanical hum that whined around them like an angry mosquito.

"Admittedly, I haven't explored all that much. But this underground runs clear to the river."

"You were right about it being like a hive. Don't laugh at me, but have you ever seen evidence that the goblins have a queen? A breeder?"

He frowned at her. "Don't take my analogy about the cockroaches too literally. The goblins are very different than mindless insects."

"I know. The fact that they can think only makes them more dangerous." Io listened to the clicking. It did sound a lot like giant cockroaches. Unnerved, she asked again: "But do you think they maybe have a queen somewhere—the way ants do?"

"I hope not! Though, a lot of ant queens will eat their own young when hungry, so it might not be all bad if they did." Jack paused in front of some burn marks on the tunnel wall. It was hard to see in the strange light, but it looked as if something liquid had splattered and blistered the paint. Jack was careful not to touch it.

"Ants squirt acid," Io said. She rubbed at her forehead. Either the heat or the constant humming was getting to her. She was beginning to feel dizzy.

"Formic acid," he agreed. "But last I looked, goblins weren't going around spraying. The little skunks stink generally, but they don't squirt."

"Yeah? But what if we haven't seen all the goblins? What if there are worker goblins who never go up top? They could be different."

Jack appeared to consider this. "Who would they be squirting at?"

"Other goblins? Intrepid junkies looking for the fruit fields?" Io rubbed her forehead. "Or maybe my stupid imagination has gone galloping down the high road to outright paranoia."

"If there are goblins who are squirting acid that can burn stone, I hope we never see them," Jack said slowly. He looked at his watch and then Io's face. He seemed to reach some decision. "Come on. I know where one of the fruit fields is located. Let's get our sample and then get you out of here. You look green."

"Well, so do you." She paused. "What about Neveling Lutin?"

"If there's time, we'll look for his place. But this may be more important—finding the fruit fields. I am beginning to think there is a whole lot down here we don't know about. Come on, the field's this way." Jack touched her arm, gently causing a brief arc on Io's skin. She pulled back quickly.

"Sorry. You startled me."

His lovely lips thinned as he pressed them together, but he didn't say anything before starting back up the tunnel.

Feeling increasingly unwell, Io followed. A part of her wanted to take Jack's hand and lean her throbbing head against his shoulder, but she didn't do it. This wasn't the time for magic pheromone sparks,

or whatever it was that went on between her and
Jack when they touched.

It was a little late for second thoughts, but Io knew
now that she had miscalculated, that the longer she
and Jack were exposed to each other's company,
the more involved her heart became. She could
fight her feelings for a while, but not if her body—
and Jack—worked against her. She'd never survive
two weeks.

And if she started getting touchy-feely now, there
wouldn't be any reasonable argument for stopping
him later—except the one she wasn't willing to dis-
cuss. So, it was strictly hands-off. Clearly, she had to
get this job done as soon as possible and put some
distance between them.

One small touch and Io had turned cagey on him
again.

Jack shook his head.

He could see that she was suffering, beginning to
get a pressure headache from the dank air and bad
light, but since she didn't want it, he didn't try to
touch her again. Under other circumstances, or with
some other woman, he might have taken her in his
arms and comforted her with a healing spell. But he
knew it would only do more harm than good if he
tried it with Io. For some reason, she was bent on
resisting him.

He had every intention of finding out why, too—

but exploring the kinks in her psyche would have to wait for a more auspicious moment.

Jack stopped at the end of the tunnel and looked about carefully before stepping into the large chamber beyond. He estimated its size at about twenty acres. This was one of the smaller fields.

The ceiling was low and ragged, having been blasted out of solid rock and never finished. There was no reason to pretty the place up. The plants didn't care what the cave looked like. They stuck their roots down into the stone and slurped up whatever the goblins brought them, and then gave birth to their addictive fruit.

Io gasped softly as she stepped into the room. "Goddess, save us! It's October, but look at the fruit! I've never seen a field this full."

Jack turned to look at her instead. She appeared horrified right to the backs of her big blue eyes. Her arms were folded across her chest. Her neck was hunched as though hiding from a cold wind. And maybe she was cold. The chamber's ambient temperature had to be at least ninety-five degrees, but some kinds of chill had nothing to do with the body. If you were smart enough to consider the implications of this fruit, then your nerves were bound to take a chill. This farm at full production in the fall represented something worse for humans than all the opium fields or coca plantations combined. If that didn't freeze the nerves, nothing would.

Jack pulled out a knife and quickly sliced through

the nearest vine. The severed stem bled red, drooling out sap that looked just like blood. He quickly wrapped the piece of nearly ripe fruit in his bandanna and dropped it into his coat pocket.

"I never thought you could actually look bad," he said unkindly, knowing the insult would be as bracing as a glass of cold water dashed in Io's face. "But right now you are the color of cheese mold."

Io blinked once and then indignation dawned. Her arms unfolded and her spine shot up. "Well, you're not looking like any sex god yourself, Mister Mildew."

Jack refrained from laughing at her return insult. He made a point of checking his watch again. "We have to go."

"What about Neveling?"

"Tomorrow night," he said.

He hadn't planned on bringing her back underground, really, but perhaps it was the lesser of two evils. H.U.G.'s mortality rate had gone way up since they'd started their policy of direct confrontation with goblins. Xanthe might have plans, but Io was one operative who wasn't going to be used as goblin fodder. Jack's job was dangerous, but Io was safer with him than being pushed around like a pawn by Queen Xanthe. He planned on keeping her far away from H.U.G.

"We need to be out of here when the topside goblins start pouring back in at dawn," Jack pointed out as he wiped the beading sweat from his brow. This, the goblin underground, was the only place where he perspired. He figured it had more to do with his body trying to rid itself of toxins than the Labyrinth's actual heat. "They'd buy the poor lost tourist shtick up there, but no way would they let us go if they found us down here. Not with fruit. Not when we are fey and packing spells."

Io nodded once. She tried to hide it, but she looked relieved they were going back up. Air down in the Labyrinth took getting used to, mostly because there was a lot less of it. Her head was probably pounding from the lack of oxygen, and even for the green light she looked exceptionally nauseated.

He gave her credit for trying, though. The thought of confronting two carnivorous gargoyles was daunting even when one wasn't feeling sick. It took a dedicated person to suggest it when she was feeling ill.

"I have some home-brewed antihistamine back at my place," Jack said as he started back toward the exit. "It's mostly cognac with a few herbs, but it will help your head and stomach."

"Antihistamine?" Io asked, moving quickly to keep up with him. He wished he could stay behind her and watch her walk. Too bad he had to take point, because her heels gave her a nice feminine sway.

"Yeah. You have goblin allergies," he said matter-of-factly. "We'll get you set up before we come back down again. A good day's sleep and a shot of my home brew and you'll feel terrific."

"Oh. I didn't know we could have allergies to anything." She sounded reassured by the explanation. "Jack? About going home with you—"

"Don't bother arguing," he interrupted. "You said you were in, little fey. That means you're in all the way."

"Zayn is going to be looking for me," she argued. "I just sort of ditched Xanthe and him without telling them anything. With ticks saying I'm stuck in some nightclub bathroom when I am clearly *not* there, they are probably going bonkers."

Jack smiled at the idea of the cool Queen Xanthe going bonkers.

"Let the pretty boy look. We'll catch up with Zayn tomorrow if you really want to see him. Come to think of it, that's an excellent plan. He can get someone to water your houseplants and feed the parakeet."

"I don't have a parakeet! And it isn't a matter of wanting to see him," she explained.

"It is now. And *wants* take a backseat to *needs*. What you need to do is become real scarce around your former compatriots. Your presence from here on out will be rarer than hen's teeth or dragon's tears as far as H.U.G. is concerned." Jack looked back at her. He made his voice flat so she would know he wasn't kidding. "You're on my team until this job is done, Io Cyphre. New team, new rules. One of those

111

rules is that you see people from the outside only in controlled situations. Another rule is that you lie to everyone at H.U.G., because the less they know about where you are and what you're doing the better for both of us. You see, there's a sort of balance of physics in this kind of work, a mathematical equation that doesn't vary. H.U.G. has spies here? You can bet the goblins have spies there."

Io thought about this. "You want me to lie to *everyone?*"

"Except me." Jack considered whether he needed to threaten her with anything to ensure her obedience, and decided against it since he couldn't think of anything dire that he would actually be willing to do to her. "So . . . you are coming back to my place tonight, and we are going to have a toast to our partnership with some antihistamine. And then you're going to bed so you have the strength to kick goblin ass tomorrow night."

He waited to see what Io would say to this highhandedness. Usually she would be angry and very inquisitive about his plans. Put some whiskers on her and she could pass for a cat in that regard. Therefore he knew she had to be feeling really wretched when all she asked was, "What shall we drink to? Confusion of the enemy?"

"That's a damn fine start, don't you think?" Jack stopped in front of the ladder. "I'm going up to open the cover. Wipe your shoes off as best you can—we don't want to leave tracks all over the street."

He thought he heard her mutter, "So much for Little Bo Peep and her sheep." He wondered what she meant.

Maybe he deserved a set of whiskers, too, for curiosity where Io was concerned.

Chapter Ten

It started to rain once they were back inside Jack's gothic retreat. Watery dawnlight pressed its way past the dirty-paned windows, edging through the bit of glass scrubbed clean by the cloudburst and sending phantom rivulets of green running down the far wall.

Amazingly, Io was feeling sleepy. Somewhere along the long walk back to Jack's she had gotten comfortable with him.

"Would you like a shower?" Jack asked. "There's water here."

Io hesitated. "Without clean clothes—"

"Use one of my shirts for now. One of us can go out tomorrow and pack some things up for you." One, but not both. Someone had to stay in the city and hold the spells they'd collected. Without someone to keep them, they would probably melt back into the earth from which they'd come.

"Okay. That sounds good." Getting clean before

bed suddenly seemed immensely appealing.

"There's a shirt hanging on the back of the door, and soap in the shower. Ignore the markings on the tap—I'm afraid the water only comes in lukewarm no matter where you set the dial."

"Would you mind if I gave your spells back now?" Io asked, turning toward Jack. The rain on the glass sent ghostly tears trekking down his cheeks, making him suddenly appear more the death fey that he was.

"No."

But she could see that he did mind. Feeling bad for rejecting him yet again she explained, "It's just that I still feel a little odd and I'm afraid of what might happen when I sleep. I've been dreaming lately. What if I accidentally morphed them into something stupid or dangerous?"

Jack's face softened. When he spoke, he sounded thoughtful. "It has been one hell of a night, hasn't it? And you're out of the practice of using your magic this way. Come here."

Prepared for the transference, Io approached, turning her face up so Jack could take her chin. She had herself schooled not to flinch when their flesh made contact, but this time he barely touched her.

"Close your eyes," he ordered. "There's no need to watch. I won't bite."

Io let her eyelids drift shut. There was a small tingling when his lips brushed her forehead and his fingers traced her jaw. There was an up-rush, like a breath of air, and then suddenly the magic and headache were gone, leaving her empty and feeling a little naked.

Io slumped, almost leaning against him.

"You're beat, little fey. Have your shower," Jack said gently. "I'll put out some cordial for you."

Io looked up. Staring into his eyes, she could feel something almost painful stir inside them. Genuine loneliness? Latent lust masquerading as lonesomeness? She was too tired to figure it out. Probably she should ignore it until she could think more clearly.

Sighing, she turned toward the bathroom door.

"Jack?" she asked, before stepping into the giant tiled room.

"Yes?"

"Where do you live when you aren't here?"

When he didn't answer, she recalled his injunction to secretiveness because it was safer for both of them, and added hastily "Never mind. I—"

"I live anywhere and everywhere that the job takes me. But no place is home. You know what I do. I can't take the risk of having a known base."

"I see." And sadly, she did. She hadn't had a real home for years either.

She closed the door softly behind her.

Jack couldn't figure out Io's mood. Perhaps she had truly hit the wall and was too tired to go on being wary. Or maybe she reacted the way she had earlier because of where they were. When one was walking on dangerous ground, it was bound to raise a hair or two on the nape and make a person nervy as a cat.

But whatever her mood before, she wasn't fighting him now. When he'd taken the magic away, she had done everything but crawl into his lap and asked to be cuddled. It seemed an ideal moment to try to seduce her—always supposing that he was willing to be his usual bastard self.

But . . . he couldn't do it. He just couldn't. Not if she was *the one*.

He was just figuring out that she could be. The magic was acting like she was the real McCoy.

He'd had many lovers, most human, and more of those than ever since the holocaust had wiped out most of his kind. There had been no expectation of finding someone he'd be with for life, so he had decided to take his pleasures where he found them. And the lifestyle of casual encounters suited him.

But now, unlooked for, and not particularly wanted, Fate had raised her ever-nosy head and thrust Io into his life. Jack's whole way of existence could be on the verge of change, and he wasn't sure how he felt about it. Intrigued, certainly. Maybe a little annoyed.

Maybe a bit frightened.

Frightened? The big bad death fey?

Jack's first impulse was to deny this. But, though he habitually lied to everyone else, he made it a policy to never be anything but truthful with himself.

Okay, so maybe he was a little nervous. He had reason to be wary. Death feys tended to mate for life. If they ever found a woman who could tolerate them, they tended to settle in like bricks into mortar. And they didn't do well when something happened to their spouses. Their humanity left them. His father had been cold as a well-digger's ass after his mother died. Nothing had moved him. Given Io's chosen path, the odds of something happening to her were higher than Jack liked.

His own calling was even worse . . .

Leaving his feelings aside, what of Io? She knew there was chemistry between them, and she was fighting for some reason. Could she sense that, in spite of the magic, they were wrong for each other? Or that they were absolutely right for one another, and she didn't want any part of it because permanence was out of the question? It would be just like that bloody bitch Fate to send him a mate whose heart had already been feathered with silver arrows and could never actually love. He'd heard that a lot of siren fey were born heartless.

Or maybe her resistance had nothing to do with being magical or fey. Was it just that she was as wary of his career as he was of hers, and she was being sensible?

Jack stared out the window. That seemed far too simple an answer.

It could have something to do with Io's mother getting tangled up with Drakkar. There'd been magic at work there too—black stuff. Could that ugly affair have permanently bent Io's psyche? Made her distrust *all* magic and magical beings?

Who could know without asking the sorts of leading questions that would likely send his wary fey running away as fast her slender legs would carry her?

Jack borrowed some of Io's gutter troll to express his feelings of frustration and then got out a glass and his hip flask.

Io emerged from the shower a short time later, smelling vaguely of coconut and plain old warm skin. Jack's shirt was huge and looked faintly ridiculous on her, but he liked seeing her in it anyway.

He handed her a glass with two fingers of cognac in it.

She smiled up at him, eyes glowing faintly. "Confusion to the enemy," she said, and then drank down the liquor.

"Hop up in the hammock," Jack suggested. "I'm going to take a shower."

"I don't want to put you out of your bed," Io said softly.

"You won't," he assured her. They would be sharing the hammock, but she would probably never know it. The cognac had valerian in it and would knock her sideways in five minutes flat.

"Okay." She yawned. "I'm suddenly very sleepy."

Looking at her drooping eyelids, Jack revised his

estimate downward. She probably had two minutes of consciousness left—tops.

"Need some help?" he asked, watching her hoist herself into the hammock. His shirt rode up her legs but stopped before the view got too interesting.

"Oh no. I sleep in a hanging bed." Io yawned again and then added in a slurring voice as she curled on her side, "I live in a tree house. I always wanted to when I was a child, so when I came to Michigan I had one built."

"That sounds about right," Jack muttered, picking up a blanket and spreading it over her.

"It's nice that you don't have rats," Io commented, her eyes falling shut. "A lot of old buildings do."

"That is one benefit to living in Goblin Town," Jack conceded. "They do tend to keep down the other vermin by dining on them."

"Mmmhmmmm."

"Go to sleep now."

" 'kay . . ."

Io tried to stay awake, but she was barely conscious when Jack emerged from the bathroom wearing jeans and no shirt. She tucked away in the back of her sleepy brain the fact that the rumor was true: He did have the letter J stitched in his chest. It was also true that it didn't diminish his attractiveness one bit.

She watched through slitted eyes as Jack approached the hammock. He lifted the blanket up and then rolled into the bed with a practiced motion.

Part of Io knew she should protest the intimacy of sharing the space, but it felt marvelous to curl into his heat and have someone hold her while she went to sleep.

"I don't suppose that there's anything you'd like to say to me right now?" he asked softly as she settled her head on his shoulder and wrapped an arm around his chest.

Eat my heart. Drink my soul. Love me to death.

"No," she answered with a regretful mumble. "I'm too tired to die tonight."

Her living pillow shook and gave a rumble of soft laughter. "If I didn't know better, little fey, I'd say that you were drunk."

"I am," she agreed, unable to resist the truth spell, but then she stopped talking as sleep came rushing up to claim her.

Chapter Eleven

Io woke sometime later when the sun had shifted over into the western sky. The heavens had a sort of acid green radiance, suggesting that storm clouds were lingering nearby.

She waited for her body to wake up to the fact that she was pressed chest to chest with Jack, and start panicking because their posture alone could practically count as foreplay. But her body remained strangely quiescent.

Io felt her hand slowly lifted, and Jack brushed his lips over her inner wrist. She could also feel him smile when her pulse leaped. He scraped his teeth over the mound of her palm and then tucked her hand back against his chest.

Io flexed her fingers and buried her face in his shoulder, pretending that she wasn't awake and therefore not responsible for anything she did.

Jack's muscles rippled beneath her, but he didn't speak, apparently pretending too.

After a moment, she reached a foot out and shoved against the wall, sending the hammock into a gentle swing. The easy rhythmic sway was like lazy sex first thing on a Sunday morning. Body stroked body, the friction of skin on skin causing those magical sparks as the hammock reached its zenith and then fell back.

"Your body's asking. Why don't *you?*" a deep voice asked.

Eat me, drink me, love me, Jack.

She almost said it. She wanted to.

"There isn't time," she said instead, avoiding a real answer. "Someone has to get my clothes, and I need to see Zayn."

"Hm. That sounds like an excuse, and a lame one, and you are being a tease." This time it was Jack's foot that reached out and pushed their bed into motion.

"Maybe. But you're big and strong. I'm sure you can take it."

"Uh-huh. The question is, can you?"

Io didn't look up or answer, so Jack continued, "Now, if you are determined on seeing Zayn, then there are things we need to do. Soon."

"Yes?"

"I'm not sending you out into Goblin Town without a full compliment of spells."

"That's fine," Io agreed, still speaking into his chest. She let her fingers trace a small pattern on his skin, tracking lightly over the thick J. She grinned up at him and then closed her eyes. "I like . . . having *spells*."

"Well, goody then," Jack said, rolling onto his side and dislodging her from atop his chest.

"Goody?" she asked, opening her eyes as he loomed over her.

"Yeah, I just love this part."

"Why?" she asked, beginning to frown. "Jack! Be nice!"

"Nice? No, I don't think so. Let me demonstrate how I feel. I do love giving spells to you. Magic." Jack leaned down and set his mouth against hers. Instantly magic ran down her body from tongue to toes, making her muscles clench at her core. Jack stopped short of forcing a climax on her as he had done that first night, but it was a very close thing.

A worse thing, she decided, as her body started howling its frustration.

"You rotten cad," she whispered, when her mouth was free. Deprived of even that contact, her body again protested its sudden arousal, and she pressed her thighs together in a useless effort to stop the throbbing. She crossed her arms over her chest.

"That's almost as much fun as the real thing," he answered, grinning at her ire and then rolling out of bed, taking the blanket with him. He kept it in front of his body so she couldn't tell if he had been affected the way she was.

The thought that he hadn't, made her almost speechless with fury—and she hated that! She didn't like the rush of strong emotion. It seemed to be blasting open conduits in her brain, pipelines for more and greater feelings.

"Of course, if you want to finish this," he taunted, "all you have to do is ask."

"Not if they were ice-skating in Hell!" she snarled. Anger helped douse her arousal. A little.

Jack turned and opened the bathroom door. Chill air rushed over her bare legs, making her shiver. Desire was dying fast under the twin assaults of anger and cold.

"Suit yourself. If you're quick, I'll let you have the bathroom first."

Io rolled off the swaying bed and glared at him. On her way to the old tiled room the floor was freezing on her socked feet, and she felt frustrated and grumpy. She said something mean in troll and poked at Jack's ribs as she passed.

"We are going to have to work on your trench mouth," Jack remarked.

"Give me time. I'm sure it can get worse with practice."

Io looked into the cracked mirror over the rusted basin in the bath, and gasped at the sight of her hair. She hadn't cared for the punk look even when it was fashionable.

"Uh-oh," Jack said, leaning in the door and grinning at her. "It looks like somebody is having a bad hair day. That's what happens when you go to bed drunk. That and waking up with strange men."

Io spun about to punch him, but he was already gone. Recalling that she had the steel fist again and could actually hurt him while goofing around, she quickly caught hold of her temper.

"I could have put my fist right through your eye!" she scolded.

"You're not fast enough." He laughed. "And, anyway, I put that spell in your left foot this morning. Today you can really kick ass if you want to."

Jack's head reappeared in the doorway, then the rest of him. He had pulled on jeans, a gray sweater, and added sunglasses.

"I'm going out for coffee—or some facsimile thereof. I'll be back in ten minutes. Try not to kill anyone while I'm gone."

"Don't worry. You're the only person around here that I harbor such strong feelings for." Her smile was all teeth.

"See! I knew you liked me." Jack pulled out of the doorway and melted into the shadows. Even without his invisibility spell he managed to open and close the door without making a sound.

"Sneaky, creeping death fey!" she called after him.

Thoughtfully, Io lifted her left foot and tested it for magic by kicking the rotting bathroom wall. Plaster and lathe shattered.

Jack wasn't kidding; he had actually managed to put her spell there. How had he done that without her knowing it?

It just proved what she had always suspected: Lust was a bad, bad thing.

Chapter Twelve

Jack's magic was in place, arranged to her liking, and Io was definitely invisible. She was walking along the wet street without a shadow, even though there was a bright orange sunset behind her and her shade should be stretched out twice her height before her silent feet. Supposedly she was inaudible and unsmellable, too—so if she didn't smack into someone, she was completely unfindable. She should be safe.

Unless someone in town had a counterspell and used it on her.

Her world had changed from yesterday. What she'd seen beneath Goblin Town had made her more nervous and untrusting, and she was therefore more aware of her surroundings. She eyed cars parked along the street, and was relieved when they were appropriately empty. Her eyes grew more restless as she neared downtown and her gaze moved from vehicles to dusty windows and then dark door-ways looking for movement.

She wouldn't be alone for long. The sun was nearly gone from the sky. The manhole covers would be popping open soon and the more human-looking goblins would be creeping out to take up their night jobs. Tourists would begin pouring through the gates looking for a party. Junkies would crawl out of their holes and be looking for things too.

Jack had elected to go for her clothes—probably so there was no chance of Io having a run-in with Xanthe and spilling her guts in a fit of dutifulness. That meant Io was loaded up with all hers and Jack's custom-built magic, and it was making her nerves hum. She didn't plan on using any of it on Zayn, but it was reassuring to know that she could if necessary.

Io sighed. She didn't like it, but Zayn had been moved from the list of reluctant allies to one of unknowns. He wasn't actually an enemy, but he and she weren't exactly on the same team anymore. Unless she could convert him to her way of thinking, get him to understand where the real danger was. It would be a hard sell, because Zayn was not a loner when it came to making decisions. He liked the security of an organization behind him.

Io arrived at The Madhouse just as the doors were opening, and eased inside as soon as the way was clear. She still didn't like the place. Even without the full compliment of patrons and their awful din, the fractured mirror wall gave back a kaleidoscope of ugly images. The lighting was not kind to fey eyes.

She slipped into the restroom behind a cocktail waitress and waited in a corner until the woman was gone.

Once she could hear the reassuring babble of excited voices and the start of SEXXX's atonal wailing, Io let go of the invisibility spell and checked herself in the mirror: spiky hair, black leather, contacts hiding the blue of her eyes. She was ready.

"Time to go," she muttered.

Taking a last deep breath of relatively clean air, she pulled open the door and waded into the club. Once again, something other than oxygen was floating in the air, and it prickled her skin and nerves.

Zayn was already on the dance floor and busy scanning the room as he slithered about with a petite female goblin. Io didn't like the way the goblin moved. Her head would draw back with each beat, just like a snake preparing to strike. Her scalp drew back with each head bob, too, taking the rest of the skin with it so her lip peeled back and her pointed teeth were exposed.

Io shuddered, wondering how Zayn could stand to touch the creature.

Zayn spotted Io at once and began moving his partner toward her. Io let herself slide into the arterial rhythm that thumped her ears and bopped her way over to her annoyed ex-partner. She kept far away from the snake-mouthed female.

"Hey, baby," she said loudly, not giving Zayn a chance to speak. She was careful not to look into the girl goblin's eyes, not wanting to know if the pupils were actually slitted. "I hear there's a big party tonight at Forty Shades of Green. Maybe I'll see you there."

"If there's a big party, you can count on it," he answered, smiling with his teeth but not his eyes. "Don't get caught in the bathroom again. I'd hate to have to come rescue you in there."

The message was clear. Io nodded and then began dancing her way toward the exit. She wanted out before Hille or Toc saw her and decided it was time to invite her down for another party in Glashtin's office.

Once outside the club, Io found a dark alley and quickly pulled the invisibility spell back over her. She waited until Zayn emerged from the club and then followed him back up the street to the small jazz club, Forty Shades of Green. Like all goblin nightclubs, this one had been decorated by someone with a severe shortage of taste and an exaggerated dislike for bright lighting. The best that could be said about the place was that it wasn't as loud as it might have been.

She let Zayn choose a table, back from the stage, but not so distant as to attract attention. He ordered a drink and then started scanning the patrons. His face was pleasantly blank but his posture suggested irritation. Io waited until the small foyer was empty and then again cast off her invisibility.

Zayn's surprised look told her that Jack's revved up spell was truly effective. Zayn wouldn't have been able to see her under the magic cloak, but with his own enhanced powers he should have sensed that she was there.

"Hi. Mind if I join you?" she asked, easing herself into a chair without waiting for an answer.

"Where have you been?" he demanded, dropping his voice. "Xanthe's been looking all over for you. And Hille Bingels wants another date."

"I've been busy doing my job." Io's voice was unusually cold, and she wondered if she had picked up some of Jack's power of intimidation.

Zayn blinked and sat back, suggesting that he was wondering the same thing. "Look, if you're having a personal party with Jack Frost then you should let Xanthe know. She's worried about you."

"I am letting her know. Through you. Xanthe and I won't be talking directly again until this mission is over."

Zayn blinked. "Why?"

Io thought about mentioning that she would be staying in Goblin Town, but changed her mind. Jack's precautions didn't look so paranoid to her after last night. Before then, the Labyrinth had just been a word, a place that wasn't real. Now she knew just how real and dangerous it was. Too much was riding on her mission to take chances with idealism.

"You might ask Xanthe that," she said instead. "She and Jack have a personal history—and Jack isn't inclined to chat about it, except to say he doesn't want me near her. Maybe Xanthe will be more talkative."

Zayn frowned. "Does it matter that they were involved?"

"That's unanswerable. It might matter a great deal—at least to me. I was the one sent to climb into Jack's hip pocket, after all. She could have told me a bit about the wolf before throwing me to him."

Zayn shook his head, automatically denying wrongdoing on Xanthe's part, but he didn't look happy with the news. "Where are the other ticks? I can't find them."

Io didn't know, either. She was willing to bet that Jack had moved them somewhere shielded, though. "They're safe enough. I'm keeping them alive in case I need them."

"You should have them on you. We might need—"

"Zayn, you want ticks, you get your own. I'm done hosting parasites. Only if you do let them tick you, watch what Ferris does when you aren't looking. He stuck a big one on my back that he didn't tell me about. Jack had to cut it out and then burn the wound closed."

Zayn blinked again. "He burned you?" He looked appalled. Feys did not use fire on other feys. Ever.

"Yep. It hurt like hell, too."

The waitress arrived with Zayn's drink and asked Io if she'd like anything. Though she didn't care for beer, she ordered something German that came in a bottle, requesting that it remain sealed until it came to the table. When the waitress looked surprised, Io smiled and said she wanted to try her new bottle-opening spell.

Satisfied with the answer, the goblin server retreated.

"Those extra arms must come in handy in this line of work," Io said conversationally, when Zayn failed to initiate conversation.

"You've changed," Zayn finally said, looking troubled. He asked diffidently, "Has Jack done something else to you? I can feel his magic all over you."

Io shrugged. "Jack's my problem. We have something else larger to worry about."

"The jewel?"

Io shook her head and sighed. "Zayn, I am only going to try to tell you this once, so please try hard to listen and not make any judgments about my story until I'm done."

"Okay. But wait until the girl brings your drink." He was beginning to look freaked.

Io stared at him. "Why are you with H.U.G.? I mean, I know what happened to your brother. But have you thought about why H.U.G. took us in?" she asked.

"Because it is illegal to discriminate against people with handicaps," he said flippantly. Like many feys, he was grateful for the Supreme Court's legal protection, but also annoyed that his basic biology should be considered a handicap. He was annoyed that the few physical manifestations of his heritage—in his case, fractal eyes and very pointed ears—he had to hide under long hair and hats if he wished to pass for human.

"Like H.U.G. cares about legalities. Get real, Zayn. We should have asked ourselves this question long ago."

The waitress returned. Io smiled a bit and thanked the goblin who put her beer on the table. She made a show of using one of the spells she had pickpocketed and blasted the bottle cap off with the force of a rocket. It stuck itself into the acoustical tile ceiling.

People at nearby tables applauded.

"Geez! Let's just call for a spotlight," Zayn muttered.

"Relax. This is what tourists are supposed to do."

"What are you going to do about Hille?" Zayn asked, his voice again lowered once everyone had looked away. He still sounded disgruntled. "She's been asking for you all over the place."

"Nothing."

"What?" Now he looked shocked. "But we need to follow her!"

"No, we don't. Here's the thing," Io explained, lowering her voice as far as she could and still be heard. "The situation is much worse here than I was told. I've been down in the hive—"

"The what?" He looked bewildered.

"The Labyrinth. Jack and I went down last night—"

"Are you nuts! You've had no combat training—"

"For the goddess's sake, shut up! Geez, Zayn, are you retarded?" she hissed, losing her temper. "What did you think would happen when Xanthe threw me at Jack? Of course I've gone down with him—and I don't mean that in any sexual sense, though that was clearly what our boss expected of me."

"Io—"

"Now, I am telling you that things are *bad* down there. There are acres upon acres of goblin fruit just waiting to be harvested. And I am asking myself what they have been feeding these plants that they could have a crop this late in the fall. You probably should be asking some of these questions, too."

Zayn began to look troubled. But when he spoke it was to address the lesser of problems. "They shouldn't have sent you in, Io. I was against it. You aren't ready for this, not trained to read the facts and make useful assessments. And Jack Frost is—"

"Jack Frost is glad to be back and ready to be out with his babe," Jack said, slipping into the chair next to Io. He leaned over and kissed her, easing the steel-fist spell out of her before she could even think to protest the extraction. "Got your clothes all packed, babe, so you don't have to borrow my shirt again."

"Thanks," Io muttered, trying to hide how disturbing his kiss had been, even without any intent at hanky-panky on his part.

Zayn stared at them, completely unnerved. For the second time that night, someone had sneaked up on him without his detecting their presence, and he didn't like it.

"Nice to see you again, Zayn. But I think we have to be going. Places to go, people to see," Jack said, his smile colder than the ice in Zayn's glass.

"Okay," Io agreed, deciding that she wasn't going to get anywhere with Zayn that night. He was too much the obedient soldier and needed time to move through proper channels. She stood up. "Tell Xanthe that I'm fine and doing just what I should be."

"Where are you staying?" her ex-partner asked, rising to his feet as Io and Jack did.

"Sorry, my address isn't fixed," Io answered. Knowing it would outrage him, she still suggested, "You can leave a message for me in the bathroom here—if you feel comfortable sneaking into the women's john. Put it in a plastic bag and leave it taped under the tank."

"Why not the men's?" Zayn asked, clearly peeved. "If you have a cloaking spell, you could retrieve it there."

Io shook her head. She didn't explain that the spell was Jack's. "Men's bathrooms are disgusting. I'm not touching anything in there."

Jack threw back his head and laughed. Normally Io liked the sound, but tonight it grated her ears like breaking glass. Something had happened to piss him off. Getting him away from Zayn seemed like a really good idea.

"Time to go," she said to both men.

"Lead the way, babe," Jack answered, dropping a possessive arm around her shoulder.

Io resisted the urge to look back at Zayn as they left the club.

"What happened out there?" she asked, once they were out in the street and moving away from the bright lights of the downtown area. Jack didn't drop his arm, and she didn't ask him to.

"Our problems have potentially gotten a whole lot bigger."

Io used a troll word, and this time Jack didn't bother to tease her.

"What now?" she asked.

"It looks like Xanthe may be in cahoots with the goblins," he said bluntly.

"What?" Io was stunned and, for one moment, disbelieving. She twisted to look up at Jack, unconsciously using the truth spell. "How? Why?"

Jack shook his head at her.

"Untrusting little fey," he said, obviously feeling the magical probe. "I wouldn't lie to you about this."

"Sorry," Io muttered, reeling the spell in.

"Xanthe has a kid sister who has disappeared. Rumor on the force is the kid is living in Goblin Town,

138

an honored guest of our favorite goblin. He's kindly making sure that she gets a generous supply of what she craves and all the partying she can handle."

Io shook her head. "Her name's Chloe. She disappeared? I don't for one minute believe she's here willingly."

"Neither do I."

"But then why didn't Xanthe ask us to find her?" Io wondered aloud, speaking more to herself than Jack. "Zayn and I are *here*. We could be looking."

"Probably because a rescue op has a damn poor chance of succeeding, and Xanthe doesn't want anyone cowboying about and getting the kid killed. There is also the credibility factor. I don't think H.U.G. higher-ups would take kindly to having a director-in-charge of the northern U.S. with a sister who is a goblin-fruit junkie."

"So, instead of asking for help and admitting that she is compromised, Xanthe is dithering about, not doing anything to directly mess up Horroban's plans, but trying to gather information and look efficient while she comes up with some arrangement to save her sister?" Io sighed. "Well, hell. I knew something was wrong when she pushed so hard for me to come back to Goblin Town. The goals were too amorphous. The mission had no shape. And the only reason she wanted me near you was so she could tell Horroban where the real danger was coming from."

"My thoughts exactly. But I'm glad you see it."

"It's a little hard not to. It's like finding a big, fat spider swimming in a glass of curdled milk." Io thought about the developments, unconsciously resting her head against Jack's shoulder.

"I don't honestly know what she'll do," she told him after a moment. "Not if push comes to shove. Xanthe is really fond of Chloe."

"I know she is. So, for sure she can't be trusted with any information. You can't pass anything along through Zayn."

"Goddess, no!" Not with how fond of Chloe Zayn was. He'd had a sort of crush on her forever.

"However, this mess doesn't change our job any. Our objectives are the same as before," Jack reminded her. "It'll take the lab a day to do the analysis of that fruit and see if the addiction content has been raised. In the meantime, we still need to find out what Neveling Lutin is up to—that is, if you're still in. Things are getting really tricky and I wouldn't blame you if you decided to pull out."

"Put a sock in it," Io snapped, without real heat. "I'm in, and I'm staying. So, we go back into the Labyrinth and find Neveling?"

"I'm afraid so."

"Damn. Want to bet the gargoyles are on duty tonight?"

"Almost certainly."

Heat began to drain from Io's body as it finally understood what it would be doing that night. The flesh of her nape began to creep, lodging its own protest at this plan.

Jack laid a warm hand on the back of her neck and stroked gently.

"Let's go by your place and I'll change shoes," Io said, proud of the calm in her voice. "If I have to run, I don't want it to be in heels."

"Okay. I have some nifty tools there as well."

"Yeah? What kind of nifty tools?"

"Well, for one thing, there is a neat little handgun that shoots bullets forged of cold iron. It even has a silencer."

"That's a really nifty tool," Io agreed, looking up at Jack. "Who gets to play with it first?"

"You know how to shoot a pistol?" Jack asked.

"Yes."

"Then it's all yours."

"Thanks, I guess."

Chapter Thirteen

They went down and in near Neveling's factory, and their first stop in the Labyrinth was another cavernous farm covered in a field of the ripening ruby goblin fruit. Io was better prepared for the sight this time, but the spectacle still left a bitter taste in her mouth and had her gut clenching. It was too easy to recall her mother nibbling on the glossy spheres as a smiling Drakkar fed them to her. Feys didn't age the way humans did when they took the stuff, but they became just as addicted to goblin fruit, and their minds became just as given over to obsession.

"Shall we find out what's feeding them?" Jack asked.

"Yes." Io swallowed hard. "Do it."

Jack knelt down at the end of a row and, drawing on a glove, he pulled back the tangle of barbed vines. The plants were being supplied nourishment by individual drippers, two tubes for each cane. One was filled with a clear liquid; the other was not. It was difficult to judge shades in the eerie green twilight, but Io was willing to bet that the other was thinned-down blood. That was, after all, what goblin fruit needed to grow: human blood, human bones.

"Where are those destructive garden gophers when you want them?" Io muttered.

"At the donut shop with the cops, probably," Jack muttered back. "Keep an eye and an ear out for goblins. I want to see where this goes."

Jack pushed vines aside and followed the plastic tubing into the field, tracing the red line to a tank located nearly twenty feet in. The thing was about the size of a coffin and sprouted a dozen spigots off its sides. He laid a gloved hand against its corroding surface and gave the tank a shove. As expected, there was the sound of sloshing liquid. But there were also several hollow thumps, suggesting something solid inside.

Io thought of the junkie she and Jack had seen and tried not to be ill. Jack's face was also grim.

"There must be what—fifty of them down here in this field alone?"

Io nodded.

They followed an ear-assaulting whine back to a small pump house at the edge of the field where the largest feeder lines disappeared. The pump sounded as if it needed oil. Goblins weren't big on mechanical items and tended to be careless about maintenance.

"Can we break in?"

"Do we need to?"

"We could do a little sabotage," Io suggested.

"Not yet. We don't want them to know—quiet!" Jack grabbed Io and quickly drew her to the far side of the pump house. Two goblins appeared out of the south tunnel and approached the pumping station, hissing dry sibilants at each other as they carried on their argument. They held long bloody scythes in their bony hands, which they occasionally brandished at one another. Apparently goblin gardening was a gory business.

Jack waited until the pair was almost upon them and then he flattened Io against the wall and plastered his mouth against hers. Magic raced over her tongue and down inside where it exploded through every cell of her body. A spell screamed through her nerves, making them wail in shock at the violent intrusion. It was like being spun in a giant centrifuge. At the moment when she thought she might cry out, the invisibility spell completed its circuit, covering up the sight, smell and—most importantly—noise of both of them.

The goblins passed so close that Io could feel the displaced air move around their gore-covered bodies.

Jack held her up against the wall, mouth to mouth and their bodies mated to the knees, until the goblins had left the cave. Only then did he gradually pull his magic back and set her body away from his.

Though he was gentle about the extraction, it took a moment for the world to right itself.

"Are you okay?"

"Never better," Io lied, her voice rough.

"Swell."

She braced her hands against the wall and ordered her knees to stop buckling.

"Did you catch any of that tiff?" Jack asked, turning away from her. His voice was calm, but Io felt what their proximity had done to his body. He was not as unaffected as he sounded.

"No." Io's voice was nowhere near as calm as Jack's. She still sounded husky enough to be a torch singer, and her breath tended to catch mid-sentence. "What were they complaining about?"

"There is some other, more important garden back the way they came. One was feeling crabby because none of the fruit was for them. It all goes to Neveling Lutin for 'the project.' The other one wanted to steal some, but his buddy was afraid to try it because Lutin's gargoyles ate the last poacher—feet first."

"An important gardening project for Neveling Lutin, *and* gargoyles too," Io mused, straightening her spine. "That would seem to have our names written on it. I guess we'd better go see it the very first thing."

"Yes, damn it, we do need to see it," Jack agreed. "But we had better make it quick. We've also got to get into Neveling's hole tonight and see what he's up to. His damned aerosols are being used all over town and we still don't know what's in them!"

Io nodded. "And I think it is high time that someone got a look at Horroban. That creature is more mysterious than Moriarty." She couldn't stop a shiver at the goblin warlord's name. "Neveling is just a pawn. We need to find the mastermind."

"Right, that's on the to-do list, too," Jack agreed. He blotted his brow. "These fields are damned hot."

"So, let's get this over with and then go have a beer," Io said, credibly faking heroic bravado.

"Yeah. A beer would be good." Feys didn't usually drink beer, since alcohol interfered with their magic, but both Io and Jack's human side found the idea appealing.

Jack set off at a fast pace, and Io forced herself to keep up. Her nerves were sniveling softly about their close call with the goblins, and her body was screeching about again having Jack inside her but not *really* inside. At least not in the physical way that counted.

She told them both to shut up, but it didn't seem to help. She was still both terrified *and* aroused.

The passage seemed to go on forever, a glowing green tunnel that might lead all the way to Hell. Jack knew that with the constant gloom and white noise, a sort of sensory deprivation could start to set in. The brain, bored with nothing to look at or listen to, started inventing things to entertain itself. Small hallucinations could quickly turn into big bogeys. The problem was, of course, that sometimes the bogeys weren't figments of the imagination, so you couldn't just go on your way ignoring them.

He wanted to explain this to Io, so she would be prepared if her brain started freaking, but he also needed to keep his ears peeled for light-footed goblins. They might not have time to share the invisibility spell again, and he needed to be prepared to clobber anything that got close enough to endanger them. He didn't want to leave suspicious corpses lying about as calling cards, but he would if there were no other choice.

Io would probably resent his protectiveness. She would point out that she had his gun with her. But Jack was not certain that his little fey would actually use it. He had found his visit to her treetop house very instructive. The place was a lot like Io—open to the sky, full of life, and well-hidden from casual passersby. On her shelves, she had a number of books on animal first aid and herbal lore, and a collection of various bird and animal foods stored in glass canisters for refilling the feeders hanging in the tree.

And he'd already seen to what lengths her compassion for the junkies would lead her. This was a woman who respected life. Given that love of all things living, it was ridiculous to have her functioning as a soldier in a situation where she might have to kill. What the hell had Xanthe been thinking?

Well, both Io and he knew what Xanthe was thinking about—and it wasn't Io's welfare.

Of course, to be fair to Xanthe, the other thing that Io Cyphre had in abundance was stubbornness, and apparently a decade of revenge mapped out in her mind. Things like the murder of a parent needed some form of closure, Jack supposed. Chances were that if she knew of something afoot in Goblin Town, Io would have found some way to be here, no matter what Xanthe said.

No, the present situation was not a happy one, but Jack still saw that there was a potential silver lining. He was not usually big on philosophical consideration, but any moron could see that it would be helpful for his future to build a relationship founded on life-and-death sort of trust. He could build just such a relationship while helping Io take care of a lot of old personal business.

And Io was definitely warming up to him. She hadn't fought at all when he pulled the invisibility spell over both of them. She could have pulled the steel-fist spell out of him, and knocked him and both goblins into next week if she'd wanted, but she hadn't done anything except press herself against him as if she were trying to crawl inside his body.

It had been a hard invitation to decline. His body still wasn't happy at being told to get back to business, but it would just have to endure. Far more important was that his wary fey continue to have faith in him. And that they stay alive, of course.

148

"I think we've found 'the project,'" Jack said softly, shaking off his musings.

The tunnel opened up into another cave, this one hung with lamps to provide lighting other than the walls' luminescence. Plants were being grown in raised tubs in an obvious if unusual form of hydroponics.

Each plant was loaded with what appeared to be enormous fist-sized strawberries that looked deliciously succulent.

"You'd never know they were grown underground. *Except for their size*, they could pass for normal fruit," he murmured.

"Only more irresistible. They're like the apples the wicked queen fed Snow White: perfect, deadly, the perfect marriage of high tech and black magic."

"And they're all organically grown in eco-friendly ways. Nothing but the finest evil fruit for our every dining need. What would you pay for one of these beauties?"

They stepped closer. The sound of trickling fluid feeding the goblin-fruit plants' basins was too thick to be relaxing. Ears knew that they weren't listening to water rippling down a stream.

"Gotta love hydroponics. No pest-control problems," Jack commented, looking at the fruit plants' enormous leaves. "I bet some salt in the water would screw things up though."

"Or an imported dose of red stele infection—or spider mites." When Jack stared at her, Io added, "I like gardening. I have my own strawberry patch."

"How fast could either of those things kill off a plant?" he asked curiously. "Could we use them as subtle sabotage of this crop?"

Io looked at the huge foliage and the nearly ripe fruit around her, then shook her head.

"They're not fast enough."

"Okay, so much for subtlety." Jack took out his bandanna and plucked off two of the lower pieces of fruit. Again, each tiny stem drooled red sap. "We have samples. Enough with our goblins' farming endeavors. We need to go see the production end of things. They have to be *doing* something with all this fruit, and I am sure it isn't going to the Saturday farmers market. Damnation! We will never make it to Neveling's factory at this rate."

"Wait. Not the farmers market, but . . ." Io thought hard for a moment, obviously trying to fit a couple of odd facts together in her mind. Jack waited patiently. Her intuitions were usually sound, if oddly arrived at.

"Jack, they said these were for Neveling."

"Yes." He mopped his brow. "And speaking of him . . ."

"Wait. I need to think." She laid a hand on his arm, probably making sure she had his attention—as if he had stopped thinking of her for a moment since sharing the invisibility spell.

"We've been looking at three things and thinking they were mostly unrelated," she continued. "But maybe we don't have three problems. Maybe we have just one."

"What do you mean?"

"We've been worried about what Glashtin is pumping through The Madhouse's ventilation system, right? We have also been wondering what Neveling is up to in his factory with this new perfume he's making from goblin musk—or at least Ferris is wondering that."

"Don't forget Horroban."

Io shook her head. "I haven't. Our éminence gris is up to his ears in this stuff, one way or another. But to me he seems a sort of a side issue. In the long term he's important, but he's not something we have to deal with right now."

Jack shrugged. "Maybe, maybe not. But go on. What is the third thing?"

"The last thing we've seen and wondered about is the increase in goblin-fruit junkies—and how sick they are. I keep asking myself—Why would so many new people be eating the goblin's poisonous fruit when they are educated against it? People aren't that dumb. And if they did start using, intending it to only be recreational; when they first saw that they were really getting sick, surely they'd go for help— try rehab or something." She turned to Jack, her eyes wide and worried. "But they don't. You want to bet it's probably because this new super-fruit the goblins are growing is being delivered in innovative and experimental ways and people don't even *know* they are being addicted? I mean, the goblins would want to test it, right? See how it is most effectively delivered?"

"Maybe." Jack began to put it together on his own. "You think Glashtin is testing Lutin's new perfume in the ventilation system of his club. And the perfume is made not just from goblin musk and some man-made hallucinogenics, but from goblin fruit—this *super* goblin fruit—as well. And all at Horroban's instigation."

"Well, think about it. What if they could make a fruit so potent that you didn't need to ingest it to become addicted? All you had to do was get a few parts per million on the skin, or inhale it. Don't forget what Ferris said: Neveling's basic perfume is a perfect biological delivery agent. It has something to do with its molecules being small enough to pass through human skin."

Jack shook his head. "Nobody would want strawberry juice cologne, though—even from a regular cosmetic company."

"No, not because it's strawberry juice. But what *would* be oh so fashionably chic to wear is the first-ever goblin musk perfume."

"It would?"

"If the media told people so, often enough and loudly enough. 'Take a Walk on the Wild Side—L'Air de Lutin. Coming Soon.' And 'Bad Girls Do—Will You?' You've seen the ads, Jack. I have."

He nodded. The ads were everywhere, even on the sides of buses.

"Then, when all fashion magazines had hyped your product, and you had the masses clamoring for a whiff, what if you did a free mass-mailing of your *L'Air de Lutin* perfume all over the country? Or the world? I mean, money is no object if you have a powerful backer. Or a lot of them. . . . Look at whom the goblins have been replacing. It isn't priests and paupers."

Jack gave a low whistle. "When you go paranoid, you go all the way."

"Is it paranoia?" Io asked urgently. "Think what would happen; then tell me I'm wrong to be worried that practically every woman in the U.S. is about to become addicted to goblin fruit essence."

"What would happen is that you'd have a huge increase in the junkie population worldwide. Just like we've had here," he admitted, not liking her theory but seeing it had diabolical merit.

"With a one hundred percent guaranteed return business for your product."

"For three or four months, until your customers all died," Jack pointed out.

"Maybe not. Maybe the aerosol version isn't as deadly as the pure fruit. Maybe you just need more perfume at, say, five hundred dollars an ounce. It would be more expensive than opium or cocaine— or any drug that has ever been on the market. It would knock out every other perfume manufacturer, too. No one would go around wearing other scents. Lutin would have the market cornered. Do you know how much money we are talking about? The government types might be largely spared, being men, but they all have families—mothers, wives, daughters. Everyone would be affected in some—"

Jack shook his head. "I've been thinking about that, and we can't even assume they'd be initially missed because they're men. There could be secondary addiction through touch or breathing of perfume sprayed in the air. And anyone the goblins couldn't get with perfume could be addicted through sabotaging the ventilation systems where they worked."

Io swallowed. "They'd become goblin-perfume users too," she said aloud. "Everyone would become a customer."

"Now take it a step further," Jack said. "We can't count on this being about cornering the perfume market and making lots of money for some goblin consortium."

"Why?"

"Because of our friend Horroban's involvement. Look at the things he has already done. He is known for being secretive and wicked beyond all normal greedy goblin behavior. I mean, Horroban could be something more than just an ambitious, unethical capitalist with six limbs. Maybe he is a homicidal megalomaniac who would be quite happy to wipe every last human off the face of the earth."

Io began to shiver. "Why would he? He could have all the power and wealth he needs here by selling—"

Jack shook his head. "You've been listening to the propaganda from the goblin apologists. They'd have us believe that most goblins are harmless little farmers longing to return to the good old days of keeping human hearths clean and looking after our homes in exchange for a fair wage. But that is all just mythological nonsense. They never wanted to just be our housekeepers. Remember the reasons for the goblin purge back in the Twenties? Believe me, the goblins do. They are angry that they missed their chance to be on top, and have been waiting for another. With humans dead or enslaved, and most of the feys gone, there wouldn't be anything to stop them from finally ruling the world."

Jack and Io stared at one another across the beautiful, deadly fruit plants, feeling cold all the way to their bones in spite of the cavern's tropical heat.

"I believe you, Jack. I do. But no one else will ever consider it—not in time," Io said quietly. "They'll think we're nuts, or that I am so bent on revenge for what happened to my mother that I am making stuff up. And if Xanthe is really involved she'll contradict anything I say."

"The police will believe me," Jack said, "but there won't be much that they can do officially—not without something indisputable to force the governor's hand. The man in the capitol has his boot on everyone below him's necks because Horroban has promised to finance his reelection campaign. He won't piss in the goblins' soup bowl until the problem is so big it bites him on the ass."

Io stared hard at Jack. "We've got to find the proof. Somewhere. Something they can't ignore."

"Yes. I hear you." Jack looked into Io's eyes. Then he said quietly, "But it might not be a bad thing to have a back-up plan for taking out this Goblin Town hive. Just in case we *can't* get the evidence pulled together in time."

Io's eyes got big and began to glow with alarm. She opened her mouth and then shut it again. For a moment, Jack wondered if he had lost her law-abiding heart.

"Take out Goblin Town? The whole underground? By ourselves?" After a moment she swallowed hard and then said, "Well, it never hurts to have a back-up plan."

Jack exhaled slowly. He hadn't misjudged her. Her love of life was coming down on the side of humans, and she could understand the need to destroy this place. "Glad you feel that way."

"You bring the marshmallows. I'll bring the beer," Io said in an attempt at gaiety.

Jack laughed softly. *Goddess! He loved this little fey! What a team they made.* He said, "You bring the beer and marshmallows. I think I'll bring the kerosene and a supercharged fire spell. Or dynamite, if I can find it."

Io's tentative smile died. "I'm all out of dynamite and fire spells this week. I guess we had better go shopping."

"First thing tomorrow morning. Fortunately, I know someone at the dynamite store who can help us out. It sometimes pays to have low friends in high places. And I already have a fire spell."

"Jack, I've been thinking." Io rubbed her forehead. "Before we do anything *final* . . . we have to try to get Chloe out. I know she's a junkie, but she's young. It may be that she can be saved if she gets treatment."

Jack sighed inwardly. He should have known that Io's conscience would eventually rear its head.

"We won't do anything for a while yet," he assured her, evading the plea. He'd try to help the kid, of course, and anyone else trapped in the underground. But getting Chloe out might not be possible. They couldn't risk being discovered here before the goblin fields were destroyed. The stakes for the world were too high. Chloe might end up being a casualty of war.

Io knew this too. She could do the math—in fact, she had made the calculations ahead of him. She just wasn't ready to give up on the girl without a fight. And that worried Jack—in this situation, a tender heart was a liability, undermining a person's resolve.

"Hey, remember that this plan is for just in case our raging paranoia turns out to be correct. Okay?"

Jack asked. "We'll try everything else first."

Io looked at him, her expression as sober as any hanging judge's had ever been. "Okay, Jack. But I have a bad feeling about this."

"It's probably dinner."

"I don't think so."

Jack didn't think so, either. He had the same bad feeling, and it wasn't confined to his stomach.

"Time to go," Io whispered.

"Time to go," Jack agreed.

Chapter Fourteen

Once past the agricultural acreage, the hive became more urban in appearance and a lot less hot. There were more goblins about, too, but more places to hide from them. Io didn't need telling to stick close to Jack. The closer they got to Lutin's place, the more the reality of what they were dealing with filled her mind. She had too vivid an imagination, and her nerves demanded Jack's solid, confident company.

"Here," he whispered. "This is Neveling's place—notice the early Anthill Revival style."

Io nodded without smiling.

They slipped into the shadow of the uneven building and waited, listening intently for any sound that indicated goblins were working nearby. There was nothing to see, nothing to hear, but . . . Io reached up and, for the first time since entering the hive, she removed her nose breather.

She sniffed carefully. The lack of expected scent

was stunning. She couldn't smell anything even remotely goblinish coming from the open doorway of the building they were hiding behind. More startling, the odors that floated on the air belonged above the ground: wet earth, rotting timber, gasoline fumes, hot tires.

Jack, seeing her arrested expression, quickly removed his own breather. He and Io took one more breath together, tasting the foreign air, then reinserted their nose filters.

Neither spoke. Just because they didn't smell goblin didn't mean that there wasn't some modified goblin goon or giant troll waiting inside to douse them with poisoned perfume. Or just to bite their heads off.

The thought was instantly undermining. Io had a short, sharp internal struggle that pitted her will against her unhappy imagination. She could feel dread trying to invade her and make her weak. It whispered about the unseen things in the dark, slinking about, waiting to eat them, or to turn them into goblin slaves that would eventually feed the fruit fields.

It took an act of supreme will to deny the images of her mother's mangled body rising up from her imagination. The corpse had not been pretty once the goblin gangs were done with it.

"Time to go," Io whispered to herself, taking a step closer to the door and then stopping when she heard a soft, mechanical *tick, tick, tick*.

Alarmed, Io pulled out her gun and held it pointed upward and tight against her chest. Jack nodded approval, pointed to his own chest and then around the corner. Io nodded back, her overactive imagination quite happy to let him go first. She knew nothing about bombs.

After the horrors she imagined waiting for them inside the building, it was deflating to discover an ordinary garage with only a strange low-slung limo as occupant. It was the car's cooling engine that was ticking like a clock.

The limo was long, black, and had tinted bullet-proof windows. It had an immaculate finish that shone like polished glass. The car was somehow familiar, perhaps something Io had seen on TV and—without any logical reason—she loathed it on sight.

She and Jack did a quick scan of the garage for hostiles, but it was empty and featureless except for some sort of electrical box and two doors. One of those doors they had used as an entrance; the second was a side door leading into the misshapen building beyond.

Jack and Io walked softly toward the car, yet the floor beneath them still rang hollowly with every step. Puzzled, Io looked at Jack.

He shook his head and kept moving. They positioned themselves outside the limo's passenger door. Jack reached out a gloved hand and eased the latch up. There was no resistance, and the door opened silently.

He and Io took shelter on either side of the car door, again listening for sounds of occupation, but other than the slow ticking of the cooling engine, all was silent.

Jack finally leaned over and looked inside. When he didn't pull back, Io joined him in the wide opening. They were both careful not to touch anything with bare skin—the goblins had a keen sense of smell when it came to human flesh and would know if the car had been invaded.

The leather seats made Io's own skin crawl. She was certain that the leather was made from human beings. There was also plush carpeting that looked suspiciously like woven human hair—dyed a uniform black—a CD player, a cabinet for liquor or whatever else the limo's owner might be drinking, and seating for ten. It was almost a standard limo in appearance, except for the guns, neatly racked in the ceiling and between the seats. Handguns, machine guns, guns sawed off and silenced—and most likely missing their serial numbers.

Io felt cold, but she didn't know if it was the cooler temperature in the garage or if her nerves had taken a permanent chill.

"It's good to be a little afraid," Jack said softly, guessing her mood. He turned his head to look her in the eyes. "It gives the body adrenaline and gets the muscles ready to work."

Io nodded. *Fight or flight*—fear would facilitate either. She knew that was true, but still didn't like

162

the feeling. She had never been one to terrify herself with scary movies just for the fun of it. Terror was a relatively new experience for her.

"You know what these seats are made of?" she asked.

"Yeah. They really make full use of those junkies," Jack joked.

Io looked back at the car, willing herself not to vomit. The interior, the guns—it all was a signal she could not ignore: *Beware*.

"Why a limo?" she asked suddenly, the question popping out of her subconscious. She seized on the distraction gratefully. "There aren't any roads down here."

Jack pointed up. "It's for above. This room is an elevator, an industrial one. I think I know where we are now. This is under the old GM plant."

Io blinked, picturing the layout of the old auto factory.

"Okay. But why a limo?" she asked again. "A motorcycle would work better here in the tunnels, and it would be way more in keeping with goblin machismo."

Jack shrugged, then said, "My best guess? It's for Horroban, so he won't be seen on the outside when he leaves. You may have noticed that our industrialist goblin is media shy. Perhaps he's really, really ugly."

"H-he's *here?*" The small hairs at the back of Io's nape began to creep. The feeling she'd been having of ants crawling over her skin intensified.

Jack nodded. "Probably visiting Neveling, checking up on his investments."

"So . . . we might be able to get them both, if we go in now." It took an effort to say the words, to suggest that they actually confront the monster. Io had never been less prepared for a face-to-face challenge in her life. "W-we could kill them here—before they can do any more harm."

"We could. Maybe. But there will be bodyguards everywhere. If we shoot Lutin and Horroban, we'll have the entire goblin nation after us. And anyway, we don't necessarily need to *kill* them—wiping out their crop will stop them, and it gives us time to bring in the authorities. Then we can do things by the book."

Io was suddenly suspicious. So much reason and advocacy toward law and order didn't go with Jack's reputation.

"I don't think Chloe will be with him," Jack added. "If we want to get her out, then we need to wait."

Io chewed her lower lip. Everything Jack was saying was true, but she had the feeling that he was only saying it because she was with him and he didn't want her involved in anything dangerous. The thought both pleased and aggravated her.

"It isn't that I want to die. But, Jack . . . if we have the chance tonight—"

He cut her off. "I thought we came to gather information. We don't even *know* that Horroban is here. Maybe he sends this car down for detailing once a week. Hell, we don't even know for sure that we are right about the goblin perfume. Remember Little Big Horn and the Alamo? Both bad judgments. Let's not go cowboy before we have to." He winked at her.

Io slumped. "You're right. I'm jumping the gun. My nerves are screaming at me to do something quick so we can get out of here, and I'm making mistakes," she admitted.

He grinned. "I don't blame them. Very sensible things, those nerves. So, we're going to take a page from their book and be sensible too. He who snoops and runs away, lives to snoop another day." He waved a hand at the car. "We'll look a little more and then we'll come up with a plan. But right now, I'm thinking that it will be easier to destroy the crops than Horroban."

Io straightened. "And once again we are running out of time. We've got to be out of here before the goblins come home."

"And we need incendiary supplies if we are going to blow anything up."

"Jack?" Io girded herself to ask a question. "These aren't nerves talking now, okay? I want to know if you're sorry I'm here."

"Of course I'm sorry you're here. I'm sorry that *I'm* here."

"That isn't what I mean," she said, exasperated.

165

"Are you sorry we met? Sorry we ended up partnered for this mission? Sorry—"

"Sometimes you say the dumbest things," he answered. "And this is no time to start acting like a girl. I know you're freaked, but shake it off!"

"I am not acting like a girl!" she snapped. Aggravation pushed her fear away; something she suspected was supposed to happen, as Jack had likely calculated his answer's effect. Grateful for his bracing treatment, she nevertheless decided to see the conversation through. She added reasonably, "I am not the best person to have along in terms of training or natural abilities. A lot of the feys have great magical powers—I've only got blue eyes."

And a real taste for fey sex. But she pushed that thought away.

"Blue eyes that can see in anything except pitch black. And you have immunity to most illness—a real plus here in Goblin Town—as well as the capacity to heal from wounds that would incapacitate a regular human." Jack added the last bit impatiently as he closed the limo door. "Besides, you are willing and available. I like that in a woman. Now quit trying to pick a fight with me and look for goblins."

Io ignored the exasperation that welled up in her at both observations, reminding herself that Jack wasn't necessarily indulging in double entendre. It could—just possibly—seem to him that she was trying to force an argument.

"You could use Zayn," she went on doggedly. "He's good with magic."

"I don't care if he's memorized Merlin's grimoire and has the Amazing Kreskin's cheat book. Zayn can't think for himself. I'd have to be on him every minute telling him when to wipe his . . . uh, *nose*." Jack straightened to his full height. "Now, are we done? We can have the relationship talk later—like after we have a relationship."

"Goddess, you are arrogant! Who says there's going to *be* a relationship?"

"I do. And it's all part of the service." Jack smiled. He touched her chin with his finger. "You know, you are *so* cute when you're angr—"

"Don't say it! I really, really hate it when men say that!" Io could tell that her eyes were beginning to glow.

"If you get to act like a girl, then I should get to act like a guy. And would you mind turning down the high beams? It's like being around Rudolph the red-nosed reindeer."

Io fumed, but she considered the validity of his argument. It took her a minute to drain the magical buildup from her eyes.

"Okay. I'm not saying that I'm acting like a girl," she warned. "But we can talk about this later."

"Or not. It's just your nerves making you try to pick a fight and let off some steam. You'll get used to the adrenaline flood with time," he reassured her. "It's

167

like your goblin allergies. You'll build a tolerance with exposure."

"I will?"

"Guaranteed. So . . . time to go?" Jack asked.

"Time to go," Io agreed. She exhaled, turning loose her annoyance completely so that she could pay complete attention to what lay ahead. It would be stupid to die down here because she was miffed at Jack.

"So, what do you think? The door? Or do we elevate up and out of here?" Jack asked, watching her, waiting for her to make a decision.

He was probably worried that her nerves were fraying faster than he could fix them, and offering her a dignified out. A part of her very much wanted to take the suggestion they depart, but she ignored the impulse. Their little spat *had* turned down the voice of dread until it was just more unpleasant background noise.

"The elevator is probably too noisy. Though it would be fun to piss Horroban off by joyriding in his limo," she added, then jerked her head at the other door. "Your ears are better than mine. Give it a listen. Make sure there aren't any gargoyles on the other side, slobbering with anticipation of their next meal."

"I'm willing to bet that the gargoyles are locked up. It wouldn't do to have them accidentally nipping the meal ticket while he's in town."

"Yeah, but who's to say they aren't locked up behind that door?"

"Good point. I'll go listen."

"Okay." Io looked at the limo again, something about it still bothering her. "Jack, have you ever seen a car like this?"

"Sure, just not in Goblin Town. You usually see this kind of armoring and bulletproof glass in Washington, DC, where the politicos go in fear for their overpaid hides."

"I wonder where Horroban got the thing. And who from."

"Where and who, I don't know. But the *why* is obvious enough."

"Sure, he knows we're on his trail and is quaking in all three pairs of custom-made boots," Io joked.

"He's a lowlife for sure, but I doubt he goes about on his belly." Jack chuckled at the idea, and then fell quiet as he laid his ear against the door.

Io stayed quiet too, listening for sounds of approach from the other doorway.

After a moment Jack tried the knob. It was locked, but not for long. He extracted a thick bent wire from his pocket and set to work on the lock.

"Bingo." He turned around to grin at her. His smile was nothing like the Mona Lisa Giaconda's. It involved teeth and a wicked twinkle in his eyes, and it did vandalism to Io's female heart and pulse points.

"I thought you had a spell for that sort of thing."

"I do. I just like to keep in practice."

"Men! They always do it the hard way."

"Of course. It doesn't work if it isn't hard."

Io didn't reprimand him. She'd walked into that one.

Chapter Fifteen

Io found that trips into the Labyrinth involved two types of conflicting time: emotional, which said she had been stuck on the wrong side of this earthly divide for long enough; and logistical, which showed with every glance at her watch that the opposite was true. Time fled at an indecent rate, and she and Jack weren't moving fast enough. Her nerves, strained by perpetual watchfulness, simply wanted it to all be over.

Jack had to jimmy another lock on a metal fire door before they were in the building proper. He did it as efficiently as he did everything, but every second's delay seemed a wasted eternity.

The building they entered was human built; the room perhaps a basement, but quite ugly anyway. It was uniformly unpainted concrete, long expanses of gray wall and ceiling broken only by florescent lighting fixtures, a few doors, and clusters of insulated pipes that punched through from above. The hall looked a bit like that of a prison, but there were no cells or barred doors, only wooden ones.

They paused at the first door, Jack laying an ear against it. After a moment he tried the handle, and finding it open, they stepped inside. There was no furniture, but the right wall had a window cut in it, which was paned with strange thick dark glass. On the other side of the translucent barrier was a conference room where a bizarre sort of board meeting was in progress.

"It's a two-way mirror," Jack said softly. "They shouldn't be able to see or hear us—but don't get too close anyway."

Io nodded, barely able to speak because of the spooky feeling filling her throat with new alarm. She took one more step toward the glass and then stopped.

"Is that Horroban?"

"I think so." They both stared hard. They couldn't see the goblin's face or body, but the back of his head looked chillingly familiar—so familiar and chilling that Io barely noticed the CEO of the New York Stock Exchange sitting across from him.

Of course, there were other reasons besides Horroban's presence not to notice the small man in his business suit and power tie. There was lots of muscle cluttering up the room, both human and troll, and all quite large enough to be in the WWF or linebacking for the NFL. To have described them as "armed and dangerous" would have been an ironic warning, for their bulging, hairy arms were hazards in and of themselves.

The part of Io's brain that clung desperately to everyday details in the hope of denying where she was, thought it was a shame that the custom-made suits fit so poorly over their guns. That they were custom made she couldn't doubt. Suits that big didn't come off-the-rack even at the Big and Tall stores. The creatures in them were almost certainly genetically customized as well.

She and Jack couldn't hear the conversation in the other room, but they felt the vibration when a modified goblin in a lab coat was thrown against the door hard enough to crack its mirror-window in two places.

"Wanna bet Xanthe just lost her mole?" Jack asked.

"Sucker bet," Io responded. Her words were flip, but she felt bad for the goblin who had tried to help H.U.G.

There was more confirmation of the reality of what Io was seeing when two trolls pulled away from the wall where they slouched and opened up on the hapless snitch with AK-47s, proving that they were thorough—if not necessarily crack—shots.

Io and Jack both fell to the floor and covered their heads, waiting for the shattered glass to tumble out of its frame and splatter them. It didn't happen, but only because it was enforced with some kind of wire mesh.

The benefit of the goblin's death and their own subsequent close call with the door glass was demonstrated a moment later when someone spoke in the other room and they could finally hear the conversation.

"Neveling," hissed a soft voice. "Fetch your pets. We have to get rid of this traitor's body—they may as well have a snack. Don't look so glum," the voice added, apparently now addressing the trolls. "This one has had some unusual gene therapy. He wouldn't taste good—especially not filled with lead."

Gargoyles. Time to go. Io turned her head and mouthed the words at Jack.

He shook his head. *Wait. The gargoyles could come from any direction.*

Io reminded herself that the best way not to become a target was to avoid acting like one. So running away screaming at the top of her lungs was not an option—however much her muscles wanted to flee. But, oh, she wanted to do just that!

She stared hard at Jack, trying to draw strength from his example. Jack was a genuine hard case with nerves of steel. She needed to start acting like one or her fears would be justified and she would get them both killed.

Once again, her nerve clock shifted over to timing eternity. She waited with eyes closed, counting breaths, not thinking of anything but lying completely still until she could hear the gargoyles bounding into the boardroom on their stony claws. There was a horrible woofing noise and then the trolls started to cheer. They began wagering about how long it would take the gargoyles to eat the goblin corpse.

Jack leaned over her, touching her face. *Share the spell,* he mouthed.

Io nodded and raised her head to meet his lips. Jack wasn't brutal, but he wasted no time shoving the magic through the circuit. Io quickly wrapped her legs about his waist and helped Jack roll to his knees and then onto his feet. She had a moment of hysteria where she worried about blocking his view as he carried her and raced for the door, but then recalled that she was invisible.

And Jack was too. She could see through his head and clear to the fractured glass when one of the gargoyles raised itself and, with a bloodied snout, pressed itself against the window, and began snuffling at the bullet holes. A long forked tongue lolled out and tried to wiggle through the glass. Its useless wings began to beat excitedly.

"What is that witless beast doing? Licking blood off of the glass?" the head of the NYSE asked, and a dozen heads turned to look at the door.

"Jack!"

"I know!"

He was running back the way they had come. He

had the door open and they were through. Io
shoved it shut behind them. They were moving
down the hall as fast as Jack could move, but they
both knew it wouldn't be fast enough if the gargoyles came after them.

Behind them, they heard the damaged window
finally shatter, and then ripping noises as the gargoyle tore into the wood of the door. A moment later
a second set of claws joined in the destruction and
a terrible ear-shredding howl filled the air.

Jack broke his connection with Io as they reached
the door that led back to the garage. He pushed the
invisibility spell into Io and then shoved her through
the metal fire door. He slammed it shut, using his
fire spell to melt the lock. A moment later two giant
bodies hit the panel and started clawing.

Stone claws. Metal door. Io had a bad feeling that
she knew which was stronger.

"Time to go—and I mean it!"

"Amen! Amen!" Jack answered, grabbing her arm.

The elevator in the garage was tempting but probably too slow. Taking it would also prove beyond
any doubt that someone had been spying down
here in the hive. They had to make an effort to cover
their tracks.

Instead, they bolted for the maze of caves and
prayed for a nearby manhole. Jack took the lead,
the steel fist spell ready to flatten anything that got
in their way.

* * *

He slowed their pace as they neared the exit to Watson Street. They had been lucky so far. No worker goblins had been in the tunnels, and there was no sign of gargoyle pursuit. It was time to take a breather and get back above ground. They were under a deserted part of Brush Park, and it was a good place to make an exit unseen.

"Slow down, honey. We're okay."

Io gratefully dropped to a walk and wiped the perspiration from her forehead.

"This is like jogging in a sauna."

"Only less healthy," Jack agreed. Then he felt himself laugh softly.

"What?" Io stared at him as if he had grown a second head.

"We're alive," he explained. "Don't look now, but we just beat some really big odds. We are now members of that great mathematical fluke club, *the lucky*."

"Oh. Yes, I guess we are. Alive." Io didn't laugh, but she managed a smile. "I didn't know if our Laurel and Hardy style of jogging was going to work. I know we were flying, but it didn't seem nearly fast enough with those things on our tail."

"It did work though. You've got strong legs, little fey."

"I wasn't about to fall off you."

Jack stopped and looked up the iron ladder to the manhole cover. There were a few minutes before daybreak.

"You know, I wondered whether being chased by gargoyles would make the spell-sharing less erotic."

"Did it?" Io asked, not meeting his eyes.

"Hell, no. It just kept me from thinking real hard about lewd things. For a while."

Io finally laughed, but the sound was an exhausted one.

"Without a doubt, this has been the longest night of my life," she said.

"Time to go?" he asked.

"And then some."

Chapter Sixteen

The weather had worsened while they were underground, and laid down a layer of slush on the street and buildings. Already the melting snow was stained and showing the wear and tear of the tourists' feet in several patches of shady, unappealing gray in the hazy, unhealthy light of predawn.

"It isn't exactly Currier and Ives material, is it?" Jack asked, sliding the manhole cover back into place.

"And snow? In October? It isn't even Halloween. We have two days to go yet." Io looked about tiredly as she put on her sunglasses. Their night in the underground had been exhausting.

"Well, it's all tricks and few treats here in Goblin Town, even when it's not Halloween." Jack also slipped on his shades, covering his telltale eyes. They didn't glow like Io's, but they were odd enough to draw attention once the sun was up.

"Do you think Glashtin had a temper tantrum? If he really blew his top it could have caused a storm."

"Could be." Jack sounded distracted as he answered. "We'll find out in the morning."

"It is morning. Almost."

"If it only snowed in here, then we'll know for sure that's what happened. Let's go, honey. Time for adventurers to be in bed."

"I wonder what set him off," Io wondered. She began pushing through the slush, wincing as the cold water seeped into her sneakers.

Jack shrugged. "Or who. I'd like to know if someone has been getting in his way and somehow thwarting plans. This may be a case of the enemy of our enemy being our friend."

"Or not. This is Goblin Town, and the natives like to s-s-squabble. Or maybe Horroban t-told him about the wrecked m-m-meeting." Io's teeth began to chatter. "Damn! It's really cold."

"Doubt the meeting was 'wrecked' for anyone except the goblin who got turned into Swiss cheese. And if it *was* anything important, we'll hear about it tonight. In the meantime, try and forget about it. Come here. You look like a popsicle."

"You say the most unromantic things," she complained. But she moved closer.

Jack dropped an arm around her shoulder and pulled her tight. His body held the worst of the chill at bay. Io didn't mind the tingle of magic on her skin anymore. She was getting used to it.

180

"Humor me, honey. I had a bad scare."

"Yeah."

"You are shaping up as a great partner, though. Damn! And to think I nearly drove you off."

Io snorted. "It's the harsh-but-effective form of on-the-job training. Wimps would never make it past their first date with you."

They moved into the edges of Brush Park. The neighborhood was deserted. There was little reason for people to go there; it was mainly all rubble now, dominated by the few remaining ruined mansions of Little Paris. It was much more a place for gargoyles to haunt than an industrial underground.

"You know, it may be rushing things, but I can't help but think that Halloween might be the perfect night for us to stage a raid." Jack's voice was again thoughtful.

"Because of all the parties?"

"Yep. We wouldn't be able to do anything about the goblins up top because of the people, but the streams of masked tourists would give us somewhere to hide until we could get out of Dodge."

"They'll be after us, won't they?" Io said quietly.

"Like the original Nemesis," Jack agreed. He added, only half-kidding, "We may have to take a long vacation in some sunny southern clime if things go badly. Or even if they go really well."

"Then we have a lot of preparations to make."

Jack looked down at her, his expression as serious as Io had ever seen it. He finally said, "I'll have to take some time for a trip outside the city. I've got to drop these strawberries at the lab and tell a buddy of mine what we think is going on."

In case we don't make it out alive. He didn't say it, but Io realized what he really meant.

"You have a buddy?" Io asked, momentarily diverted.

"Yes, I have one or two. If we don't end up with a goblin bounty on our heads, I'll introduce you."

"Okay." It made no sense, but Io began to feel more cheerful. Jack having friends made him seem more normal.

"Anyhow, I'm always ready to travel, so this isn't a problem for me. But can you be packed and ready to leave by Halloween night?" he asked. "Just in case we have to go straightaway."

"I'll have to be," Io answered, feeling a pang for leaving her tree house and her animal companions. This was her first home that had actually ever felt like one; it was the first place she had even felt inclined to put down roots.

Jack frowned at her answer. "Look, little fey, I'm sorry—"

"It's okay, Jack." She reached up and squeezed his hand and then leaned her cheek against it. "I learned early that nothing in this world is free, especially not if it involves goblins. These creatures have taken away everything I ever held dear. I'm willing to pay almost any price to stop this son of a bitch."

182

"Let's hope we can put it on the installment plan. This probably isn't a bill we want to pay all at once," Jack joked.

"I think I'd rather pay at once than go on paying forever. That's why we have to stop him. The interest on this mess just keeps compounding. And I don't know about you, but I don't want to live in a world run by goblins. Anything compared to that is cheap."

"Having a goblin king wouldn't be my first choice of governmental systems, either. We'll just have to make sure it doesn't happen."

Jack walked with his arm around Io and pondered the mystery of where all the lovely—but entirely superficial—sexual draw had gone. When had his plans switched over from getting laid to taking on a new partner? Here he was, never actually having had sex with Io, and their magical chemistry absolutely demanding they do it, but she still felt more like a best friend and longtime lover rolled into one small but powerful bundle—

Maybe it came from actually sleeping together at night. Or sharing magic. That was a large step up from sharing a toothbrush.

Not that he didn't want to have sex with her—he did. Goddess, yes! And badly enough that he was considering foregoing the matter of the ritual where she asked to be his lover. Did they really need those words? If she didn't actually say 'no,' wasn't that as good as 'yes'?

Who was he kidding? They needed the ritual for safety. He had to get her to say the magic words.

Well, if they didn't make love before sundown today, it wouldn't be from lack of trying on his part. Yes, their schedule was full—what with trying to rescue a kid junkie, escape man-eating gargoyles, and foil a plot for world domination—but a man had to have priorities.

"Jack? You are looking awfully serious."

"Was I? I can't imagine what for."

Io giggled. He looked down at her, amused, never having heard the sound before.

"Come on! What's on your tiny little mind?"

"Truthfully?" he asked, surprising himself. "I was thinking about us—how we've become rather instantly intimate. No dates, no sex, but it's like we're married or something. We may have to go into business."

Io nodded, also serious. "Being in each other's minds is a little like walking around in front of each other without any of the usual emotional clothing, isn't it? And I'm not sure if I like being a nudist on such short acquaintance."

"I am fairly sure that *I* like your being a nudist," Jack joked. "Or will once I have the opportunity to take a long look. Of course, I'd be willing to trade stripteases—real clothes for emotional ones—if it would make you feel better."

184

Io didn't giggle this time. Her arms were wrapped about her waist as she hugged herself either against the cold or his words. Her face was both wistful and a little frightened as she looked up. Snow was beginning to fall again, flat gray flakes that looked like a plague of dying moths fluttering in death spirals as they crashed to the ground. They caught in her hair and on her cheeks, hiding the flush of her skin.

"Is this the time for the relationship talk?" she asked, turning her gaze away, her eyes once again scanning the doorways and windows for lurking figures.

She stared at one sign for a long moment, causing Jack to also look up and see what had her attention:

FUSS & PHILPOTT
ATTORNEYS-AT-LAW

Jack snorted and then answered her question.

"Hell, no. This is the time for a sex talk. And it can be kept short and sweet."

Io nodded once. "And all I have to say are the . . . um, ten? Ten magic words?"

"Yeah, ten." *Eat my heart. Drink my soul. Love me to death.*

Jack had to admit that they sounded rather ominous. In her shoes, he wouldn't be enthusiastic about saying them.

"However, I've been thinking about that," he

amended. "I think perhaps we could get by with two words—if they're the right two. And my name. I'd like to hear you say my name."

Eat me. Drink me. Love me, Jack. Yes, any of those would do.

"The words wouldn't be 'me, me, me,' would they?" Io asked.

"No. Not unless this is just about riding the adrenaline rush." Jack looked down into her sunglasses, wishing he could see her eyes. "If this is about lust, then 'Oh, God' will do just fine."

"Hmph! I like 'me, me, me,' but I didn't think it would be that easy."

"Nothing worthwhile ever is."

"The timing of this sucks," she told him. "I don't want a lover right now. Frankly, I didn't want a fey lover *ever*."

"The timing sucks," he agreed. "Unfortunately it may be the only time we have."

"I know. And I'm definitely thinking about that." Io slid an arm about his waist, sinking into his body and letting down her barriers so the feelings he was trying to elicit could come. "I'm thinking hard, Jack. And I don't believe this is just adrenaline."

"Neither do I."

Io paused. "But we can't really know, can we? I've never been in a situation like this before—getting almost killed every night, sharing magic several times a day. What I feel could just be some hormonal, magical, specie-survival thing."

Jack wanted to disavow the idea, but answered honestly, "No, we can't *know*. Not yet, anyway. But I can tell you sincerely that almost being eaten by a gargoyle doesn't usually turn my crank."

"But how about sharing the hocus-pocus? *Mmmm.*" She sighed as his magic lapped at her in a warm gentle wave. Jack was very careful not to let anything get too strong. It was time to be mellow.

He rested a cheek on the top of her head. Her hair smelled like verbena and was as soft as any silk ever spun, if a little cold and clammy.

"I like the way you think, little fey. At least, most of the time. But maybe you could stop thinking now. We've had plenty of insights for one night."

She chuckled and remarked, "You're really good with the juju, Jack. I don't even feel my wet feet now."

"Some women see stars, some get warm feet," he said lightly, stopping to look up at the parapets of his building. No gargoyles were glaring down at them, at least no living ones.

They climbed the stoop to Jack's appropriated manor and he fiddled the lock with a short spell, letting them in. He carefully warded the door behind them once they were through—it wasn't a night for taking any more chances with the outside world.

Chances with each other were another matter. Those he was up for. Eager for them, actually.

Though the building felt empty, Jack and Io went

quickly and silently up to his room, and didn't speak until the lamp was lit and the flame turned high. Dawnlight was stealing in the windows, but it was cold and comfortless. Io didn't like fire, but this felt right since it came from Jack's power.

"What are you thinking now, little fey?" Jack asked quietly. "Reached any decisions about adrenaline and magic words?"

"What am I thinking?" She laughed without much humor, then quoted:

'DO NOT STORE UP FOR YOURSELVES TREASURES ON EARTH, WHERE MOTH AND RUST DESTROY, AND WHERE THIEVES BREAK IN AND STEAL. BUT STORE UP FOR YOURSELVES TREASURES IN HEAVEN, WHERE MOTH AND RUST DO NOT DESTROY, AND WHERE THIEVES DO NOT BREAK IN AND STEAL. FOR WHERE YOUR TREASURE IS, THERE YOUR HEART WILL ALSO BE.'

"Matthew Six: nineteen to twenty-one." Jack nodded, smiling a bit at her surprised look. "Hey, it's not my religion, but I respect strong magic wherever I find it."

He pulled off his sunglasses and then his sweater. Firelight played over his marred chest. "So, does that rather long Biblical passage mean the answer is *yes*?"

"I'm trying to find an argument against it," she said earnestly. "Because a week ago it would have been out of the question for us to be lovers. I don't do sex

188

with feys—ever! But knowing that we almost died tonight—that we might very well be dead two nights from now—has sort of put things in a different perspective. So . . . yes."

She took off her sunglasses and let her eyes fill with emotion. "Yes, it means *yes. Love me, Jack.*"

"Little fey, I thought you'd never ask."

Jack reached for her, this time holding nothing back. But he didn't force anything either. Magic flowed, connecting them, and soon grew luminous. Between them, they created a different kind of enchantment—not one of fire, not water, not air, not earth. It felt familiar, like something he should know but—

Love.

No, that was ridiculous. It couldn't be. Death feys did not love. *Love me, Jack*, was only a ritual phrase of consent that would keep the encounter from being one-sided. It would keep it from being a rape when the moment came for their hearts to join and her life would be placed in his hands.

So it was just adrenaline?

No! Damn it—it wasn't that either. He didn't have a label for it and didn't want one. Whatever the source of this magical fascination, it was the start of *something* magnificent. Analyzing it would just kill the joy. It was like he had told Io: It was time to stop thinking.

Jack's voice had gone low and delicious and deep. His power reached for her, calling to the magic that was inside her softer, small body. It was magic built into her blood, flesh, and bones—and it answered. The fascination he conjured with his voice was something rich that Io wanted to wade into, to pull over her entire body and roll in it like a cat in a bed of catnip.

She would have been angry as well as frightened if she thought he was using his stronger magic on her in some casual seduction, but she knew it was something much more for Jack too. For better or worse, the attraction between them was not something to be dismissed as careless itch-scratching.

Io shied away from using the word "love." To name a thing gave it power, and she did not want to empower this attraction lest it overwhelm her. It was way too soon to begin thinking this way. And way too dangerous.

"You're thinking," he growled.

"Not with this brain, I'm not." She sighed, finally letting go of reason and fear. She leaned into Jack, allowing him to take her weight.

"What do you say that we move this party into the shower?" Io blinked, so Jack explained, "As much as I want you, I don't want us stuck in nose breathers for the night because we reek too much of goblin to stand each other without them. I'm saying that I want to start things off right."

"Let's start clean and new," she agreed in a murmur. "Good idea."

"And let's hope it's the first of many beginnings."

Chapter Seventeen

Rebirth begins with baptism. Io didn't know why this thought occurred to her at such a moment. Perhaps because she had quoted from the Bible earlier and some of its images had wedged in her mind.

The shower was not the River Jordan, but if the water was less than warm and holy, she never noticed. There was too much fascination in seeing Jack without clothing. She had *seen* him before, but that had been only with the eyes of a wary stranger. She had not looked with the vision of a lover. A lover's eyes saw much, much more than just the surface skin that wrapped the true person.

His body was not flawless. It carried scars as reminders of past battles. But while marred, it was still beautiful. Those wise eyes, the heat of him, the clever hands! She watched in a sort of helpless fascination as they ran over her bemused flesh, undressing her and then smoothing away the salty traces of old fear.

More astonishing still was seeing her own arms raise and feeling the pads of her fingers trace the outline of Jack's body. The musculature looked like any man's but it felt wildly different. Beneath the skin and hard, flat muscles, Jack was a different beast—a creature not simply possessed of magic, but made of it.

Desire reasoned faster than prudence. It was dangerous folly, a potentially fatal recklessness, but Io wanted most urgently to know who and what Jack really was. In that instant, she might even have sold her soul if it was the only way she could have him.

He understood this and kissed her. *Ah! Such a kiss.* She fell into it, twining arms about him and then legs, locking them about his waist as she had earlier. She pushed back with her own magic, willing the desire to compound.

Jack's arm wrapped about her hips and another circled her back, protecting it from the cold of the tiles when he leaned against them. His hand fisted in her hair and he pinned her, stilling most of her maddened squirming. He lowered his head and nipped at her throat.

Io didn't want to be stilled. If she could have reached the wall in front of her she would have pounded on it with her fists. But as it was there was nothing but Jack's slick body within reach, and that was hardly a help in restoring calm. Pinned and helpless, she felt the excitement in her body with no place to go and nothing to do but race ever faster as it ran through her, driven by the ever increasing tempo of her heart. She moaned in frustration and ran ungentle nails down Jack's back.

"Temptation is good, but don't drive me to insanity just yet," he warned as he lifted his head from her throat. His eyes were deadly serious. "It isn't wise to push too hard too soon, little fey. We are both carrying a lot of spells, a lot of wild magic."

Shaken by his words, she stopped struggling and hung suspended and helpless. The magic rushed through her. As reason drove back the blindness of desire, she realized for the first time how very strong Jack was. She could unhook her legs and let go with her arms, but it would make no difference. She was pinned against the wall by a body and will far more powerful than her own.

And he could have made this happen at any time. She had never had any real control beyond what he had given her. Her eyes widened as she realized this, and met Jack's with her astonished observation plain to see.

Yes, now you understand.

And she did. She was helpless. What would be, would be—because Jack willed it.

Seeing the wariness that filled her mind when she understood her vulnerability, he made his kisses lighter, his touch more tender, assuring her with his body that his passions were strong but not violent. *Trust me now.*

She heard a voice cry out, and knew it was probably her own, but her ears were not familiar with the sound. It was a noise that was neither all passion nor all pain, but some strange mix of both.

He slid into her—a physical shock, as he had not been kidding about his body's dimensions—and then the real possession began.

Their hearts began to syncopate; she could feel it happening, her body adopting a rhythm that was not her own. It was all Jack's! He slowly moved through her, controlling her heart, the flow of her blood, perhaps her thoughts and her very soul—and in the next few moments he would decide if she lived or died. He would decide whether she knew the little death, or the big one.

Eat my heart, drink my soul, love me to death.

"How about a pretty big one?" he murmured, obviously hearing her thoughts and doing his best to see her past the fear. "Trust me, Io. We will live and enjoy this moment. You just have to trust."

He needn't have asked for permission. She gave it anyway, and the tightness in her chest suddenly eased.

"Love me, Jack."

And he did. Bodies pounded, hearts pounded, the rush of tangled magic and emotions scalding them with something immeasurably sweet yet dangerous. Io watched, eyes wide, as the passionate finale rushed at them. Jack's eyes were open, too, and shone with a sort of exaltation.

Magic lit the dawn in a blinding flash, and for a moment Jack and Io's hearts stopped beating as their released souls decided whether to flee with the departing ecstasy or return to their earthly bodies.

Chained by Jack's will and Io's dreams and ambitions, their spirits finally returned to their fleshly houses. Reason returned too. Jack and Io's entwined bodies slowly sorted out whose heart was whose and where the magic belonged.

Finally, Jack reached over and turned off the tap, the noise loud in the silent aftermath.

Feeling drained and weaker than at any time in her life, Io slumped against Jack, her face buried in the curve of his neck, again content to let his arm take her weight, for him to carry her to their bed.

"So," he asked quietly. "Was that big enough?"

Io didn't answer, but she knew he felt her lips curve as she smiled.

"We'll get to the 'eat me, drink me' part later. It doesn't do to rush these things."

"Be still my heart," she murmured in response. And this time she meant it.

They lay cuddled under the hammock's blanket, Jack content to watch Io sleep while he thought about what had occurred.

Io had been right to be wary of what was happening between them. Sex with magic was a dangerous thing—wonderful beyond anything of this world, but not to be taken lightly. He had somehow—stupidly—forgotten this since meeting Io.

Grainne, one of his first lovers, was gone now, as was so much of the world he had known as a child. But until today, her lessons had lingered strongly in his mind and kept him from committing most acts of supreme folly.

Jack didn't usually spend a lot of time looking back at his past mistakes, but decided that maybe this was the moment for a bit of sober review.

Much of his early life had been lonesome after he turned six. Before that, he had lived very much as any fey child in the United States. He'd gone to school with the other neighborhood children and then come home to the real schooling, where his parents taught him what he needed to know to control the potential magic that grew in him with each passing year, and that would one day—though they could not guess when—blossom into full power. Only when he passed through this *Oicheanta Si*—a faerie's magic night—would he know if he was of the Twyleth Teg like his half-fey mother, Ciaran, or whether he was his father's son and an Ankou death fey.

The matter had never worried him, though he knew his mother was concerned about which magic line he inherited. He had loved both parents, and with a child's faith in the rightness of the universe, he saw nothing to fear in either of their powers.

Then one particular sunny day, when he was outside playing goblins and dragons, his universe was abruptly overturned.

He had been creeping about with a burlap sack stuffed with a sling and rocks, and using extra stealth as he stalked through the bushes because he was planning to beat the evil imaginary goblins to the dragon's golden hoard and keep the prize for himself. While he stole through the shrubbery, searching for the hidden entrance to the magical lair, he was suddenly disturbed by a faint, painful mewling that he heard with more than his ears.

Diverted from his game by the pained voice, at the edge of the property he pushed through the thick hedge that he was never supposed to cross because of the dangerous road beyond. He emerged from the shrubs at the side of the busy avenue where he found his pet cat, Soot, lying in a bloodied ruin.

Horrified, he had dropped his sack and rushed to her on hands and knees, not feeling the gravel and glass that cut him as he crawled. The moment he touched her bloodied body, he realized that she was going to die, that she was passing out of life even as he held her.

Unable to accept this, he had unconsciously reached inside and found his true magic and tore it out where he could use it. Because he could not accept the loss of his beloved friend, he had kept her heart beating while he petted her and wept over her mangled body.

His father had appeared soon after. Though not usually demonstrative, the man had put his arms around his son and comforted him, even as he told Jack the hard thing he would have to do.

"She hurts, Jack. She wants to die. You have a great power—a gift that is almost godlike. But the problem is that though it seems divine, it is not. Ours is not the gift of healing. We can decide—quick death or slow, easy or hard—but we can't stop death when it comes. You only hurt her with this delay. If you love her, son, you must let go. You must stop her heart and let her soul free."

And because Jack did love Soot, and felt her suffering, he did what was kindest.

That was the last time he had wept, crying out a lifetime of tears as he followed his father's instructions and stopped the cat's laboring heart, feeling her tiny soul depart from her battered body.

That was also the last time he had ever loved unreservedly, deciding with his six-year-old heart and mind that he would never let himself be hurt that way again. Never, ever, was he going to be put in a position where he had to hold someone he loved and make the decision that it was the greater kindness to stop their heart.

His mother had offered other pets, but he had refused them. Soon his magic grew stronger than either of his parents had ever expected, and by his early teens he developed a frightening charisma that attracted the opposite sex. Soon, other half-feys were offering him their hearts and bodies. Though he took the latter, he never touched the former. Never. The subduing of his natural magic during relationships left him isolated, especially in the most intimate of moments, but he didn't care. He would not be responsible for taking another loved one's life.

Grainne, older than the others, had understood— but many others had not. Their willingness to love him in spite of his nature was a constant, unknowing trap. And since his desires had a habit of outwitting prudence, instead of settling into a normal existence, he had taken up a career that guaranteed that he would never have the option of wife and family. He kept his affairs with lovers short and superficial, and he stayed on the move so there was no chance of setting down any more roots.

Once his parents were gone, he ruthlessly cut off all ties to the people and places he had known before. And he'd never looked back—not until today.

So what had happened this time? Against all reason and better judgment, he had hooked up with a stubborn half-fey who was bent on personally seeing through a possibly suicidal mission where there truly were things to face that she would believe were worse than death.

His most terrible fear could take place again. He

could end up holding Io in his arms and, out of kindness, stopping her heart.

Jack looked down at Io and the soft pulse fluttering in her delicate throat. She was so soft, so breakable!

And so stubborn.

He shook his head.

"Damn. *Damn, damn, damn.*"

This wasn't supposed to happen.

Chapter Eighteen

Io awoke, noticed the slow rhythm of her lover's breathing, and curled happily into the warmth of Jack's body. For years she had lacked this basic pleasure: cuddling with someone in the morning— *or afternoon,* she amended, looking with one eye at the sun's high position.

Time was short for them, and there were a lot of practical things that needed doing before Halloween. But there were other things just as important, though less sensible, that should be seen to as well. And right now she had the energy to do all that she hadn't managed earlier, beginning with a leisurely hands-on inspection of Jack's body.

There were scars on the skin that sheathed those lean muscles. She had seen them with her eyes, but now she let her fingertips examine them one by one—the puckered indentation of a bullet's graze, a close call with an iron knife, some sort of a magical burn that left the skin smooth and hairless and snowy white, and of course Jeerith's ill-fated bit of embroidery. In time Jack's body would heal these marks completely, but for now they were sobering reminders of the dangerous life he led.

"You have a soft touch for some rough terrain," he said softly. "I don't know about your choice of real estate to invest in though. Surely there is something more attractive that would interest you."

"I was being nosy about your scars," she confessed, burying her face in his neck. He smelled like Jack and it made her smile.

"I've always believed that curiosity is a good thing. Please, don't let me stifle you." He sank his fingers into her hair and tugged gently.

Io looked up. Jack's face was as close as it could be without kissing, but she could still read nothing in his eyes. It was frustrating that he could remain so blankly enigmatic when she was certain that everything she felt was written plainly on her face. She wondered if this emptiness of expression was some trick of the lighting, or if he was deliberately shielding his thoughts from her. And if so, why? What could he be thinking that required such reserve?

She looked him over carefully, assessing his other features. He had a square chin and a jawline that could only be described as firm. His lips were thin, but sensual. And stubborn. His body was at ease but not boneless with relaxation. Jack was still on guard.

202

He looked hard and reckless and ruthless, ready to take on the world or any part of it that got in his way.

He *didn't* look like a man on the verge of falling in love, or experiencing any other soft emotions. It was fairly safe to say that he didn't have flowers and valentines on his mind.

She wanted him anyway. Without promises or softer passions, she wanted to curl up against the warmth of the fire that burned in him and lose herself in the ardor that lived there. And she had a bad feeling that this new want would be with her forevermore.

The thought caused a moment of despair. Was she lost after only one night? Could a fall from grace happen that fast?

"I always know when you're thinking, but I'm damned if I know *what*. What do I see in your eyes? Desire? Despair? What emotion is riding you now?" he asked, voicing the very questions she wished to ask him.

"Desire," she answered. "Not really despair, but . . ."

"But?"

She sighed. "Just make love to me."

Jack's mouth crooked up at one corner. "My pleasure. Which shall it be—'eat me,' or 'drink me?' "

Once again, his outrageousness saved her from gloom. Io rose onto her knees and carefully shifted herself over Jack's body. The hammock began to sway, but not alarmingly. She curled her fingers into the cotton knots of their bedding and lowered herself until their chests met and Jack's face was going out of focus. Their noses all but touched, their breath mingling.

"Thank you for reminding me. I really do think that this time it should be 'drink me.' "

Jack's eyebrow rose and she could see that he was getting ready with another smart remark.

"Be a good boy and say it nicely," she urged with a wicked smile before he could speak. " 'Drink me, Io.' "

Jack paused, perhaps to think, but didn't hesitate for long.

"Go ahead. 'Eat me, drink me, love me to death'— or any other way."

Io leaned down and touched their lips together, a light graze, no more. Magic would distract her if she lingered, and she wanted this to be a moment purely of the flesh. She began a careful retreat down his body, peeling back covers as she went, rubbing cheek, chin, hair and lips down his torso, the indentation of his navel, all the way to his—

"Jack, is this real, or a spell?"

He laughed even as he stiffened. "I'm hurt that you have to ask."

"Hurt! Ha! The strongman in the circus couldn't bend this."

"That's fine because I don't want the strongman to bend it," he pointed out. His eyes began to gleam.

"You, on the other hand, are welcome to do anything you like."

"Naughty, naughty," she chided. But pleased at his light response and willingness to let her take charge when he was so clearly designed to be on top of every situation, she smiled at him before turning her head away.

Jack was abundant, ready, and not resisting. *And for what we are about to receive, let us be truly thankful.*

He tasted of salt, of the sea. His flavor mingled with the ever-present magic, which refused to stay politely buried and calm. Io knew that he burned as she suckled, a rare sweat sheening his skin and his breath going immediately ragged.

She burned, too, down to the deepest root on every nerve in her body. But she didn't hurry. She let her hands and mouth explore, gentle at first and then with longer, slower, firmer touches reaching with fingers where her mouth could not. She was descended from siren feys; she had her own magic to call and knew exactly what she was doing. It wasn't decent, wasn't decorous, but it was oh-so-effective when one wanted to tease.

Io watched through slitted eyes as Jack bent his knees and tried to find purchase on the slippery cotton ropes of the hammock, knowing he wanted to quicken the leisurely pace. It was a useless effort and almost made her chuckle. He was helpless and she refused to be rushed.

"Io!"

She hummed an answer.

Jack muttered something under his breath. Io flattened her tongue and pushed him against the roof of her mouth, pressing her lips tight.

"Okay, that is probably enough!" He gasped and his tone grew a little wild. "I don't think the 'drink me' thing is a good idea. Great in theory, but this isn't enough—Io! Damn it!"

Io finally took pity on him and slid her left hand below, cupping and then stroking upward the root of him. Hammock, or no hammock, Jack managed a splendid back arch that lifted his body and Io's as the delayed climax rushed up through his body and to an escape.

After a long moment wracked in an incredible posture, he collapsed back into the swaying bed.

Io touched her slightly swollen lips and turned to look at Jack's face. She climbed back up him.

"You forgot to say thank you," she teased.

"Tricky little siren fey." He rolled her beneath his body, shaking his head in mock admonishment. His eyes weren't blank now; they made her heart roll over. She wasn't afraid, but Jack looked just a tiny bit dangerous, looming over her. And, of course, he was. That was part of the attraction.

"What a bad girl." He touched a finger to her inflamed lower lip.

"And I thought I was being good," she murmured. "I was certain I did that right."

"You were being a tease."

"I don't think, technically speaking, that can be called teasing," she defended, trying to shift, but being defeated by the weight of Jack's body and the infirm nature of their bed. "Now, if I'd stopped. . . . But I didn't."

"Hm. I'll let you slide on the technicality, but we both know that you were enjoying tormenting me. I should probably tickle you until you admit what you were doing. I know the backs of your knees are vulnerable. I was paying attention last night in the shower."

"Well . . . maybe I enjoyed teasing you to a modest degree. But only a little, and not for so awfully long," she admitted, flattening her legs as much as she could, but knowing such precautions were useless if Jack did decide to tickle her.

"*Uh-huh.* Even if I give you a pass on this, we are still left with one other bit of unfinished business." Jack's right hand slid down her leg, pausing halfway.

"Yes?"

Eat me.

"Jack!"

Io knew that she colored, and the sight made Jack smile. It wasn't the kindest thing she'd ever seen, and it made her heart beat wildly.

"Um . . . is this wise in a hammock?" she asked. "I'm pretty sure a chiropractor would advise against it unless both parties are double-jointed."

"I'm not sure it is even possible, but we'll see." Jack's hand reversed itself.

"Do I have any say in this?" she asked.

"Of course. Say anything you like, but it's this or the knees."

She pretended to think for a moment.

"I really hate the knees," Io confessed.

"I know. I was counting on that."

Jack smiled as he slid down her body. He didn't bother trying to keep the magic contained.

"That's cheating," Io gasped as her abdominal muscles contracted. "I was merciful and didn't use magic on you."

"How foolish of you. Next time you'll know better," Jack murmured the words shifting her up the hammock without causing it to sway.

Io could feel his breath on her belly and marveled that he was so close. It didn't seem possible, but Jack Frost was her lover. He had kissed her, been in her, was planning on—

"Jack!"

"Beg if you want," he murmured against her thigh. "But I have to warn you that mercy isn't one of my primary character traits."

Sparks flew, caught hold of her body and imagination both, and started a fire.

"I'm very ticklish," she said breathlessly, reaching up behind herself and grabbing the large eyebolt that held the hammock in place. "Be a little rough."

Jack laughed silently and then pulled her legs over his shoulders.

The hammock never moved, but the world certainly swayed. Io was glad that she had been doing yoga and was flexible. She stared for a moment into Jack's beautiful eyes and then closed her own against the sight. It was too embarrassing—or would be, when she was back in her right mind—and too intimate. *Was that possible? Being too intimate?*

His hands were hot, his breath, too, the instant before he laid his mouth against her. Clever Jack! He found new nerves even as he started her to burn. The fire would have her—yes! Let it burn . . .

Sweat poured off her body and dampened the cotton, making the knots prickly beneath her. Io's super-sensitized skin made note of the new stimulation, unsure if it liked it or not.

Jack's head lifted as he slipped a finger inside her.

"You will tell me when I'm doing this right, won't you?" he asked, his voice a teasing growl.

It took Io a moment to find the breath to answer him. Passion clogged her throat and stilled her tongue. "You'll probably be able to tell when—*yes!*" she hissed as he slid a second finger inside. "That's definitely right."

She felt him laugh, his amusement another sort of thrilling vibration that sent magic running over her. After that, she had trouble sorting out what was Jack and what was sorcery. Io dropped her arms and clapped hands over her eyes, giving herself to the fire, no longer caring which was which and what would happen.

Arousal twisted tighter, tighter, tighter—*Jack please!*—until it could wind no more. She would break, die, be torn asunder if she did not escape the rack!

And then finally she broke free. The coil unwound, throwing her into the living, glorious fire. She shuddered against him—beyond her normal emotions, embarrassment, pride, concern, or even fear.

"So, do you need a doctor?" Jack asked, as the last spasms left her body. He carefully slid her boneless limbs off of his shoulders and onto his thighs. He rolled back, facing her from the opposite end of the hammock, his legs dangling on either side. "I know this orthopedist . . ."

Io pried an eye open and took in his self-satisfied expression. She considered making a bid for a more modest posture, but abandoned the idea immediately. Movement simply wasn't a possibility yet. Her brain would have to reconnect the dissevered synapses and remember how to make her limbs function.

"I don't know," she finally answered. "Ask me again in an hour."

"You don't need a nap, do you? That is usually a guy trick—and we get scolded for it."

"I know it is a postcoital bit of rudeness, but yes."

Io closed her eyes. "And you can't blame me. It's all your fault."

"Yeah, I know."

Io made a note to deal with Jack's smugness later.

Chapter Nineteen

The place that Jack and Cisco had chosen to meet was a Chinese restaurant that didn't deserve the one-star rating it would have gotten in Michelin's or Fodor's, had any of the guide books ever found the no-name place down in the maze of narrow streets where it churned out its strange cuisine. The food was bad, the ambience under the fluorescents and Formica was nonexistent, but it had the benefit of not being frequented by anyone that Cisco or Jack was likely to know—cops or criminals. They'd been meeting there for years whenever Jack blew into town.

Chang, the old man who waited tables, showed Jack to his seat with the sort of bowing that was usually reserved for deities or at least their high priests. Jack gave him the finger, a show of disrespect that made the old man laugh and stop his mocking servitude.

TRAVELER

"You want to see specials?" the old man asked. It was another joke. The old man always served the same thing, no matter what they ordered.

"Surprise us," Jack said, slipping into the seat across from Francisco Vega. The old vinyl creaked under his weight but didn't split. Jack didn't take off his shades, and Cisco didn't ask him to.

The old man wandered away chortling. He disappeared behind the bead curtain that spanned the doorway between the large plastic light-up Buddha and the red, broken wall-mounted pay phone that were the restaurant's only decorative items.

"Wondered if you would show, *amigo*," Cisco said, pouring out tea for both of them and shoving one of the cups Jack's way. "Big storm in Goblin Town last night. Somebody must of tread on old Glashtin's shoes."

"Wasn't me," Jack answered, wondering if it were true. He offered, "Might have been Zayn. He's been around Goblin Town a lot lately."

"If it was Zayn, he got out alive last night. Someone saw him bolting through the gates just after dawn like the hounds of Hell were chewing on his skinny ass."

"I hate when that happens," Jack answered, his face completely straight.

"Yeah, me too. Probably because I got more ass to chew on than I used to."

"A lot more," Jack agreed.

Cisco called him a name. Then, "I suppose it

213

could have been the gargoyle trouble that pissed Glashtin off and sent Zayn flying."

"Yeah? What happened?"

"I hear Hille Bingels's stony pet got loose during the show and bit a few stoned patrons who didn't figure out it wasn't a hallucination."

"Maybe he chewed on Glashtin, too."

"Maybe. But he's a dead gargoyle if that's true. Old Glashtin is supposed to have poison skin and a worse temper."

"Wouldn't surprise me," Jack agreed. "Lots of people around Glashtin end up dead. I hear he's half curare toad."

Chang appeared with a large plate of steamed-to-death vegetables and a bowl of sticky rice. They waited until he was gone to begin discussing business.

"So, you weren't real clear on the cell, but you've got something else for me?" Cisco asked, taking up his chopsticks. He and Jack had learned to use them because Chang didn't bother with standard silverware.

"Yeah." Jack reached into his pocket and pulled out the two samples of goblin fruit he had wrapped in a bandanna. It had been off the vine for a day and still looked succulent. There was no sign of wilt or rot. "Go ahead and have the boffins test it, but I already know what it is."

"This is the super-fruit you were looking for?" Cisco eyed the items for a moment and then carefully stowed them in his own coat pocket. "That's bad news then."

"Yep, and I'm afraid that means it's going to have to be a Sherlock-Holmes-and-Moriarty type of *final solution*, and soon. This is an act of terrorism. There are fields of this stuff down there all ready for picking. If Neveling Lutin is to make his perfume launch date, then they'll have to begin harvesting shortly."

"So Lutin is involved."

"Right up to his antennae," Jack answered, thinking of Io's insistence that the goblins really were bugs.

"You're suddenly smiling, amigo. That always worries me. Is it the girl? The fey you told me about?"

Jack nodded once. His tone was reluctant, but he volunteered "Her name's Io."

"Tigre Cypher's daughter? And you're letting her in on this party?" Cisco didn't bother to hide his amazement. "Man, you always did have the biggest *cojones*."

"She's nothing like her mother. And I couldn't stop her—not without . . ." Jack shrugged. "Anyway, I need her help. She can do some incredible things with even average spells. I've never met anyone who fine-tunes the way she does. It's like putting a killing edge on a knife."

"Good. You're going to need a lot of help, amigo, if you're taking on Horroban and all of Goblin Town. And a little extra firepower would help, too." Cisco spoke persuasively.

"That's why I'm here," Jack agreed.

Cisco leaned back, further surprise showing in his dark eyes. "It isn't like you to be so reasonable. This mess is really that bad then?"

"Yeah. The goblins aren't kidding." Jack finally took off his sunglasses and looked his friend in the eye. "We stop it here, or we're all screwed."

"You'd better tell me everything. Could they really addict the world with this stuff?"

Jack nodded and began talking.

Io knew that Jack would not be happy with her for answering Zayn's note and agreeing to this rendezvous while he was gone from town, but she was loaded with enough magic to wipe out a regiment of goblins, including a truth-resistance spell. Surely that was sufficient to protect her from any tricks Zayn might try to get information out of her.

As she walked, she was careful to keep an eye on the imps chattering up in the trees. They were part of the park landscape, though not as charming as squirrels, or as pleasant to look at—and they were certainly more dangerous.

A pitiful screech from the base of a park bench drew her attention. Someone had set a wrought-iron leg down on top of a gray imp's tail. Probably the imp had been annoying and deserved its fate, but Io found that she couldn't leave it there suffering to starve or be tormented by the others. If it kept whimpering, something was going to come along and eat it.

Io put down the two cups of coffee she carried. Flexing her fingers inside her gloves, she bent down and quickly wrapped a hand around the leathery jaw so it couldn't bite her with those tiny, razor-sharp teeth. She then quickly lifted the bench and pulled the imp out. A fast look assured her that its tail wasn't broken.

She put it on the ground and, releasing it, stepped back smartly. The imp, though it couldn't see her, knew she was there and set about repeating the sort of screechy begging that had likely gotten it pinned in the first place.

"Go on, beat it," she said.

The imp ratcheted up his whining and the others of his kind paused to see what the fuss was about. They began to creep closer.

Sighing in exasperation, Io reached inside her pocket and flipped a stick of gum down onto the sidewalk. The creature would probably devour it, paper and all, but that wouldn't hurt it. Imps ate anything. They were like buzzards.

Delighted with his minty prize, the imp picked it up and scurried off, his hairless and featherless body shivering with delight. Other imps began chasing after him, shrieking with jealousy.

Io waited for them to rush by her, then picked up the coffee and moved on.

She finally pulled off her invisibility when she

reached the park bench where her fellow agent provocateur waited and there Io sat down next to Zayn. He flinched when she appeared, his whole face twitching.

She had never seen the fey look so nervy.

Io gave him one of the cups of coffee as a peace offering, and then looked into the distance at the beds of dead flowers while he collected himself.

"Okay. Spill it," she finally said. "Hurry up. It's cold."

She pulled her sweater around her with her free hand. The snow had melted, but it was still unseasonably cold in Goblin Town. The sun was well up, but just didn't seem able to warm things. It was as though the heat of the city was being sucked straight down into the earth.

And maybe it was.

"We had some excitement last night. Hille's pet gargoyle somehow managed to swallow your dish of ticks along with some bits of tourists when it got loose at Glashtin's club." Zayn took a gulp of coffee, wincing at both the heat and the taste. Io didn't blame him. No one in Goblin Town seemed to have mastered the art of making drinkable java.

"That explains Glashtin's temper tantrum and the sudden snow." She was relieved to know it was this and not the foray into the Labyrinth that had been responsible. "I wonder how much he had to lay out in bribes to shut everyone up about the gargoyle feast."

218

"Yeah, I guess that's what made him mad. Deke said he went storming out of the club just after midnight and didn't come back." Zayn didn't seem to notice that he named another H.U.G. operative. Or maybe he assumed that Xanthe had told Io who else was working in Goblin Town.

"And then what happened?"

Zayn looked about nervously. There were no shrubs to speak of, and all the trees were bare. There wasn't any place for a goblin to be hiding, even if they were so bold as to be out during the day, but his eyes kept moving fretfully from trees to shrubbery and back again.

"All but one of the ticks were expelled. I couldn't figure out at first which signal to follow . . ." His voice trailed off, and Io had a flash of him stumbling into gargoyle poop while he followed each tracker.

She managed not to smile. It was hard because somehow, in spite of what she and Jack were facing, she found it difficult not to feel wonderful. Bits of the new magic they had built between them still lingered in her body, reminding her of Jack and how spectacular she could feel when her magic was charged with his.

"But the other tick kept moving, so I followed it instead," Zayn continued.

"That was the one Ferris put on my back, I bet. That wasn't just a goblin tick. I think that sucker could bore into anything."

"Probably." It cost Zayn something to admit the

next statement. "Ferris is a little fanatical and sometimes oversteps the bounds a bit."

"Yeah, I noticed. So where'd the gargoyle go after it snacked on the tourists?"

"Back to Hille. She finally went down into the basement and started for the lake, so I followed her down below and tracked her—*all the way to Horroban*," Zayn whispered. His face was white and he kept licking his lips, but his mouth was so parched that there was nothing to moisten them with. He tried a second sip of coffee, being more cautious this time. "I don't know how you stood it down there. I was only under for a couple of hours and thought I'd die from the heat while I hid in the tunnel and watched the two of them make it."

Io sat up, ignoring Zayn's complaining about the heat or watching goblin sex, and she asked urgently. "You saw Horroban? Well, who is he?"

Zayn turned his head to face her. His eyes were huge and looked like broken glass. He was terrified.

Her voice dropped to a whisper as she asked again, "Zayn, who is Horroban? What does he look like?"

Zayn inhaled deeply and then exhaled as though preparing for a deep dive. He inhaled once more, and then said the name of the man expected to win the presidential election that next Tuesday.

Io went white too. Goblins had tried for the White House before, but fortunately for humankind they had never been able to mask their underlying oddity

220

and therefore hadn't had any real chance of succeeding. This time, humanity's luck had seemingly run out.

"Have you told Xanthe yet?" she asked.

Zayn shook his head, the motion jerky and completely lacking his usual grace.

"Don't tell her, Zayn. You can't."

"Why not?" he asked, frustrated. Then "Something is wrong, isn't it? I can sense it. I almost told her, but at the last minute I . . . I stopped."

Io did some deep breathing of her own. She had to make a decision. Did she confide in Zayn, or try to blank his mind? She might be able to bend the truth spell enough to do it.

Or she might not. Zayn carried his own magic, and it was a completely hostile act, a form of rape, to use magic on one another without permission. He would probably fight back.

"Yeah, Zayn. Something is very wrong," she finally answered. "Xanthe is working with Horroban."

Zayn looked stricken, as though someone had taken a knife of cold iron and plunged it into his gut, but he didn't deny her contention.

"Why?" he whispered. "How could she?"

"It's Chloe," Io answered, knowing this would upset Zayn even more. He was fond of Xanthe's little sister. *Very* fond. "Horroban has her, in the underground probably. He's turned her into a goblin-fruit junkie and is holding her hostage to Xanthe's good behavior. As long as we go chasing after the jewel,

221

no problem. But if we get near his crop of goblin fruit or Lutin's factory, Chloe gets the chop and Xanthe's reputation gets smeared. Or at least that's what we believe."

"That son of a diseased water moccasin!" Red rage bloomed in Zayn's pale cheeks. He looked at Io with hot eyes that glittered angrily. She had never seen him so passionate about anything. "What are you and Jack going to do?"

Io looked at Zayn and thought some more about how much she should tell him.

Jack headed back for Goblin Town, pleased with the day's work. He had two new pistols, both made of a light polymer, compact and silenced, and fitted with laser sights. They made him feel a bit more on top of things.

Trolls could batter a man to death, given even half a chance, and goblins liked to strangle. Those were their traditional methods of killing. However, even tradition had to bow before practicality. Guns were a great equalizer when you were smaller than the people you hated, and the goblins had apparently learned that through the years. Jack had seen so firsthand.

He would have worried about bombs from the bugs, too, but he knew they had discovered that technology and magic didn't go real well together. Goblins got the whole *point-bang* concept, but were less comfortable with finicky timing devices that tended to blow up when brushed by careless magic.

Guns weren't traditionally fey, either, but bullets could outrun most magic, so Jack too had to be practical.

He patted his bag. The goblins had guns; now he and Io did too. It kept things more even. Murder wasn't the most elegant solution to their problem, but it seemed the only effective one.

If he pulled it off.

The ammunition in the clips he'd packed was staggered—cold iron and then hunting rounds, designed to blow big messy holes in the body. Not knowing what he and Io would be up against, and some beasties not responding well to certain types of ammo, it seemed prudent to be packing both. Gargoyles, goblins, trolls—who knew what the night might bring?

It also felt damn good to know that Cisco had his back covered and would take out Lutin's factory while he and Io ruined the underground and its main bad guy. Demolishing the factory was secondary to eradicating the crops, but it would help foil the goblins' plan. Jack would take the help either way, especially since nothing else was being offered in the way of official assistance.

He shifted his duffle bag into his left fist as he neared the iron gates of Goblin Town. He wanted his right hand free in case he needed to do a quick draw with his new pistol. He was ambidextrous, but slightly faster with his right hand. It was just a precaution, but one he took because the stakes they were gambling were astronomically high, and he had every intention of getting back to Io alive.

The thought of her attempting to destroy Horroban's empire on her own made his blood frost. Her fate, if she was caught, didn't bear thinking of. Horroban would probably turn her into a humanskin lampshade and a new belt. And the goblin warlord wouldn't be so kind as to stop her heart before he started working either.

The troll on duty that afternoon hung back deep in the shadows of the toll booth, and didn't question Jack as he paid his admission fee and stuck his hand into the basin to draw an entry spell.

Jack fished about carefully until he found what he wanted: an enlarging charm. With this new magic—modified, of course—and the hair spray in his duffle, Io would be able to make one hell of a firebomb. She'd be able to go through the hive with a flamethrower and take out everything standing more than an inch above the ground. The spell would work on his canister of salt, too. Io could multiply the little grains until there was enough to sterilize every field down there.

At least it would sterilize every field they could find. Jack didn't kid himself that he knew where they all were. He and Io would keep looking as long as they could, but the hive was vast and something would escape them. That was Murphy's Law as applied to goblins.

Of course, he didn't like sending Io down alone to deal with the crop, but she'd proven herself resourceful and there was something even more important and dangerous that he had to do that night. It wasn't something that Io would like, and not what Cisco could ever officially acknowledge was good policy, but everyone understood that Horroban had to die. The goblin warlord had too many powerful friends in too many powerful places. Jack and Io might wipe out this crop of goblin fruit, but there would be others again and soon, because no one in authority would ever put Horroban away. As long as the goblin warlord lived, humankind would be in peril.

That was what Jack had really meant when he said he was choosing the *"final solution."* It wasn't just the hive that was going to be taken out.

The acknowledgment of what needed doing was unspoken, but it was a cause that Cisco had been ready to risk his badge and life for. He had a wife and two kids to think about after all, so he'd been willing to help Jack in whatever way he could.

And it didn't hurt Jack's cause that Cisco was a bit of a pyro and just plain liked blowing things up.

Chapter Twenty

Jack had the frightening capacity to stand in utter stillness when he was either angered or assessing. He paused inside the door, inhaling deeply, taking in the scent of Io's fear and perhaps seeing some of Zayn's magic clinging to the edge of her aura, and then froze. An eternity later he said "You told Zayn about Chloe, didn't you?"

"Yes," Io admitted, looking him in the eye, though it was difficult because his expression was remote. The new coldness after their morning together made her heart twist. "It was the lesser of two evils. Either I gave him a reason not to go to Xanthe or else I had to blank his mind."

"And telling him everything seemed the lesser evil?"

"I didn't tell him *everything*. But, yes." Io swallowed. "Jack, things are worse than we thought.

Worse than we even imagined. We will probably *need* Zayn."

"I don't doubt that things are worse than we imagined," Jack said calmly, putting down his duffle. His expression was annoyed. "This has been a pain from the start, but we haven't had nearly enough trouble."

Apparently their brush with gargoyles didn't count. Jack's nonchalance about that helped Io stay calm.

"Zayn found out who Horroban is."

Jack looked up from his bag, his expression momentarily arrested. "How did Zayn manage this?" His voice was cool.

"He followed Hille's gargoyle. It ate my ticks." Io pulled her hair back from her face and exhaled. "Look, I know you don't trust Zayn—"

"With cause."

"But you don't understand something about this situation."

"Quite probably. So why don't you stop fussing with the small stuff and explain what I don't get?" Jack asked politely, trying hard not to let his exasperation show but failing.

"Zayn is in love with Chloe," Io blurted out. She regretted her words almost as soon as she uttered them.

"What?" Jack looked revolted.

"You heard me. They were lovers once upon a time, but Xanthe intervened. She asked him not to see Chloe until she was older and through with school."

"And this helps us how?" Jack was obviously un-impressed with her logic in regard to Zayn's moti-vations, or perhaps didn't believe the truth of them. "Assuming you're right and he does actually love her, you don't think his first loyalty is to Chloe's sis-ter, his boss?"

"No, I don't. Jack, listen to me. I was there when his brother died. Zayn hates the goblins—and he knows exactly what happens with goblin-fruit junk-ies. He might not have listened to our theories about Lutin's perfume being an addictive agent as long as Xanthe wasn't interested, but he damn sure listened to the fact that Chloe is being turned into a junkie—and that Xanthe isn't doing anything to stop Horro-ban because she would rather have a drug-addicted sister than a dead one."

"I see." Jack's voice was still neutral, but he was listening.

"He also knows that after next Tuesday, it won't matter anymore. None of it will. Horroban will prob-ably cut his losses and kill Chloe." Io tried to fight down her returning agitation, but it was difficult with Jack's annoyance and magic crawling all over her. He had obviously picked up some strong spell on his way back into town and been tweaking it.

"I see. So you haven't got to the crux of the matter yet, have you? What's the punch line?"

"What?" Io blinked.

228

"Who the hell is Horroban, and why will he kill Chloe after Tuesday. Nothing is going on in the next week except—" Jack stopped cold. "Are you saying that Horroban is one of the candidates for the senate?"

Io shook her head.

"Governor?"

"No."

"Not the presidency. It can't be."

"Jack, Horroban is *William Hamilton!*" Io pulled back her hair again. "William Hamilton. The polls say he'll take it in a landslide."

Jack muttered something really bad in troll.

"I hadn't heard that one before," Io said, trying for a note of lightness. "I'll remember for the next time I find myself in an appropriate situation. So, any constructive thoughts about what we should do with this new problem? Zayn wants to help, but I haven't told him anything definite."

Jack nodded. "Yeah, I have thoughts. We do exactly what we always planned to do—and we do it very, very well. And you let me talk to Zayn from here on out. I don't trust him not to sacrifice you if you get between him and Chloe."

"Fine. But you will have to talk to him or he'll go in after Chloe alone. Soon."

"Moronic hothead," Jack muttered. "Nothing like a fey in love with a human to make bad things even more difficult. There is no stupider animal in the annals of history than a love-struck faerie."

"Maybe so, but—"

"I'll talk to him before he screws us up. Don't worry about it. Actually, I suppose the news could have been worse."

Io stared at Jack, unhappy with what his words implied but not arguing. Fey-human romances rarely worked out well in the long term. And Zayn *was* talking wildly. He might very well do something stupid that would endanger everyone. The fact that Io sympathized wouldn't interest Jack. It would probably make him further question her judgment.

Jack lifted his duffle onto the table and unzipped the central compartment. His movements were easy and his magic had folded back in on itself.

"Come here, little fey." Jack's eyes had lost their cold cast and he smiled as he looked over at her. Relieved that he was through being annoyed, Io stepped closer.

"What's in there?"

"Oh the usual—salt, hair spray, handguns. That isn't what I wanted to show you, though."

"No?"

"No. I brought you a present." Jack slid off his long coat and threw it down on the table. He began un-buttoning his cuffs.

"Yeah?" Io looked up at him, wondering if he was flirting with her. With Jack, it was sometimes hard to tell. "And what might that be? Candy? Flowers?"

"Come here and kiss me and you'll find out."

"How about a hint?" Io suggested, running a finger

230

down Jack's shirt. She stopped at his belt buckle. "I can feel the spell sparking all over the place. It isn't standard issue. You've been playing with it."

"I've been supercharging it," Jack admitted. "But I'll let you do the final customizing."

"Uh-huh. And what kind of spell is it?"

"An enlarging spell."

"An *enlarging spell!* Now that sounds interesting— not that you need to be any larger." She let her fingers drift lower. Her heart turned over and her nerves trilled, but this time it wasn't with alarm. "Or maybe you want *me* to be a little more *gifted.*"

Jack's thin lips twisted in a smile. "We'll play that way later if you really want to," he promised. "Right now, I want to show you how to make a flame-thrower."

She gave him a coy look. "Is that what you call it? Well, everyone should have a pet name for it, I guess."

"Pay attention, Io. I mean it." He tried for properly stern, but somehow fell short.

Io looked up. "I'm all ears."

"You're all hands." Jack stepped back from her. "I'm not joking, honey. With this spell and a can of hair spray, you have something better than napalm. But you'll need to practice so you don't hurt yourself."

"If it's that dangerous, why don't you handle it?" Io asked. "This is more your speed anyway. I'm kind of a slug-'em-and-run sort of girl."

231

"I *can't* handle it." Jack paused, then added, "I won't be there."

"What? Why not?" All urge to tease fell away. Io stared at him, trying to read his face and failing to, as she so often did. "Where exactly will you be?"

Jack met her gaze squarely and said precisely what she had been fearing to hear ever since Zayn had revealed Horroban's identity.

"I'm going after Horroban."

"No." She shook her head. "Not alone."

"Someone's got to take him out, Io. We both know it," Jack explained gently. "But we have to get those fields, too, or it's a Pyrrhic victory even if Horroban dies."

"No," she repeated. But she knew Jack was right. Someone had to get rid of Horroban—permanently. And before next Tuesday.

And after tomorrow night they would have burned their bridges; Horroban would have warning after the attack on the fruit fields that someone was onto his plans, and would disappear behind a wall of Secret Service men until it was too late to stop him. Once in the White House, killing him would be next to impossible—supposing he actually allowed any humans the opportunity to live long enough to attempt assassination.

He would also loose his dogs upon her and Jack in retaliation. Between the goblins and the resources of the U.S. government, there wasn't anywhere on earth that she and Jack would be safe from his retribution.

Horroban had to die, or they would. They *all* would.

It was Io's turn to use bad troll. She put real feeling into it, hoping it would keep tears from pooling in her eyes. Macho goblin-fighters did *not* cry.

"Sorry, honey." It didn't change anything, but Jack seemed to regret the pain he was causing her, to regret that she would have to destroy the crops on her own. And if she cried he might drink her tears, swallow her sorrow. She couldn't do that to him. He was already carrying a terrible burden.

Io stopped swearing. It took a little longer to make her body halt its trembling and for her heart to calm, but she stayed at it until the last of the symptoms left her.

"I'm all right now," she said. It was a half-lie, but she knew she would have to make it the truth before they went back underground that night. This was their last chance to scout the hive and find fruit fields that needed destroying. It was also their last chance to find Horroban's bolt-hole.

He would be somewhere in the city, Io was certain. All Hallows' Eve was a powerful time magically, and the goblin would want to be close to the source of his dark power.

"So, give me my gift and show me how to make a flamethrower." Io rose up on her toes and deliberately pressed her mouth against Jack's.

He hesitated for a moment and then began transferring the spell. His hands found her waist and held her up while the powerfully charged spell spilled into her, making her muscles tick and spasm.

"Goddess!"

Perhaps it was just her mood, but it seemed to Io that besides the spell she had also being filled with cold purpose and a sort of grim determination. The feelings were foreign and yet familiar. Jack was doing his best to protect her by giving her some of his relentless fortitude.

She didn't know what she could give him in return.

"Hope," he whispered as the last of the spell left him. He stood looking into her eyes, which she knew were blazing with cold blue fire. "You've already given me it. Hope."

"Let's pray it was a fair trade."

"It was." Jack's lips crooked. "I never do anything to my own disadvantage."

"Really? I do. All the time," she answered, thinking about how much emotion she had invested in Jack and how it might all be taken away.

"You'll learn."

Io nodded sadly. She was very afraid that he was right.

Chapter Twenty-one

Twilight moved in early, helped by a new front of storm clouds coming down from the north. There were great banks of them whose deeper shadows crept silently over the city, blotting out the lesser shade of buildings, and making the world go flat metallic green before surrendering completely to the night. The eve before Halloween had arrived in a mood of sullen brooding, a gathering wrath in the sky, and it sat, holding its rain as though saving up its malevolent energy for the coming All Hallows' Eve.

Or perhaps Glashtin was still sulking over his guests' unexpected medical bills, and that kept the weather cold and glowering. Io preferred to believe it was this lesser magic at work than that Nature herself was turning on them.

As soon as the sun set, she and Jack slipped on their shades and moved out into the colorless world.

The tide of events was bearing them along now, accompanied by the crunch of the dreary rubble beneath their feet, bones of old mansions shifting slyly beneath them. The sound put the need to hurry in their soles and—when they let it—worry in their hearts.

The Labyrinth seemed just as it always had, but Jack and Io chose a new place of ingress and entered with a fresh caution anyway, just in case their previous visits *had* been discovered and some new traps were laid.

"What do you think of Death Valley?" Jack asked as they started down the echoing corridor.

"I don't. This is quite close enough to a valley of death for me. It's hotter than Hell down here."

"But out west they say it's a dry heat."

"Yeah, right. And it never rains in California, either." Io knew she sounded bitchy, but bickering kept her mind occupied and her hands steady.

In another situation, she would have preferred to think about Jack, because thoughts of him were enough to overwhelm anything, even fear of goblins. But the memory of what they had shared, and any speculation of what might come later, was dangerously distracting. What was it Donne had said? "Love all alike, no season knows, nor clime." That seemed about right. If she started thinking deeply about Jack, she could walk smack into a pack of goblins before even noticing they were there.

"Damn it! There is green goop everywhere. It's going to ruin my shoes."

"Fresh plaster job," Jack said. "Now, I wonder why."

"To impress visiting goblin dignitaries," Io guessed randomly.

"Don't joke, honey. Horroban isn't the only ambitious goblin in the world. No reason they shouldn't finally get smart and unionize. H.U.G.'s feared that for years."

"Maybe so, but he's the only one I'm prepared to worry about tonight. I can't cope with the idea of a worldwide goblin organization."

"Good point. We'll worry about the goblin mafia later. I am just wondering if this is the route they will be taking the fruit. It leads right to Neveling Lutin's factory."

Io looked around. "Well, skids would slip right along, if they move the fruit on pallets."

"The cupped bottom and irregular walls of this tunnel would screw up the average truck, that's for sure," Jack pointed out.

"Tires would slip too. Besides, I haven't seen vehicles down here—excepting our favorite goblin's limo."

Jack grunted and fell silent.

There was no music in the grave and none in the underground. There was no silence either, just the infernal humming of the water pumps that set Io's teeth on edge, making her think again of Hell. It grew louder as she and Jack neared the place that Zayn said was Horroban's subterranean hidey-hole.

Jack, who was on point, held up his hand and waved her to a quick halt. Before she could ask what was wrong, he pulled on the invisibility spell and then eased around the corner of the tunnel. Io went as far as the curved bend and then stopped, listening.

At first her ears could discern nothing over the motorized hum of the pumps, but eventually her ears distinguished the separate sound of low moaning grumbles. It was an unattractive noise, similar to what a wolverine might make when sitting down to devour a particularly tough bit of carcass.

Jack reappeared beside her and raised his brow, asking if she wanted to use the spell to take a look.

Io nodded and bent her head back. She tried to tell herself that she was allowing this spell-transferring kiss solely in the interest of thorough investigation, but knew she was lying.

Once cloaked with invisibility, Io pulled herself away from Jack and forced herself to peer around the corner and see what manner of creatures were making this awful growling noise.

The first thing she had to do was look down about two feet lower than expected. There were probably two dozen of the creatures moving through the field, snuffling and grunting.

They had to be goblins of some sort, perhaps children, or else the worker class she and Jack had spec-

ulated about earlier. Whatever they were, they were
small even for goblinkind, and had withered third
and fourth limbs that were little more than bony
claws. Their faces were also particularly unlovely
and they had no defining sexual traits that Io could
see. And she could see a lot because they crawled
about naked on hands and knees, licking the fruit
in the fields with long black tongues that left a gloss
of saliva behind. Io tried to think what they could
be doing, but the only explanation that occurred to
her was that they were on some sort of polishing
detail.

Saliva seals in freshness.

They were revolting and pathetic, and also dam-
nably in the way since she and Jack wanted to get
to Horroban's place and the only route they knew
of was through this field. They didn't have any
choice about where and how they went. They had
to know their enemy's defenses and weaknesses—
if any existed—and this was the only sure path. It
was also hers and Jack's only opportunity. This was
a case of dog eat dog. Their job, on this last night of
reconnaissance, was to see that they came up with
a plan that guaranteed that the right dog got eaten.

Io eased back around the tunnel's curve and re-
joined Jack. Without saying a word, she wrapped
her arms about his neck and placed her lips against
his. His hands lifted her up as they began to share
the spell.

Io curled her legs about his waist as Jack began

making his way through the goblin fruit field, careful to avoid the grunting workers. She closed her eyes on the sight and told herself that this was a necessary action and she wasn't enjoying the moment at all—and knew that she was lying about that too.

Liar, liar, pants on fire. Only it wasn't the lying that was making her burn through the cotton of her jeans. It was Jack. Io opened her eyes. Her body's attempts at recalling past passion had to be short-circuited. Her mind's eye had to stamp it down, too, before it started making stuff up. She hadn't ever suspected it, but her imagination had an erotic streak that was miles wide and very active when given the right stimulation.

Instead, she concentrated on outside irritants—the infernal noise and the hot, damp air that brushed over her skin like rough wet wool. And the ugly, drooling monsters. The combined unpleasantness was almost enough to keep her from grinding herself against Jack's body. Almost. She compromised with only a small wiggle and a little deep breathing.

Why didn't he *feel* invisible? They might be moving like specters through the hive, but Jack was solid beneath the invisibility cast by the spell, and Io could feel his body change as he too was affected by magic, proximity, or unstifled imagination. He had more discipline, though. He didn't wiggle.

They made it safely through the field and into another tunnel before Io had to break their embrace and suck in air at a greater rate than she could manage through her nose. At that, she didn't know whether to breathe or moan. Though they were hidden from the workers' view, Jack was slow to break their clinch, letting her slide down his body in unhurried inches before pulling away his spell and freeing her.

"I am so glad that you are female. As much as I like Cisco, I wouldn't be carrying his ass through a goblin field doing a liplock," Jack said, surprising one short gasp of laughter from Io.

"I also wish that I liked baseball," he continued. "It's the traditional thing to think about in these moments when control is a potential problem." His voice was low and rough.

"Or England," Io suggested, her own voice far from its normal tone. "That's supposed to work too."

"This is ridiculous. We need to be thinking about our goblin friend." Io knew that this wasn't a sudden expression of new affection. Jack would be careful not to mention Horroban's name down deep in the Labyrinth when magic might carry it to the goblin war chief's anxious ears.

"I have been," Io answered as they again started a slow creep down the sticky tunnels. She was careful to keep her arms away from the walls. Seeing the goblins licking the blood fruit to a high sheen had put her off *touching* anything down there. Even thinking about the possibilities of what they used for plaster had the effect of killing her burgeoning de-

241

sire for Jack—which was probably just as well.

"Our *friend* is bold and sneaky—but in a way a childish braggart. We've been making him into an exotic boggle," Io went on at a whisper. "He isn't really the inscrutable Fu Man Chu."

Jack looked back and raised an eyebrow. "Go on. I'm listening."

"There are many subtle ways to gain power, but our friend has chosen the route with the highest possible degree of visibility," Io explained. "He *wants* to be noticed. He wants people to know him, so they will feel especially shocked and betrayed when he tells them what he's done. He's flipping us non-goblinkind the bird before he kills us because he's pissed off about something."

"And you think he will tell everyone?"

"Oh, I think so. It fits the profile—at least the profile of a human thrill killer." Io frowned. "Do you think there are goblin psychopaths?"

"I think the more pertinent question for us would be, are there any goblins who aren't?"

"You're right." Io shook her head as though still unable to believe the evidence before their eyes. "Every goblin in this city has to know what is going on under here. It's the attempted genocide of the human race. And they are content to let it happen. I doubt there's a goblin *Greenpeace Let's Save The Humans Organization*."

"No. Not with hive mentality. They don't feel they owe humans anything. We aren't their kind."

"But we have helped them," Io objected. "The United States gave them a home when three-quarters of the world wouldn't have them. We also forced the world into amending the Geneva conventions to include goblins and other feys under the articles of fair treatment for prisoners."

" 'Give me your tired, your poor, your huddled masses' . . . But they don't see it that way. You know they don't."

"I know. Only, there was one who tried to help us."

"Xanthe's mole?" Jack asked.

"Yes. He died trying to help. That should count for something."

"*Maybe* he was trying to do a good deed," Jack allowed. "He may also have been in it for the money. Goblins love gold. Xanthe could have hired him to get word of her sister, and Horroban found out about the double-cross and snuffed him."

Io sighed. "We'll probably never know."

"Probably not. And that is just as well. This isn't the time to start humanizing our enemies. Whatever they are, however moral they are within their own belief systems, the fact remains that they are planning to bring about the end of humankind and our way of civilization—at least, civilization as we have always known it. We are at war. Compassion and mercy have no place until the battle is won."

Io thought of her mother and then of all the other blank-faced, blank-minded addicts she had known, the mindless ones who turned their backs on all their principles and everyone they ever loved because they prized their drug more. Zombies weren't half so dead or dangerous. Yes, this was war.

"Don't worry. Conviction won't fail me." Her voice was firm. "We'll put an end to this madness tomorrow night," she promised.

Chapter Twenty-two

Io stood inside her small tree house and watched it brighten as the dawn hit the skin of a nearby grove of white birches and backwashed through her living room window. A few of the last shivering leaves sent tiny sparks of reflected gold fire dancing over the floors and walls. It was pretty but cold, flames without warmth, a chimera.

She hadn't been gone from here but for a few days—a small number; hardly any, really of those "rags" that Donne said time clothed itself in—but already the place felt abandoned.

She was tired. Their night in Goblin Town had been long and at times terrifying. She was now convinced that it was more exhausting sneaking about than simply engaging in stand-up battle. It was almost a relief to know that the showdown was finally here.

Jack had wanted her to rest before leaving the

city, but Io had a lot to do before she could leave her home, and she knew she wouldn't be able to sleep until this job was done.

Shaking herself out of her growing melancholic reverie, Io went first to the canisters of bird food and set about refilling her feeders. The remainder of the seeds and nuts she poured on the ground below, a small consolation prize for the gathering avians and squirrels who would have to find a new patroness, or else return to hunting grain and on their own.

"Sorry, guys. This is the last of it. 'Eat, drink, and be merry, for tomorrow. . . .' Tomorrow ye may not."

Packing came next. Her books, the irreplaceable ones her mother and grandmother had written out by hand, went into a duffle with her few mementos. Her favorite clothes were piled into a suitcase. Seeing how little she had accumulated in her thirty years made Io realize how terribly, achingly lonely her life had been.

She looked around a little after ten A.M. and said a soft goodbye to her nest. It was doubtful that she would ever come back. Her home was just one more casualty of the goblin wars. It would seem impossibly horrible to be losing it, but the thought of Jack—as unlikely a source of compassion as he was—still offered her some compensation. Somehow, he alone made the loss bearable.

Io tossed her bags down onto the spongy grass below and then clambered down her tree's trunk.

Her next stop would be the bank. The people

there wouldn't be happy to see her withdrawing her savings, but this also had to be done. No institution was safe from the goblins. If Io tried using an ATM or credit cards while she and Jack were on the run, the goblins might know of it and start following her. There was probably some way to drag a financial red herring across their path—Jack would know— so she wouldn't empty the account completely, but she needed most of her money in hand in order to feel safe.

She picked up her bags and started hiking toward the road through the crunchy leaves that littered the woods' floor. She tried not to remember that tonight she was supposed to take her flamethrower down into the hive and watch the goblin fields go *boom*. She tried even harder not to think about Jack taking on Horroban.

Jack looked up. Io's movements were brittle and birdlike as she laid her suitcase and duffle on the table and slipped off her concealing glasses. She had picked up a new spell, but hadn't done anything to it. It was just a tiny ember waiting patiently to be breathed to life. It was too faint for Jack to even guess at what it was.

"I had to go through twice. Once over the wall with my suitcase, then I went through at the gate to get my spell. I'm glad I didn't pack all my books," she said lightly, finally looking at him. Her eyes were almost lusterless enough to pass for human. "They seem to be making walls higher these days, and I am no good without my beauty sleep."

Jack could tell from Io's face that she was troubled by more than mere physical exhaustion. Saying farewell to her life had exacted a hard price. He'd known that it would, and it angered him that he hadn't been able to do this task for her. But that was the trouble with farewells. They had to be done in person.

"Come here, little fey," he said, offering what comfort there could be in a pair of arms. It was inadequate reparation for her loss, but it was all that he had. "I think you need a rubdown and then a nice long nap."

It said a lot for the growing trust between them that Io walked into his embrace without any hesitation. Of course, they were walking into battle together tonight. If they couldn't trust each other now, they were out of luck.

"Did you talk to Zayn?" she asked, head drooping onto his shoulder. "The cell phone worked today?"

"Yes. He and Cisco understand the timing. They'll be out of the Labyrinth before midnight."

Jack ran his fingers up the back of Io's neck and buried them in her hair, alternately tugging and massaging. She groaned softly.

"That's so nice."

"Come on." He led her to the hammock and lowered her over it crosswise, her face down. He patted her bottom.

248

"Jack, if you make one lewd remark—"

"I wouldn't dream of it," Jack assured her sincerely. But he was thinking lots of things. Tight jeans and the posture would have wrung lascivious thoughts from a plaster saint.

Nevertheless, he was all business as he set out to rub down her legs and back. Resisting all temptation, he knelt and began at her ankles, working his way back up slowly. He began to trickle some of her magic back into her body, but kept at the repetitive slow strokes until he felt the tension finally letting go of her tensed muscles. When he paused, her small humming noise encouraged him to go on.

He slid the hard outside edges of his hands up the length of her spine beneath her sweater and then circled her shoulder blades, stroking down her sides to her hipbones. He began kneading the small of her back. More magic came, warming his hands and making her body glow softly. The transference of power between them was getting easier.

He moved onto her arms, so small yet strong, and then stroked down to her hands. Those fascinated him because they were so diminutive and soft, her fingers curling in like the cup of a five-petaled flower.

Eventually, in spite of his best intentions, his body and magic betrayed his impure thoughts, and Io raised herself back up off of the hammock to look at him.

"Such a dirty mind. I can hear you thinking, you

know." She reached for him, eyes recharged and gleaming.

"You don't have to . . ." he began, but lost his breath when her hands slid over him. They were tiny but not weak, and she was at her core a siren fey. Even death had to answer the call.

Magic arched suddenly between them, a current so strong it nearly dropped them to their knees.

"Jack?" Io's voice was shaking. "What . . . ?"

"Damn."

The internal, inborn magic a faerie carried within its body was a fey's only protection from the world, its shelter from the throngs of humanity they were far too sensitive to live among comfortably.

But their core magic wasn't adequate protection for him or for Io, not anymore. Their inborn magics didn't shield them from all-consuming intimacy. The two different powers mated and made bigger magic that was harder to control. It got stronger every time they touched. And the magic wanted more all the time—body, heart, mind, and soul.

Neither Io nor Jack was ready to give that, though, so the fierce desire also brought internal war. The struggle, the hunt, and Io's attempted emotional aloofness just aroused him more. It made him want to pillage.

Then she looked up at him with those blue eyes stunned by the power, her body soft under the onslaught, her lips slightly parted, and he found he could temporarily resist the basest of his impulses that said he should take her whether she agreed or not.

Oh, but it was hard! He could hear her heart leaping. The sound maddened. He wanted to hold her, to say it would be all right, that he would protect her from everything—even himself.

But more than that, he wanted to have her. Now. He knew that it was a magical, emotional sort of craving that rode him, one that no amount of physical intimacy could fulfill. He could have her and have her and have her again, and he would still want.

His magic didn't care about logic or feelings. It was like an addiction.

Jack hesitated at the thought, knowing it should disturb Io, but she did not pull away.

"Tell me to stop," he whispered.

"No."

It wasn't a cure, but touching helped. Yes, it definitely did, he thought, lowering his mouth to hers and kissing her with intent, all gentlemanly impulses discarded for the moment.

The magic was cunning and helpful now that they were cooperating. It had clothes unzipped and unbuttoned with barely any effort on their part.

Jack lifted Io into the hammock, stepping between her stripped legs, and began leaning into her. Magic didn't want foreplay, it wanted to join up the parts that were separated and grow itself into something huge. That required that Jack be inside her. Now.

She was tight, but yielding. Her body wanted, too, and he shuddered with pleasure as she wrapped her legs about him and pulled him deeper inch by relentless inch.

He curled his fingers into the cotton mesh to anchor it and began a slow retreat. His body protested and stopped its moaning only when he retook lost ground. He began pounding into her, each thrust inside getting hotter and hotter.

Io arched, her magic lashing out with bright blue hands and pulling him in after her, calling his climax out of his body against his will and inclination.

Jack collapsed over her, his body setting the hammock into a short swing. He was stunned. No one had ever been able to reach inside and take power from him.

When the shivering finally stopped and they were able to speak again, Io cleared her throat and said softly: "Jack? The magic . . . *wants something from us*, doesn't it? This isn't enough."

"Yes, I know."

"And it won't stop doing this . . . this . . . lust *thing* until it gets what it wants, will it?"

"Probably not."

She swallowed. "I guess we'll have to figure out what it's asking for when we have more time."

Eat my heart. Drink my soul. Love me to death.

"I know what it wants," Jack said, levering himself

upright. A part of him wanted to retreat from her, but he kept himself from doing so. "Come on, let's take a shower and then catch a nap."

He offered her his hand, which she accepted warily. The magic had subsided but wasn't gone. He understood. With any encouragement the growing enchantment would compel them to another round, and Jack didn't want that to happen. Not yet. They *had* to sleep. Maybe after they rested they would regain some control of themselves.

"What does the magic want?" Io asked. Her question was even tighter than her grip.

"Just the usual," Jack answered shortly, making sure she had gained her footing before letting go. He'd had Newton's apple dropped on his head a while ago and was used to the idea, but he wasn't at all sure how she was going to take the news about the magic's laws of evolution and gravity applying to her as well.

"And that would be?"

"For us to fall in love and then make baby feys. It knows our kind are all but extinct, and it's protecting itself. Without us, it dies." He turned his head to see how this news was being received, but couldn't read anything in Io's expression. Her lids were lowered, her eyes veiled.

Was she considering the fact that they had never practiced any kind of birth control while having sex? It was rarely necessary among feys because they almost never conceived without magical aid. Of course, magic *had* been aiding them.

"It doesn't want much, does it? Personally, I don't think I can do all that tonight," Io finally said. "My social calendar is completely booked with mass destruction and arson."

"Yeah, mine too. The magic will just have to learn to live with frustration just like we all do," Jack joked. But his voice sounded short, because for some reason he did not like her answer, even though it was the only sensible one.

The magic didn't like it either and sent a shaft of desire through him, jerking his eyes down to Io's body so he would be confronted with her nakedness.

She nodded and stepped quickly into the bathroom. She had color in her cheeks, but whether from renewed desire or embarrassment he couldn't tell.

He decided it might be best if he didn't follow her.

Chapter Twenty-three

The sky was blanked out with heavy clouds, so Io could not see the moon, but she didn't need a lunar clock to tell it was nearly the witching hour. The Halloween crowds were growing manic, almost impossible to control, high on drugs, high on booze, high on mischief and dark magic.

"Time to go," she whispered to herself.

Io left the shadowy doorway where she'd been loitering and pushed her way into the throngs, heading for her chosen hive entrance on Edmund Place. She wore a cheap black cape that covered a tool belt outfitted with gun, knife, salt and hair spray instead of the usual screwdriver, pliers, and wire cutters. Her face was hidden behind a latex troll mask. Jack had chosen it for her.

He really did have a morbid sense of humor.

Her most important evening accessories were not visible. They were the enlarging spell that Jack had picked up while entering the city on his last trip out, and the fire spell, which, after careful tuning, could ignite almost anything she touched and burn it to ash. Of course, she hadn't been able to try the spells out on any magical beings to see if they worked with supernatural beasties like gargoyles. Not that she wanted to! Io shuddered and pushed the thought away.

With these two magics, she planned to take the can of hair spray and turn it into a flamethrower. The salt in her belt would also be multiplied until it covered the underground in sterile snow. Looking at the crowds, she hoped fervently the havoc would all stay belowground. She wasn't trying to burn or purify the topside city—but the crops and the soil they grew in had to be destroyed-forever. She was going to march through Goblin City's underground like General Sherman going to the sea.

There might be casualties up top. She had to accept that.

Fire and salt were good for another reason. They were effective goblin-stoppers, should keep the beasties from creeping up behind her as she retreated. That meant she only had to watch her front and sides.

She was hoping passionately that most of the goblins were topside for Halloween. They seemed to be. The streets were full of them. She was quite happy to be a saboteur, but as the night went on and she saw the monsters reveling with the tourists, she was less enthused about being their executioner. They were buglike, but bugs that seemed to have feelings too.

She checked her watch to confirm what she felt, and then lengthened her stride. She began using magic to get people out of her way. Jack's bit of death-fey intimidation juju worked like a charm on the distracted partyers who split like the sea on the prow of a ship.

Io tried to psych herself up as she would before a game, but of course this wasn't just sport and it made the task harder. In a game there would only be two ends of a field or court to worry about, and only two teams to keep track of. But tonight she and Jack were after many goals. They had many enemies. And there were at least three teams in the field, possibly a fourth: tourists, goblins, those on the side of angels—Io smiled at the idea of her and Jack in wings and halos—and maybe H.U.G. The home team had the advantage of numbers and ruthlessness, and there were no referees to keep the fight fair. Io doubted the goblins would be using Marquis of Queensberry rules, so she, Jack, Zayn, and Cisco, couldn't afford to either.

Synchronicity would be an important player too. If Io began or ended her arsonistic distraction too late, her friends might all be caught and subdued through sheer numbers of goblins returning to the hive at dawn. But Io still had to give enough time for Zayn to rescue Chloe—and for Jack to get to

Horroban, deal with him, and then escape topside—
before she fired the tunnels and trapped their enemies inside. Both she and Jack were loaded with
lots of protective magic, and Jack had the steel fist,
which should be able to remove any obstacles that
blocked his path. Yet the fire she was about to loose
was a magical one, fed with two supercharged spells
that had never been mingled before, on a night
when raw magic rode the air in nearly tangible
waves of limitless fuel. There was no way to predict
accurately what it would do once she unleashed it.

She was especially worried about Zayn and Chloe
being slow to escape. *Chloe* . . . Even career criminals had a certain system of ethics they honored. A
thief or confidence man would abhor a child-
molester or rapist as often as anyone did. That often
wasn't the case with goblin-fruit junkies.

She'd warned Zayn, "You've got to watch Chloe.
She has probably been brainwashed to hate all of
us. Horroban would have done this right off. And
she knows if you take her away from here she'll
never taste goblin fruit again. She may very well turn
on you the first chance she gets. And she'll drag her
feet all the way."

Zayn nodded, but hadn't changed his mind about
rescuing her.

Poor Zayn—he had it bad. But . . . Io shrugged.
There was nothing she could do about it now. It was
in the lap of the goddess, who'd have to look after
the ill-fated love affair; Io was busy saving mankind.

The last part of the night's plan was to have Jack's buddy blow up the perfume factory. Casualties, Cisco had assured Jack, would be minimal because it was in the business quarter and would be closed for the night. Besides, most tourists would be rushing down to the red-light district—for once quite literally full of red light—to see what the underground fires were about.

Looking at the packed streets, Io wondered if this was realistic thinking. People might be too drunk to think clearly about what to do in an emergency or pay any attention to where they were. Of course, on the plus side, the factory wouldn't go up until three A.M. That would give tourists a chance to tire and go home, and the worst of the raw magic would have subsided back into the earth, returning some wits to those who were overwhelmed by its power.

In spite of her earlier, impulsive words to Jack about having a weenie roast at the bonfire of Goblin Town, Io would have objected to this part of the arrangement because of the remote chance of hurting the Halloween tourists—except for one thing. There was no way of knowing how much of the addictive perfume might have already been bottled from earlier harvests or where it was stored. If they had had more time, they could have gone in again and investigated the factory more fully, but the hours and minutes of preparation time had simply run out. Finding Horroban and the fruit fields had been their first priority. They hadn't discovered any stash.

All Io could do was hope, and remind herself that the people reveling around her were dead anyway if Horroban succeeded in his plans. They might already be addicts if they had been to Glashtin's club.

" 'scuse me." A drunk reeled back from Io, staggering into the street. His glazed eyes showed traces of fear as he looked at her mask. The man *should* be afraid. Tonight she was more dangerous than any real troll.

Io nodded once but didn't answer. Her throat was too tight. Bottled-up fear and revved magic were both trying to escape, and slowly strangling her as she kept swallowing against them. It was painful, an all-but-intolerable burning in her throat, but all she could do was ignore the fear and the magic until it was time to let them free.

So, here was the team. Here was the plan. Io thought again of Jack, already on his way into the hive. Of all of them, he had the hardest job, and the most dangerous. He needed every bit of power and luck that Fate could spare.

Jack. . . .

Instead of continuing to try and psych herself into battle mode, Io bowed her head and began praying to the goddess for his well-being. Her lips moved behind her mask, perspiration beading on her forehead and running down her cheeks. She was nearly certain it was perspiration and not tears.

The *please, please, please,* of her prayers matched her footsteps and thudding heart as she marched down the increasingly deserted street.

Goddess! Why hadn't she listened to the magic and told him that she loved him? Her fear of love might kill him.

Jack passed through a more formal arch that marked the start of Horroban's home—*goblinium grand* in style perhaps—and went under the structure he thought of as the clock tower, though it actually was more of a lopsided cylinder and had no clock in it, just a half-formed ugly face crossed with sticks jutting out of the south side two-thirds of the way up. What its purpose was, he could not guess. It seemed ornamental, but goblins as a rule did not go in much for art.

Next there was a moat ringed with torches. Io hadn't liked this place at all. Jack understood. It was impossible to judge just how deep it ran because the water was quite black and tarry, showing nothing but the flickering orange fire on its black surface. Yet, he was convinced that the circular lake ran very, very deep. It *felt* deep.

It didn't seem possible that anything could live in it, but Jack was willing to bet that something did. Horroban wasn't the type to do things solely for aesthetics, and there weren't any other watchdogs about. At another time, he might have been curious enough to toss in a stone and see what happened, but whatever was down there could just stay down there. Jack didn't plan on making any social calls on swamp monsters that night. One should always let sleeping dogs and monsters lie.

The ceremonial entrance to Horroban's stronghold had been stolen off of someone's Moorish castle. The door was thick, studded with iron nails, and it was barred—but that wasn't a problem. Finally calling upon the spell he'd been charging all day, Jack wrapped himself more deeply in his muffling invisibility and then jammed his fist through the old oak portal. He shoved the inner bar aside, doing his best to keep the sound to a minimum.

Little pigs, little pigs, let me come in . . . or I'll huff and I'll puff, and I'll blow your house in.

As Jack shoved his uninjured hand deeper into the wood, he blessed Io for her craftwork that had altered the spell into something so useful. She was a master at making silk purses out of sows' ears. Jack could make spells strong, but it was simply brute force prevailing over weaker magic. If he pushed too hard, he could break spells, collapsing their structures like aluminum cans. Io coaxed and charmed and bent subtly. Her spells were flexible and strong. They stretched. Look what she had done with his own core magic. *Love me, Jack*, she had said, shifting the ancient protective word charm into something else.

And he did love her, goddess help him. Against all will and common sense, he loved her.

The timing of this revelation sucked, but it did add incentive to finish this job quickly and safely.

Jack pushed more power into his spell and shoved harder on the wedged bar. There was some noise when the brace hit the floor and when the hinges creaked open, but no one seemed interested in seeing who was destroying Horroban's door. Most likely everyone was up top partying. It was nearly midnight. Most magical beings would be higher than kites.

And Io would be in the tunnels now, getting ready to loose her magical conflagration.

Jack moved on through the black arcade, being just one more shadow among all the other shades that crouched there in the windowless mansion. He went slowly because the magic was thick here— thick and evil and waiting. There were no lights of any kind, and there were certain to be magical trip wires and other more physical traps. Jack was betting that that was the unwelcoming kind of guy Horroban was.

The corridor had been built all out of bad angles and uneven surfaces that had no sympathy for the preferences of human height and clumsy feet. But Jack had no trouble knowing where he needed to go. As he had told Io, a magical being's inner sorcery always knew where to seek out other sorcery. No darkness was deep enough to obscure that path.

Following the psychic slime trail of Horroban's now familiar black art, Jack went down a narrow stair cleft into the stone. Naturally, this would be Horroban's choice of locale: the deepest, darkest, closest spot to the upswell of magical power, which would peak at midnight. Sorcery Central.

Jack wiped the sweat from his face.

Goddess willing, there'd be no peak for the goblin king tonight, no nasty magical climax to make him shivery with wicked delight. Death would call on Horroban instead, and he wouldn't offer the goblin king a chance to use the mitigating charm he had donated to Io. This was one goblin whose heart was going to stop. *Eat it, drink, love it*—it didn't matter. Horroban was about to die. He'd die so the world would be safe. So *Io* would be safe.

Io didn't put the manhole cover back in place. She wanted her retreat left open since she probably would be heading back at a flat-out run, quite possibly with half the goblin population from beneath the Motor City on her heels. There would certainly be fire chasing her.

She walked silently, but boldly, heading for the fields outside Horroban's headquarters. She would start there and retreat back to Lutin's special hydroponics project, and then take out all the fields back to Edmund Street.

It would have been nice to take her mask off and allow the sweat on her face to run free, but a bit of concealment would buy her a measure of safety and time if she were spotted from a distance.

Chapter Twenty-four

"Where are Xanthe's pet spies?" the voice, familiar from television, asked. *William Hamilton. Horroban.* He didn't speak in goblin. Perhaps all the surgery had altered his vocal chords so that he could no longer produce the proper sounds.

Jack finished checking for wards on the chamber door, disabling the ones he found, but knowing there would be more inside the mirrored room beyond where all the reflective surfaces would increase the goblins' power.

He was ready, and it was time, but . . . he decided to watch and listen to his prey for a moment before sending spells and bullets into the magic-charged space.

It was an odd moment—*the moment*—brought about by Fate, and it seemed that the occasion should be marked somehow. If nothing else, Jack thought it was likely that he would never be this close to true evil again.

Also, he might learn something useful for later on. Information was power and the second coin of the realm. And Jack wanted info in a bad way because, though he doubted that Horroban had actually uncovered the magical generator, the goblin warlord had gotten hold of something very powerful, very old, and very magical that was allowing him to focus the magic that dwelled down here.

"No one's seen 'em lately," several warped Glashtins answered. The halves of the weather goblin's face that Jack could see in the multiple mirrors were all green iridescence under the glowing plaster ceiling. He sounded drunk and held a brandy snifter loosely in his upper right hand. "Figured they'd go back to Lutin's after sneaking around down here, but they never went back. They haven't been in the club either. Hille's real disappointed about that. She had plans for the little fey girl after the show tonight."

"I see. Neveling?" the calm voice asked next. "You are *quite* certain they haven't been in the factory? Jack Frost's reputation among our contacts in law enforcement does not suggest that he is the sort of man to simply abandon a project."

"Oh yes, I'm quite sure," a new voice said. "I've left Slav and Plait there to roam at will. He'd have been eaten if he came back." The goblin perfumer's voice was high; his surgeon had not been as skilled as Horroban's in manufacturing the perfect human tenor. Or perhaps the goblin was nervous. "I think they have given up. Our contacts in the police department haven't seen Jack in days and believe he has left town. And, anyway, there wasn't anything to find at the factory. Since her spy got eaten, Xanthe has been most cooperative about discouraging H.U.G. from doing anything *active*. The perfume release will go as planned."

"It is nice to know that Xanthe has cooperated. Not that it will do her any good. The little sister dies tonight. *Ah, but how?* Let's see. Give her to the trolls? They've been very patient. Would you like that, Toc?"

"Sure. Thanks, boss!" a troll, presumably Toc, said. His several long-nosed reflections grinned, showing double rows of jagged teeth. "Me and the boys appreciate it. We ain't had us a girl for a long time."

"She's at the factory," Neveling spoke up in a fretful voice. Several misshapen versions of the perfume maker pulled at their identical bow ties. "She'll have to be fetched and taken elsewhere. I don't want the mess at work. The last killing ruined the carpet!"

Horroban sighed. "Fine. I don't think Toc is particular about where he takes his meals. But be quiet now. It is nearly time. How I have waited for *thissss* night!" Horroban's tongue flicked out quickly. He closed his eyes and began 'mainlining power—that was the only word that Jack could think of to describe what was happening.

Jack watched, fascinated, as Horroban's modified

skin began to glow and his dark hair grew large, perhaps raised at the roots as the current of swelling magic contracted his scalp muscles. His perfect, capped teeth appeared as the lips pulled away in an unnatural grin. His eyebrows and cheeks drew back as well, making his lower jaw appear longer and even more pointed.

Everyone obediently fell silent, bowing their heads. They looked respectful, but unable to enjoy the magic the way Horroban did. Lutin, in fact, appeared rather ill and kept swallowing convulsively.

Time to go.

Jack shifted a bit so that he could better see where the troll Toc was standing. Neveling and Glashtin were dressed in formal wear and didn't seem to be armed, but the troll would be. Yes, he had a gun holstered on his left side, but he wouldn't have a clear shot at Jack without moving. Trolls were slow.

Satisfied that the mirrors hadn't deceived him and that he knew where everyone was, Jack shifted his attention back to the creature he was planning to exterminate.

Evil had chosen a less than prepossessing face. It was not extraordinarily ugly, nor extraordinarily beautiful. It was not extraordinarily anything. Yet however modest his wrappings, Horroban *was* extraordinary, and Jack respected that fact even as he detested what the creature was doing.

Horroban had aimed high and succeeded—the best law school, then the state senate, next a seat in congress. And his final stop was the White House. It seemed inevitable. The public loved his southern witticisms delivered in his soft, slow, drawling style. He was homely as all modified goblins were, but still looked good in the spotlight. His supporters felt sure he would look even better standing behind the presidential podium.

It was hard to imagine how he had gotten where he was. His pedigree was impeccable, seemingly impossible to forge. Yet somehow it had been stolen at some time in the real man's life without anyone noticing. Horroban had slipped into this man's shoes without a single misstep and without leaving any betraying footprints behind as clues. He'd taken William Hamilton's identity, his power, his wife, his children, and almost certainly his life.

Horroban sat there in his wing-backed chair, seemingly a man of wealth and authority, dressed impeccably in an Italian wool suit, dark red tie, and handmade shoes. Of course, it was anyone's guess as to what sort of animal the leather for those shoes had come from—Xanthe's mole would be Jack's first bet. Or maybe the man whose identity he had stolen. It would amuse a goblin to daily tread on the man into whose "shoes he'd stepped."

Worst of all, Horroban was smugly certain he was going to get away with poisoning the whole human world. It could happen, too, if Jack failed.

Horroban was surrounded by protection both physical and magical. Jack knew beyond any doubt that his own death spells wouldn't be enough to kill the goblin king so close to midnight, not unless they touched—and that was not something that Jack wanted. But a long-distance, nonmagical hit was fine with him. He'd prepared for this eventuality. Jack's hand slipped inside his jacket and he unholstered his gun and aimed it in one smooth movement.

Time to go.

Still, he hesitated with a finger on the trigger, waiting for a last miracle, a trick of magic that would allow the cup of cold-blooded murder to pass his lips without him having to drink. Jack had killed— many, many times. But never in cold blood. It was more difficult than he'd imagined.

As he hesitated, a small foreign doubt entered his mind, and finding fertile soil, it blossomed insidiously. Its petals of misgiving unfurled like an umbrella, getting between Jack's body and the light of his will.

What if Horroban wasn't a goblin? What if he was just a benevolent human who was trying to unite the species in peace? He didn't look like a goblin, did he?

Jack's eyelids began to twitch and his palms to sweat.

No! That wasn't true. Horroban was a goblin, a killer. He'd just heard the monster say he was going to feed Chloe to the trolls!

How could he think that? It was all a misunderstanding. He had no proof. None.

270

No, but—

Something popped open in Jack's mind, sending small ricochets of pain bouncing off the interior of his skull.

He should put the gun down and reconsider what he was doing. Jack was the one who was planning death—not Horroban. He was a death fey, an evil carrier of doom. He should maybe even turn the gun around and point it at himself. That would be the best thing. He should do it now! Now!

Horroban's eyes flashed open, staring into the space Jack occupied. In that instant, Jack could see the goblin inside the man. The pupils were slits, each iris running all the way to the eyelids. The entire ocular cavity glowed with black sorcery. It was sorcery that the goblin was using to invade Jack's mind, the white noise of his mind-rending scream causing some form of neural jamming.

The goblin's mouth opened, ready to speak words of power that would force Jack into turning the pistol on himself. Part of Jack wanted that, believed he deserved it. The rest of him cried out for help to finish the job before it was too late.

Jack! Jack, what's wrong? Io's voice cut through the manic screaming, breaking through the magic blanket that was blotting out his brain and will, and giving him something to hold on to. He blessed the telepathy that had grown up between them. *Jack Frost, answer me! Right now, or I'm coming in after you!*

Io! He couldn't let her near this!

Jack's hand steadied. Not giving Horroban a chance to articulate any part of a suicide spell, Jack ignored the brain-ripping screams of Horroban's subliminal voice and carefully put two rounds into the goblin's head, and then one in the monster's chest for good measure. He doubted the creature actually had a heart, but in case he did have something there, it was better to pulp it into something that couldn't be eaten or used in some spell by other goblins.

Immediately, the foreign voice stopped screaming in Jack's brain, the echoes slowing dying and leaving Jack's mind blessedly empty, a crater blasted clear by a searing bomb.

Jack let out a slow breath, his gun hand lowering to his side. His whole body was trembling, awash in adrenaline and foreign magic that was no longer being guided and therefore rushing about purposelessly.

Jack? Io's voice was louder now.

It's okay. I'm all right now. Don't come here.

Swear by the goddess! she demanded.

I swear.

And he was all right. It had worked. Jack's invisibility spell had stifled the soft sounds of the gun that the man-made muffler had not. Standing five feet away, the others hadn't heard a thing. With their heads still bowed and their eyes down cast, no one seemed to notice Horroban slumping deeper into his chair, his eyelids lowering halfway as the light faded from his eyes.

Jack stood shaking and amazed, and again blessed Io for the tweaking she had done to his spell. It felt like a grenade had exploded in his head, but no one had heard Jack cry out. No one moved. They hadn't felt any of it, not the mental battle, not the directed magic, not the death. The spell had held its shield even when Jack wasn't in control. It had held fast in the face of the strongest sorcery he had ever encountered.

And thanks to it, Horroban was dead.

Horroban was dead!

Jack realized that he could leave right then and it would be several seconds—valuable seconds—before anyone grasped what had happened. Wrapped in invisibility, Jack could be out and away, and no one would ever know that he had been the one to off Horroban. He could hook up with Io and they could escape at once—go far away, and neither of them would have to confront this awful magic again.

He wanted to—with all his heart, he wanted to flee, to run away from the awesome magic that Horroban had used to try to kill him.

But that would be leaving the job half done, and the rest of the merry band of mass murderers still alive and plotting. There'd be no White House, but they'd still have fruit, perfume, and a plan.

Damnation!

And they knew about Io and Zayn. Goblins hadn't heard the one about carrying vengeance to the grave but no further. They wouldn't shrug off Horroban's death as a casualty of war. They'd hunt Jack and Io and Zayn forever. Chloe as well, if she weren't already dead. And they would go right on with their arrangement to poison the world with goblin-fruit perfume. Why not? There was nothing to stop them.

But he could put an end to their deadly stratagems tonight. If all the conspirators died, and their genetically altered fruit went with them, there wouldn't be anyone left to carry on Horroban's legacy.

All he had to do was confront one more time the black magic running wild in that room. Go into that maelstrom, keep a hold on his sanity for a few seconds, and let his gun do its work. Without Horroban to direct this city's magic against him, he could probably manage the task.

No! Io protested. *Whatever it is, Jack, don't do it!*

Sorry, little fey.

Jack didn't want to do it, but he'd have to go into the room to get Toc, Glashtin, and Neveling. He had no clean line of fire from the doorway—and that meant he'd have to leave his own protective magic outside the door. The ravenous power welling up in the room would try to strip his brain and gather up his magic as he stepped inside. It might even turn his own core magic against him. He had no defenses

274

against his own magic—none. Jack couldn't risk it. That was rule one of magical self-defense: Don't go into battle with any weapon that could be turned against you.

You won't be able to hear me! Io said, apparently doing the math and realizing what he was going to try. *Jack, don't do it. I'll get the fruit. We'll stop them later. We'll get the fruit, the factory. We'll have time to make another plan.*

He wished passionately that it were true.

The odds were three to one against him, and the troll was definitely armed. Glashtin had strong internal magic and might be able to use the power in the room. That made him dangerous. Lutin was an unknown, but that didn't mean he could be discounted.

Jack thought of Io, conjured a picture of her face. Then he pictured her body after the trolls had been at her.

Three to one. And free-ranging, carnivorous magic was surging through the room, looking for a place to manifest itself, looking for someone to use. Not great odds, but he had to see this through. Even if he didn't make it out alive.

Fate and the goddess be with him. For Io's sake, for her future, he had to stop them.

Get going, little fey. Horroban is dead and I'll be there in a minute. Burn this son-of-a-bitch hive down. Jack made his thoughts calm and forceful.

Jack!

I love you. Now do it.

Not giving her a chance to answer, in case the reply wasn't the one he wanted to hear, Jack broke his connection with her.

Regretting the loss of fine spells they'd accumulated, Jack slipped off his invisibility and other protection.

Taking a breath, focusing his energy and thoughts on what he had to do, he stepped into the magical maelstrom.

"Trick or treat," he managed to say, the sound of his voice fighting off some of the magical surges that were still trying to find a place to jack into his brain and electrocute him.

Toc looked up and gasped as Jack appeared in the doorway.

"The faerie's here. And he's got a gun!" Then, events began to sink in. "Hey, look! I think he shot the boss!"

Neveling Lutin squeaked and hid behind his chair.

"Don't shoot! Don't shoot! I didn't want to do it! I swear I didn't." But even as he pleaded, his hand fumbled into his pocket and he pulled out a canister of what looked like mace, but was probably loaded with something far more addictive.

"Shut up, you coward! He's not shot. This is just more Halloween bullshit. Anyway, faeries don't use guns!" Glashtin insisted, apparently stupefied as well as drunk. His eyes were open, but his brain was not comprehending the visual message that Horroban was dead.

"This one does." Jack said quietly as he put two rounds into the cowering Lutin who had pointed the canister at him, and then several into the charging Toc. True to troll-form, the beast had first chosen fists over bullets and was too slow to get his guns lined up before the deed was done.

Jack didn't like people who pointed guns at him, and trolls in general since they ate people. Toc's long shiny teeth and long shiny guns both offended him, and the thought of what they could do to Io filled him with enormous, cold rage. It was enough, when combined with the last of Jack's own core magic, for him to shove back the foreign sorcery and command his body to act.

When Toc didn't fall quickly enough, Jack gave him a roundhouse punch to the head to help him on his way. It would have been better with the steel fist, but his own hand seemed up to the job.

"Did you really just call me a fairy?" he demanded, turning to the unarmed Glashtin. He aimed his gun at the nightclub owner and pulled the trigger again, but the gun was empty.

Looking down the silenced barrel of Jack's pistol, the weather goblin at last woke up to his danger. He jumped to his feet and fled into the dark stairwell before Jack could reload.

Annoyed at his own slowed reflexes, Jack slapped

another clip into his gun and started after the scuttling goblin.

Behind him, the magic of Goblin Town began its midnight crescendo, not caring that its audience was dead. Jack shut the door on the billowing sorcery. He hated being magically naked, but didn't try to pull any of the raw power out with him to shape into a quick sight spell. The sorcery in Horroban's little dungeon room was fierce but unwholesome, and his own magic was too spent. What spells he'd shed in the other hallway were likely corrupted now, too. He'd never show himself to Io with such taint inside him. Bad enough that it had touched his skin and bombed his brain. He'd have to do a cleansing before he touched her again. He couldn't risk that any lingering bits of such contamination would try to mingle with her own pure magic and structure itself into something even more powerful than it already was.

Jack stepped cautiously onto the narrow stair, hoping all of Horroban's horror palace wasn't as dark as his dungeons. Finding his way back out of this funhouse would be a lot harder without any sorcery to aid him.

Maybe, if he were lucky, Glashtin would find any booby traps before Jack stumbled into them. And if the goddess smiled on him, the drunken goblin would fall in the moat and get eaten by whatever lived down there, or get caught in Io's fire.

"Time to go." Then, though he knew Io couldn't hear him anymore, he added, "Go on, little fey, burn it all down."

Chapter Twenty-five

I love you, Jack had said, and then disappeared before Io could answer.

I love you, too, she responded, but knew it was too late. Something had happened to the power flowing between them, and whatever it was, it had shut off her unexpected mental connection to Jack. She was alone again.

Io stood outside Horroban's gardens, hesitating. Jack had said to start the burn, but perhaps she should wait.

Heat and magic were shimmering in the green air, spreading out in concentric rings from Horroban's windowless mansion. The waves were getting stronger, hotter, and brighter with every passing minute. The atmosphere was growing unstable and beginning to distort the world before her eyes. Breathing was almost impossible. Io pulled off her troll mask, stuffing it into her utility belt. It didn't help much. There was no fresh air to be had.

Io knew she shouldn't wait. Another few minutes and she might pass out from heat and lack of oxygen. It was time. She *had* to start.

Terrified at what she was about to do, and feeling like a novice trapeze artist about to make her maiden jump without a safety net, Io looked inside for her enlarging spell. She pulled it out carefully. In spite of the heat, her skin wore a chill and her hands trembled, making her fumble when she reached for her can of hair spray.

A part of her wondered where Jack had found an aerosol spray can. They had been outlawed years ago because they were bad for the environment. Certainly this particular can was going to do a lot of damage to the ozone.

She popped off the cap and pointed the container at the part of the garden that was farthest from the mansion's entrance. Channeling the spell, she began forcing the hair spray into a long arch that stretched over the acres of fruit, raining down a deadly mist.

Next came the tricky part, igniting Jack's fire spell without blowing up everything in the cavern. Io concentrated on the stream of fuel, willing it alone to burn. Almost immediately, fire of fiercest blue raced toward the mansion's walls.

"Damn!"

Io hurriedly lowered the can to the plants' level, adjusting the fire's trajectory and, finally satisfied with the range, she began searing the crops.

With her left hand, she reached into her belt and pulled out the canister of salt. She had to use her teeth to open it, but once the spout was clear, she had no problem sending part of the enlarging spell down that arm and into the salt, which she began dumping on the ground.

She covered the stony soil in fire up to the mansion door, but then fell back, leaving a clear path to the rear tunnel. Maybe Jack had found another way out of the mansion, but if not, she couldn't close off his only route of flight. There were Zayn and Chloe to consider, too. Some of the plants would probably escape the fire if she didn't finish the job, but so be it. She would not take the chance of trapping either her comrade or her lover in the inferno of this cavern. Io stopped her flamethrower, first by turning off the fire, letting up on the button, and then pulling back the enlargement spell.

The air was very bad now, every breath a pain to pull into her lungs. Her nose breather was filtering out poison gases but the heat was awful, and the oxygen was burning up at a terrible rate. The air was also growing thick with greasy smoke from fruit that didn't shrivel but rather burned like meat on a too-hot grill.

Still, Io hesitated to leave. She was dizzy and feeling sick, but she lingered, eyes tearing in the heat, waiting for Jack. He was coming. She was sure of it.

Fire largely obscured her targeted area of sight,

but she saw Jack when he emerged from the mansion's doorway.

Something was strange about him: he was staggering and even from a distance she could see that there was something wrong with his eyes. They were flat, lifeless.

He was without magic, she realized with a shock. He had no magical defenses at all. This was the first time she had seen him without some kind of supernatural power and it was frightening because it made him look vulnerable.

"Jack!" she yelled, enlarging her voice so he would hear her over the roar of the fire. She tried to circle closer to him but was stymied by flames. "I'm over here by the tunnel. What happened?"

Jack lowered his hands and squinted at her over the sea of blue fire. He shouted back what sounded like, "Lutin and Horroban are dead. But I can't find Glashtin! Maybe . . . the moat."

"Where are Zayn and Chloe?" Io called back, feeling uncomfortable about yelling their plans across the cavern where the echoes could escape and warn others in the tunnels. Still, she was profoundly thankful that Jack was there to yell at, and didn't neglect the chance for them to speak again. "Did they make it out?"

Jack shouted back something about Lutin's factory and gargoyles. He said he was going to take the elevator near Neveling's place because it was more direct.

Overhead, the ceiling cracked and glowing green plaster began to fall. Io stared at it in dismay. They had to get out before the cavern collapsed on them—but not yet! She had something more she had to tell Jack—something that might give him some power back.

"Jack, I love you," Io called, beginning to cough. This wasn't the way she had planned on sharing this revelation with her lover, but she was not putting it off any longer. They might be wasting escape time, but hopefully to good effect. If nothing else, it should make the magic happy when it returned to Jack again. "Be careful. I swear if you die, I'll never forgive you."

The rising heat distorted his features, and his narrowed eyelids made it hard to see his emotion. But she knew when Jack grinned at her. His white teeth were a beacon.

Staring at her lover across a blue inferno, Io could only be amazed. He was stripped of magic and caught in a conflagration that could kill him, but still he seemed in control. Io wondered what it would take to crush him.

Then, horrified that she might have called a jinx on them, she said a quick prayer that she would never find out.

". . . Love . . . too." Jack called back. "Careful not . . . cut . . . line of retreat."

A tower of flame shot straight into the air, stopping only at the cavern's ceiling. The growing blaze forced Jack back a pace. The thing Jack called the clock tower was burning now. It was impossible to know for sure, but it looked as though there were a sort of giant skull under the plaster that grinned at Io with searing teeth.

What the hell had Horroban been conjuring down here?

"I'll be careful. Get out of here while you still can! I'll meet you at the factory!" Io shouted as the fire found a crack in the cavern floor and began to bellow its happiness at the discovery of new fuel. Fresh flames reached for the ceiling, their fingers contorting as they clawed at the fracturing stone and started crawling their way to the surface. It looked like a fire demon being born.

Jack gave her a thumbs-up and then was gone into a tunnel. Barely able to breathe, Io also retreated from the hellscape blaze she'd ignited.

Jack! Be safe!

Resolved to finish as quickly as possible and get back to her magically impaired lover, Io ran toward the next hydroponic garden, spending her physical and magical strength recklessly. She began organizing her spells so she could attack again the moment she reached the room. There was much less moisture in the air now; the fire was devouring it along with the oxygen.

Io erupted into the hydroponic room, igniting her blowtorch and spraying crops as she ran. She flung out salt with her left hand, making wild expenditures of her magic to get the job done as quickly as possible. She didn't see any of the crawling workers in the fields, but didn't stop to search for them. If they were there, they would perish. Her priorities were now crystal clear. Jack topped the list.

The goblin fruit exploded like bombs, hand grenades of juice that burst into fireballs. The cavern became a war zone of organic shrapnel, but Io never slowed, even when bits of burst fruit fell on her cape and began to sizzle like napalm. If it reached her skin, she would stop to deal with it. Until that happened, she would run with Jack's spell and burn down all evil.

Jack ran through the door of the garage and pulled up short, saved from a fall only by the corrugations in the metal floor that grabbed the soles of his shoes.

The goddess was still with him. Not only was the elevator there and humming with power, so was Horroban's limo.

Jack dropped to a quick crouch, pulling out his pistol. It was frustrating not having any spells to draw on. He had to rely on the sensitivity of his ears to tell him if anyone was about. With the tunnels filling up with oily and possibly poisonous smoke, he didn't dare remove his nose breather and hunt by smell.

He circled the limo, moving like a crab until he came to the driver's door. Taking hold of the handle, he jerked up and then rolled to stay behind the protection of the door.

Nothing. No one was inside. His luck held.

Not daring to get trapped in the interior, Jack circled the car again to the passenger door and repeated the jerking-and-rolling routine. No one. The car was empty and conveniently full of guns.

Jack went quickly to the control box and started the elevator on its way. He jumped into the driver's seat and had a bit more luck—the keys were in the ignition. He wouldn't have to remember how to hot-wire an auto manually.

Jack began to frown. This was a great deal of good luck in a very short period and it made him nervous. He didn't like it when things went too much his way. The scales always balanced in the end, and so far he had been bloody fortunate. A big bill was coming due.

The elevator rose slowly and he began to feel new tension as he closed in on the surface. The new apprehension showed itself in his tightening stomach and in the muscles of his neck.

The limo's engine was cold, but it didn't argue when Jack turned the key. He adjusted the seat backward to accommodate his long legs and clipped on his seat belt, listening carefully to the motor as it idled. Goblins were terrible about maintenance, but this engine was humming nicely by the time the elevator stopped on the ground floor of the old General Motors building.

Quite carelessly, someone had left the bay doors open, so Jack could drive right out into the night.

Or maybe it wasn't carelessness. Perhaps it was a trap. Could Glashtin have come this way? What to do, what to do . . . ? Jack looked at his watch, but his hopes weren't answered in a happy way.

"Damn it."

Time to go.

Not trusting the situation, Jack nevertheless gave the car the gun and rocketed out into the night. He had to get to Neveling's factory. Zayn didn't know about the scheduled three A.M. bang. There'd been no reason to tell him about it when they thought Chloe was being kept at Horroban's. Jack wasn't a fan of Zayn's, but he didn't want the blood of innocents on his hands. He had to get Zayn and Chloe out of the building before it blew. He also had to warn Cisco to watch out for Lutin's gargoyles. One man, even armed, was barely a match for a pair of attack-trained gargoyles. An unwary man was nothing but dinner.

The streets were deserted around the automotive plant, and Jack took the car up to nearly top speed. There'd been no reason for the tourists to party down here. Horroban had seen to that. Yet things would be different as they neared Lutin's factory. There shouldn't be many people down there, but junkies did like the neighborhood. Jack had to make time now while it was safe.

Lights appeared suddenly in his rearview mirror,

coming up fast. They were a dangerous dazzlement to his already assaulted eyes. Jack slapped down the rearview mirror and punched the accelerator.

So, here was the expected scale balancer. Cursing, Jack reached into his pocket and pulled on his shades. Squinting into the lowered mirror he made out the shape of the car. It was a two-door Jaguar convertible sport model in gleaming red. There was only one XKR 100 in Goblin Town.

Glashtin. The thing in the moat hadn't eaten the goblin after all. Wasn't that too bad!

Lightning blasted the road ahead of Jack, temporarily blinding him with a white hot sheet of energy. The car-shaking thunder was instantaneous, telling Jack the strike had been close.

Damned weather goblin!

It was bad enough that he had to cope with a short clock and a faster car driven by a maniac; lightning strikes were a nasty icing on the cake. Or, more accurately, icing on the road.

The thought was no sooner conceived than hail began to fall. It wouldn't be long before the roads were impossible and treacherous.

Jack deliberated hard, calculating odds even as he picked up momentum. He had the advantage of a heavier car with better traction, and the fact that Glashtin had to expend tremendous effort to throw lightning at him. But Glashtin's Jag was built for speed—its V-8 engine was a screamer—and being close to the ground, it would corner well at fairly high speeds. Both Jack and the weather goblin knew the city, so geographic familiarity wasn't a factor in this fight. It would probably come down to who was the better driver—and who got lucky.

Jack grinned, his core magic slowly drinking in his racing adrenaline and beginning to awake from its swoon. Io's declaration of love had helped, too, allowing an exponential growth that had never been possible before.

It was his often-deplored human side that made him enjoy non-fey things, but he just loved fast cars! And he had a better grasp of what they could do than the goblin nightclub owner. Goblins were wary of machines, filled with distrust and fear of things mechanical. Glashtin wouldn't adore his car, wouldn't know how to coax her to perform. He would probably be gripping his wheel with all four hands, all twenty of his knuckles white.

And Jack was lucky.

Glashtin didn't stand a chance.

The only hitch would be if pedestrians got in the way. Glashtin wouldn't hesitate to play pedestrian pickoff with junkies. Jack still had a few scruples.

Cursing at the delay, Jack turned away from the factory and headed east where streets were likely to stay deserted. He rounded a bend and, for a moment, lost the goblin's hail and had a good look at the road ahead.

He glanced at his watch. Two-thirty. He had half an hour to lose the goblin, get to the factory, rendezvous with Io, warn Cisco, and make sure Zayn and Chloe were out before the big blow.

His reawakening magic answered confidently: *Piece of cake.* Jack wasn't certain that he could trust its assessment.

The street ran straight and empty, nothing but dark buildings lining the sidewalks.

Another lightning strike came dead ahead, buffeting the air, but Jack refused to swerve. At these speeds that was as good as suicide. Better to fry from a bolt than smash and burn slowly. Anyway, Glashtin had missed by thirty feet; he was having trouble driving and also throwing lightning around. A side benefit to not avoiding the storm was that driving through the electrical aura also fed Jack's magic, giving it juju food. Food was good. Jack needed his reflexes in top working order for what he was about to do.

He checked his mirror. It really was a shame that the Jag was going to have to be destroyed. Beautiful car—sexy, fast. It deserved better. But that was all he could do in this situation. Glashtin had to be eliminated, and Jack had no time for anything requiring long planning or finesse. It was all about math. This limo was built like a tank. It could stand a fairly heavy crash. Glashtin's Jag couldn't.

The smash would have to be soon, too; the limo's engine was beginning to starve for oxygen. The cold air helped, but the limo wasn't made for driving at high speeds for long distances and couldn't cram in the fuel the way the Jag could.

Jack began to slow, not using his brakes so the goblin wouldn't have any advance warning of his intentions. He watched the rearview mirror where Glashtin was coming up fast. The road in front of him was four lanes wide, empty, and as perfect as it was going to get for suicidal maneuvers. It was time for the coup de grâce, to plunge his vehicular knife home.

Now!

Jack killed his lights and hit the brakes, wincing as the limo's tires howled a pained protest. He spun the wheel about, demanding the long car make as tight a turn as possible and accelerate back the way it had come.

As soon as Jack was turned around, he hit his brights and aimed the car straight at Glashtin.

The goblin panicked at the sight of the onrushing limo, just as Jack expected. He stomped hard on the brakes, making his Jag swing crazily from side to side. Each sway brought a frantic overcorrection, further eroding Glashtin's control.

Jack watched with morbid fascination. Where would they hit? Right fore? Head on? Or would—yes! Glashtin's nerves failed him and he tried to turn the car. A better driver might have coaxed the Jag into doing it, but Glashtin hadn't the skill. Jack wasn't back up to more than forty mph, but it was enough. He slammed into the Jag's side door, tossing the lighter car into the air.

He saw Glashtin clap two hands over his eyes, the goblin's mouth open in a scream as he rolled out of sight.

Then the impact threw Jack against the seat belt, cutting hard against his chest and giving him a mild concussion as he hit his head on the wheel.

No air bag. Bad goblin maintenance struck again.

The next few moments were a confusing jumble of lights and tearing metal, but Jack quickly stomped on the brakes and turned off the engine, doing his best to control the limo's slide before he crashed again. He didn't want fuel in the engine if he did hit one of the buildings.

The brake pads howled all the way, but the limo came to rest standing diagonally across the road, its tires sending up small plumes of black smoke.

Jack looked out the side window and watched Glashtin's Jag roll twice more. He watched to see if Glashtin was somehow thrown clear, but the car was smashed flat, and a moment later burst into flame. Goblins could take a lot of damage, but not compression and incineration.

Exhaling slowly and feeling a bump rising on his forehead, Jack checked his watch. Two-thirty-eight. He had to get moving.

His fingers were not entirely steady as he reached for the keys and restarted the limo's engine.

He liked cars, and he liked excitement, but it

would be Hell in Antarctica before he ever tried something like that again. He was glad Io hadn't been there to see it; she'd have had fifteen different kinds of fits.

Thinking of Io, he began to smile again. It was probably too much to hope that she liked fast cars, too. Feys just didn't.

But on the other hand, she'd seemed to like guns. So, maybe his luck was better than he'd ever imagined.

Chapter Twenty-six

After the light of the fiery tunnels, the street above seemed as dark and empty as outer space, and about as cold. It took a moment for the afterimage of the magic inferno to fade from Io's retinas and for night vision to reestablish itself.

Io prayed that there wouldn't be any goblin goon squads getting between her and the perfume factory. It would ruin her bloodless record if she had to start shooting now. Nevertheless she pulled out her pistol and had it ready beneath her singed cloak. After all, she had just burned out the goblin hive, destroying their fall harvest and inflicting economic as well as social and psychological ruin. And Jack had killed their leader. She'd be welcomed as warmly as a dose of leprosy. Probably less warmly, because leprosy could actually be seen as a perverse form of beauty enhancement here in Goblin Town.

Io was tired and feeling debilitating cold creeping into her bones to spread its dulling ache, but she reached inside for the reservoir of will to make a quick sprint for the perfume factory. She had forty minutes before it went sky-high, and she had to be certain that Zayn and Chloe had gotten out—if that was what Jack had shouted at her.

In any event, Lutin's was where Jack would be. It was time they hooked up and made their getaway. They had pushed luck as far as Io was willing.

The air was cold in her lungs, painful as she pulled in the long breaths needed to give oxygen to her fatigued muscles, but like all her other bodily discomforts it had to be ignored. The mission fuse had been lit, and it was heading surely and swiftly toward final detonations. There was no turning back or calling for time-outs now.

Io slowed half a block from Neveling's perfume factory as alarm bells began to ring out in the darkness.

Someone had disconnected the lights in Lutin's building.

Or perhaps the fire found a path upward and caused damage to the electrical system.

No. That wasn't likely. There should be smoke alarms going off if that were the case—even the goblins were not so careless as to forget smoke detectors in a place of business. Also, the two adjacent buildings and the old church were lit up like Times Square on New Year's Eve.

Unhappy, Io looked about for Cisco—for *any-one*—but couldn't find the slightest hint of movement on the ground, or even up on the roof where Lutin's stone gargoyles leered down at her with life-like faces.

Io shivered under their stony gaze. In spite of everything she had known about gargoyle habits, until the night she had seen the gargoyles in action, she had thought of those statues as being cute—harmlessly amusing with their idiot doglike expressions. She would never feel that way again. They were a warning of actual danger that she and Jack should have heeded.

Not caring for the ants of fearful anticipation suddenly marching up and down her spine, Io nevertheless forced herself to continue on into the foyer's cold shadow.

The main doors were standing open. Just inside the doorway was a dark puddle of what might be blood. A trail of tiny droplets led to the stairs.

The decor of a company's lobby said a lot about what image the corporation wished the public to embrace. As often as not, the decor prevaricated a bit, shading the truth in the company's favor. Lutin's certainly did. The comfortable human-sized furnishings, plush carpet, and lush ferns were an out-and-out lie. There wasn't a skull and crossbones anywhere on the first floor.

But danger was nearby. Io could feel it.

Her nerves shrilled. She had the urge to take out

her nose breather and see if the blood smelled of Jack, but she squashed the notion before it could blossom and cause full-blown panic. It was just as likely that the puddle was some noxious substance of Lutin's that should not be smelled or touched. She had seen the way the goblin fruit bled red sap.

Her muscles resisted, but Io forced herself to step over the mess on silent feet, being careful that her shoes sent up no betraying echoes as she crossed the ground.

She paused again at the front desk and listened carefully, but heard nothing on the first floor. Not happy with going any deeper into the building, she paced over to the twisting stairwell and looked up at the open space that led all the way to the skylight in the roof of the building. It was only thirteen floors, not a bad climb.

Of course, she couldn't see if anyone was lingering in the stairwell's shadows, flattened against the wall, waiting to pounce on her.

Those annoying ants reached her nape and began erecting the small hairs there in case she had not received their earlier message of alarm.

The night was cold, but Io suddenly found her body slicked over with sweat. With her empty hand, she pulled down her sleeve over her fingers and then wiped her face with the smoky cloth.

She should leave the building. It seemed empty. And she had only half of an hour before fireworks time, and that was assuming that all went well and nothing exploded prematurely.

But what if that *was* blood on the floor? What if it *was* Jack's? A cruel hard hand clamped down on her heart. The organ still hammered its loud alarm, but it felt as though it were bruising itself on the bars of a new cage.

Io tried for a magical connection to Jack, but could feel none. He was still closed to her, perhaps because he was too far away.

Or maybe because he was unconscious. There was only one way to know for certain.

Io switched her pistol over to her left hand and wiped her right one on her jeans. Both hands had developed a tremor. Apparently her body was running low on courage and blood sugar.

Time to go.

Taking a low, slow breath, she started up the stairs, watching the shadows with fearful eyes.

Jack turned off the headlights and the engine, allowing the limo to coast to a stop in front of the perfume factory. Reaching up, he popped the bulb out of the overhead lamp and then quietly opened the car door. He listened intently.

Nothing, not a sound, not so much as a dry leaf being tickled by the wind.

While he was relieved that the street wasn't filled with throngs of drunken tourists or gun-toting trolls, the complete silence and desertion did not reassure him either. There should be addicts about.

Nor was the darkened interior of the perfume factory to his liking. Cisco hadn't said anything about cutting power to the building as part of making it go boom. Why were the lights out? Who wanted the cover of darkness for their deeds?

And where was Io? She should have been here by now.

Jack glanced at his watch, confirming the time visually since his body clock was still not completely recharged and might cravenly be giving in to a growing sense of urgency. Feys didn't like bombs any more than goblins did.

"Damn." Jack wasn't usually hesitant, but in this case, he didn't know what to do. Should he backtrack to Io's intended exit and make sure that she wasn't trapped inside the Labyrinth? Or did he stay and find Cisco and Zayn and Chloe? If only . . .

Taking the risk, Jack inserted two fingers and pulled out the nose breather. He inhaled slowly, sampling the cold air.

Blood. Not Io's, but female. Probably Chloe. Breathing the wounded scent a second time, Jack turned toward the old church. *That's where the woman was, still bleeding, though not at a lifethreatening rate. Had the trolls gotten to her after all? She had to be pretty bad if he could smell her so clearly.*

Where the hell were Zayn and Cisco? And Io? Where in the sweet now and hereafter was she?

*   *   *

Io's muscles grew tighter with each floor she stopped to explore. Her hair felt as though it were completely vertical, and her heart was dancing to some funky seven-eight count music of dread. She couldn't shake the feeling that she was walking into some sort of trap, and it kept her as silent as a ghost as she padded through the deserted factory. It would save time, and wear and tear on her nerves, if someone sang out the view-halloo, but she wasn't going to be the one to do it. No, sirree.

Tenth floor. It was empty too. Not a soul, not a guard, not a loyal employee burning the midnight oil—and no Cisco, Zayn, Chloe, or Jack.

Io looked at her watch. Eight minutes left and three floors to see. She'd have to hurry now and risk blundering into someone—or something.

Back in the stairwell, Io laid a hand on the cold metal railing and forced herself to mount the stairs two at a time. Just three more floors, and then she'd be assured that the building was empty.

It wasn't a friendly gesture, but Jack entered the church with his borrowed shotgun held at the ready. The interior was ablaze with candles, a sight that he might have enjoyed before that night, since he was not as disturbed by fire as many feys. But after Io's destruction of the hive with her magical blaze, he'd never be able to see candle flames as anything other than mini-carnivores waiting for their chance to devour a magical world—for good or for evil.

"Where's Io?" Zayn's voice came from the dark nave.

"Good question," Jack answered, looking away from the light and stepping toward the kneeling fey.

Zayn was busy binding up long wounds on Chloe's arms and legs. He'd already been at work on her with some sort of healing spell, because the wounds were closing much too quickly for any human healing.

Jack's eyes ran over the girl. Not trolls. Gargoyle attack. She was lucky to have survived. She was too tiny to have much padding between flesh and bone. Without immediate magical intervention, she would have bled to death. As it was, she would probably have scars no matter what Zayn did for her.

"Where did they get her?" Jack asked, frowning at the tiny, limp body. It was too easy to imagine that it was Io lying there. Jack tried to remain calm, but rage and horror made it difficult to think and started a sort of pressure building inside his skull.

"In the factory. Two of them. They broke into the office and attacked. We ran, fighting, the damn things on our ass the whole way. I'm glad we were only two floors up, or we'd never have made it." Zayn's voice seemed distant and droning, and Jack shook his head trying to clear it. He quickly reinserted his nose breather, wondering if he had inhaled something hallucinogenic. Drugs did odd things to feys.

Or maybe it was that lump on his head. He could have a concussion.

"Your friend, Cisco, barely got out ahead of another one," Zayn went on, apparently oblivious to whatever was in the air, if anything *was*. "Hille's pet. It ate one of his boots and a couple of toes. He's next door getting ready to blow those things to kingdom come. Under the circumstances we didn't have much time to chat, but I get the impression that he's going to enjoy flattening the factory and everything in it."

Zayn looked at his watch, then added.

"Five minutes to go. I don't like fire, but I can't wait to witness this. I hope I see those monsters cook. They were up on the roof last I looked, spying on something or someone down in the street. Damn! I wonder where Io is. She's going to miss the show."

Dread punched Jack in the stomach and a sudden fear burst open in his brain.

"The gargoyles are still loose in the factory? Cisco didn't kill them? Bloody hell!" Jack spun for the door and raced for the street.

"Io!" he yelled at the top of his voice. "Get out of the building!"

The answer that came wasn't the one he wanted to hear. Gunshots exploded from far overhead before he could reach Lutin's factory.

*   *   *

Some careless janitor had left out a pail of soapy water. Io jerked it over, hoping that it would serve the same role as the banana peel in a Laurel and Hardy film. She didn't pause, though, to see whether the gargoyles actually hydroplaned in the puddle or not. Taking the time to look back would have been a colossal mistake. Those gargoyles were impossibly fast.

As it was, the scrabbling claws were gaining on her. She'd run out of hall, floors, and unlocked doors, and hadn't any hair spray left—not that fire would necessarily deter the things.

That left bullets. Jack said the guns were real stoppers, and they had felt deadly when he took them out of the bag, but suddenly her handgun didn't seem adequate for the task of punching holes in living stone.

Gasping for breath, Io turned at the end of the corridor and dropped to one knee. Using the other as a brace, she leveled her pistol at the lead gargoyle and started firing. It took four shots to shatter its stony head. Even with that, it didn't stop running immediately. It lost direction and began trying to shove its body through an interior wall—which was better than eating her, but plaster and plasterboard began to buckle under the assault, and the walls groaned ominously around Io. The building's shoddy goblin construction wasn't up to gargoyle assault.

The second beast, undeterred by its littermate's

demise, just kept on coming, its razor claws ripping into the tile floor as it ran. Though her nerves screamed at her to flee, to jump out the window and scramble along the ledge, Io remained still, aiming carefully and emptying her clip into the charging beast. Less than a dozen feet away, its snarling face and shoulders finally disintegrated and it collapsed on the floor in a pile of oozing rubble. Even in bits, the beast's claws kept trying to run, and its black tongue whipped about looking for prey.

Repulsed, Io reloaded and emptied her pistol into the beast's body a second time.

Scrrrape. Scrrrape.

For a moment, after the beast's pieces finally stopped shuddering and the gun's echoes died away, Io thought she was having an auditory discrimination problem. It seemed as though she could still hear gargoyle talons, running up the stairs and down the hall. Only they were getting louder with every galloping step instead of dying away with the other reverberations.

"Goddess, damn it!" she yelled, jumping to her feet and casting the empty pistol aside. "Jack!"

A third gargoyle rounded the hall corner and began hurtling at her with its jagged jaws held wide. It leapt over the first gargoyle, which was still digging its headless body between several two-by-six studs.

Jack watched in horror as a window burst open on the thirteenth floor, and Io scrambled out of it and began running along the ledge.

He had been almost certain that the gargoyles were dead. He'd heard her empty one magazine, have time to reload, and then empty a second one. She was a good shot, and those bullets were designed to knock the snot out of anything. She should have disabled them both.

Except she hadn't planned on there being three gargoyles. Zayn had said that Hille's beast was in there, too.

There was only one way left out of the building.

"Damnation!" Jack didn't wait to see the monster chase Io out onto the ledge, but instead turned and ran back into the church. He mounted the stairs to the bell tower, taking them three at a time.

He knew what she was going to try. If he were very lucky and the angle was right, he might have a chance at getting a shot off before the gargoyle got to Io. This shotgun couldn't kill it from this distance, but it would hurt like a son of a bitch and might buy Io some time to make her jump.

She had just run out of ledge and safe options. Hille's gargoyle was oozing down the outcropping after her, gripping the stony ledge with its prehensile claws, its ugly mouth agape and tongue lolling. Its bright black eyes tried to snare her mind and paralyze her into inaction.

Io shuddered and looked out into the night, hoping for a reprieve. But the answer hadn't changed in the last fifteen seconds. She was out of time and out of ledge. Cisco was about to blow up the factory and the next building was too far away even to consider attempting a jump.

That left the power line two floors below her. It was humming, still ferociously alive. The sound scared her. But not as badly as the stalking gargoyle.

A shotgun exploded behind her and the gargoyle howled in protest. Its steps slowed but didn't stop. The shotgun exploded again.

"Io, run! Try for a window! You can make it to the other side of the building and jump there!"

Jack! He'd come to save her. He'd keep the gargoyle pinned down while she tried to escape.

Only it wasn't enough. Jack didn't know it, but there wasn't any ledge on the south side of the building. She had already looked. And she was out of time. If she went back in the building, she'd die there. Nothing could save her from Cisco's bomb. She had to get out now!

Taking a last, inadequate breath, Io stretched out her hands and leapt into the dawn. She poured all her magic into her fists trying to form a shield. The wire was there! Her mind screamed not to touch it, that she would die, but Io ordered her hands to clench around it.

Wire bit into her skin. Sparks showered around her and she heard Jack cry out a late warning.

But the magic worked. It worked better than expected, covering the whole swaying wire in smothering insulation and making it go temporarily dead.

Immediate danger past, Io jerked her head around, searching for the gargoyle. She was just in time to see it leap out into space after her. The shotgun erupted again but it had no effect on the stony body traveling down toward her.

Io knew she'd scream the moment the gargoyle's talons grabbed her.

The noise never escaped her throat.

Genetic memory had betrayed the gargoyle. The goblins, living underground, had bred out the beasts' wings until they were merely ornamental. The creature tried to flap its limbs, but it was futile. The gargoyle was made of stone, and like a stone it plummeted. The thing missed the wire altogether and hit the street with shattering force, exploding its body into a thousand pieces.

"Oh goddess! Thank you, thank you!" Io gasped. The view from so high up was sickeningly vertigous, but she still savored it.

"Move it, little fey!" Jack's rough voice came from the top of the church. He leaned over the parapet, extending a symbolic hand. No sight or sound had ever been more welcomed. "You aren't some damned gargoyle, and a protection spell won't hold forever."

He didn't say anything about the building being set to blow at any second, but Io knew that was what he was thinking.

Muscles trembling, she began climbing hand over hand along the wire, ignoring the pain in her fingers as the cable bit through her skin. She'd recover from cuts, but not from a thirteen-story fall, or from being blasted into billions of separate molecules by a fire-bomb.

Chapter Twenty-seven

Io's power line didn't lead into the church itself, so she followed it to a pole and then began a careful descent to the ground. Her hands were bleeding and her muscles were clumsy with cold and ebbing adrenaline. She worked slowly and carefully, not taking the chance of vaulting to the earth. It would be more than ironic if she broke an ankle in the last minutes of their mission and ended up dead because she couldn't run.

"Jump, Io!" Jack commanded. "I'll catch you."

Io wanted to protest, but she could suddenly feel a magnetic current traveling along the ground, heading toward the bomb with its lethal set of instructions.

I don't want to jump again, her brain sniveled. *Don't make me!*

"Io!"

Sorry, body, time to go.

She pushed off from the pole, closing her eyes and trusting that Jack would catch her.

Seconds later, hard arms snagged her and then lowered her to the ground. She caught a glimpse of Jack's white face and blazing eyes, and then both he and she began running flat-out for the cover of another building. Beneath their feet, Cisco's messenger of annihilation passed by, racing on its way to the factory.

They turned the corner of the nearest brick-and-mortar shelter and Jack pulled her to the ground, laying himself on top of her. Around them, the world went nova and filled with choking dust.

The next few moments were a kaleidoscope of horrible noises, reverberations, and smells, but Io remained anchored through it all because of Jack's hard body pressing her into the ground.

An eternity later, the shaking stopped and the air began to clear.

"Get up," Jack said, hauling her to her feet. It wasn't the lover's greeting she had longed for, but she was still glad to hear his voice. Actually, she was glad to hear anything. "We have to get out of here," he added.

As if given a cue, a man pulled up in a dirty black van. Zayn threw open the back door and held out a bloodied hand to Io. She scrambled inside, given a boost by Jack's hard fist as he crawled in after her. They were careful not to step on Chloe's prone body. The girl was shivering violently and was the color of paper.

"Io, give me your hands," Zayn said, catching her palms and pouring a healing spell over them so the bleeding would stop. The cure was painful but quick.

"Hey, amigo. You were late. Thought maybe you'd miss the show," the man in the driver's seat greeted them. "This your lady?"

"Cisco. We were a little too close to your pyrotechnics for comfort," Jack answered. "But what a bang! Yes, this is—for a few minutes more—Io Cyphre."

"Pleasure, ma'am." Cisco tossed the greeting over his shoulder.

"Likewise," Io muttered. Taking her hands back from Zayn, she added, "Thanks."

"Do we go with the original plan?" Cisco asked. "We are a little behind the time. There might be reinforcements at the gate by now."

"*Compadre*, get us to the limo and then you go on. We'll meet on the other side of the wall," Jack announced. "We'll go out through the gate if we can. If not, we'll go over the wall. The key here is that we *go* immediately, even if we have to go heavy."

"I read you loud and clear, amigo. He who kicks ass and runs away . . ."

"Exactly. You've got more boomsticks if you need them?"

"Always. I'll have the gate open one way or another."

The van turned about quickly, taking them all back to Horroban's limousine. In the distance, a tardy alarm began to sound. Io wondered if Goblin Town actually had a fire department, and if they did, what was more important, the crop or the above ground factory.

They pulled up beside the now gray and brickchip—dented limo. Io didn't question Jack when he climbed out of the van and pulled her after him. She was too dazed to think clearly.

"Get out of here," he said to Cisco, his words turning to ice as they hit the air. The temperature had dropped below freezing in the last few seconds. "I mean it. Get Zayn and Chloe out of here."

"I'm already gone, amigo. But don't worry. This place is more like Ghost Town than Goblin Town."

"Somebody's up and ringing the bell, and it isn't the imps."

"You have a point." With that, the van sped away.

Jack opened the passenger door of the long limousine and urged Io in.

"I know you're tired, but search the car," he told her, squeezing her shoulder once for comfort. "Choose a new handgun—something with lots of ammo. And look for any papers, bugs, radios—anything. This is our last chance to see what else any of the world's most powerful goblins are up to."

Too shocked to argue at this further effort, Io

313

merely nodded and started to work as Jack slammed the door and moved around to the driver's side. Her hands were sore but flexible. Zayn had done his work well.

Jack drove fast, but not recklessly, and Io was able to move about without tumbling. The back of the limo yielded very little: a small vial of something nasty-looking in the refrigerator, and a selection of weapons. Io chose a pair of Glocks. They had a tendency to jam when using nonstandard ammunition, but there was plenty of the factory spec brass casing stuff in the car. The polymer pistol was also nice and light. It had the added benefit of being easy to conceal.

She began loading magazines into her cape's pockets, praying they didn't rip out. The garment had seen better days.

"Find anything?" Jack asked.

"Guns. Lots of guns. And maybe a sample of Neveling's perfume."

"Good. I'd like *some* proof of what they were up to. It'll help Cisco." Jack paused then added conversationally, "Io, do you like cars?"

"Like cars?" she repeated, looking at Jack's reflection in the mirror. His chalk-covered face grinned at her and his eyes sparked. She realized that he was probably still riding the adrenaline wave that had beached her a few minutes ago. "I don't like this one much."

"No . . . no, of course not. But what about Jaguars?"

Bemused, she stared at him. She turned over thoughts in her brain until she found one that seemed logical if outrageous.

"Are you trying to decide what car to steal next?" she finally demanded. She fought a nervous laugh that had little to do with humor and everything to do with incipient hysteria. Her crimes were adding up fast: felonious breaking and entering, arson, conspiracy, treason—though she might escape that one on a technicality because Horroban hadn't actually been elected yet—and then there was illegal use of magic in the commission of a felony. Law enforcement was not fond of that one. Why not add grand theft auto? They were never coming back to their old lives anyway.

Still, this was different from the other things they had done. Jack was talking about committing crimes outside of Goblin Town.

"Well, we'll have to steal something," he said casually, once again giving her the hysterical urge to laugh at words that suggested he hadn't a scintilla of respect for the law that had hired him. And maybe, in that moment, he hadn't any. The law had failed them. Maybe he didn't feel he owed it much.

"We will, huh?" Io looked again at Jack's eyes. They contained the same sort of unfettered glee that she'd seen at The Madhouse when Glashtin was pumping drugs through his ventilation system. Only

Jack would never—not ever—use goblin drugs.

Not voluntarily.

She stared as Jack pointed out with cheerful mania, "We can't rent anything until we are out of the state. And even then we'll have to use fake IDs. You have yours, don't you?"

"Yes, but can we trust it?" she asked, thinking of how H.U.G. had been compromised by Xanthe. She had taken the ID when cleaning out their pied-à-terre, though she had worried even then whether it was compromised. In fact, she was sure that she had mentioned this to Jack—

"Maybe not." Jack sounded suddenly grim and more like his normal self. "We'll use mine for now. Man! I think I have a concussion."

"What about Zayn and Chloe?" Io asked, crawling up onto the seat nearest the front of the car. She desperately wanted to curl up on the soft leather and go to sleep, but instead she watched Jack's profile, trying to understand what was different about him. It wasn't just the bruise on his forehead.

"I don't know, little fey. I think it's up to them. If I were in their shoes, I'd be gone before dawn."

"Chloe's hurt," Io pointed out. "She needs a doctor."

"She's not as hurt as she will be if the goblins get her again. They planned to feed her to the trolls, you know. And I don't think a doctor can fix what's wrong with her, anyway."

Io nodded, not liking the answer, but not refuting it either.

"You know, it's total madness, but I am having an attack of basic bestial urges," Jack said cheerfully, the odd glitter returning to his eyes. "How about you?"

"You can teach me to steal cars later," Io answered as the limo slowed to a stop half a block from the city's main gate.

"That wasn't what I meant." Jack killed the engine and then swiveled around in his seat. "Though I am always happy to be the one to show you new things."

"Uh-huh."

"So, you got something for me?" He grinned at her—and goddess help her, she wanted to grin back. His mania was contagious. She could feel his magic reaching for her. No, Jack didn't have a concussion, or at least that wasn't all that he had.

"Only this. Behave now. And be careful." Io handed him one of the Glocks along with a spare magazine. She'd had enough shooting for one night, but was willing to take out a troll guard if he tried to stop them from leaving. And she might very well have to be the one to do it. In his present mood, Jack probably couldn't be trusted to keep an eye on things.

"Relax, little fey," he said, reading her mind. "It's a walk in the park from here on out. Fifty yards and we're gone."

Io shook her head in disbelief.

"Jack! You must be high on something. What happy drugs have you been taking?" she muttered, reaching for the car door.

"You know, I've been wondering about that myself," Jack answered. "I took my breather out at Lutin's when I saw the blood, and I think I got a snootful of joy juice. There was also something funky inside Horroban's cave. I've never felt magic like that. It was slimy but so powerful—like sticking your finger in an electrical outlet. I lost all my protective spells when I went in after Horroban and I think I got magically slimed. It's getting stronger all the time."

"Swell. Well, we'll fix this later. I don't think it's too bad yet. You are coherent and rational."

"We could fix it now," Jack suggested with a cheery leer. "Just a quickie here in the car and I'd be good as new."

"Get real." Io again reached for the door handle.

They climbed out of the limo and looked at the sky. There was a faint glow in the east, but above them all was black and cold. Orion and his sparkling jeweled belt were falling toward the horizon, and bright Andromeda was still fleeing monsters with a glittering Perseus racing toward Cassiopeia and winged Pegasus. The heavens at least were unchanging.

Io looked up the street and saw Cisco's abandoned van parked at the curb. It occurred to her that, like the limo, it was probably stolen. Nothing moved. It was as if the town had been abandoned.

"You may want to take a second to try to comb your hair," Jack said. Then, with cheerful heartlessness "Or do you still have your troll mask? That would be easier."

"How bad is it?" she asked, belatedly becoming aware of how filthy and conspicuous they both must be. You didn't have a building fall on you and not get dirty.

Jack looked at her ruined cape and snagged sweater poking out beneath it. Io followed his downward gaze. The yarn dangled in an uneven fringe of dreadlocks that suggested massive and irreparable unraveling.

Jack's eyes moved on to her hair.

"Well . . . you always look wonderful to me, really. Don't worry, little fey. The buffalo pelt look is all the rage. And it will grow out."

"Buffalo? Do you mean my sweater, or my hair?" she asked, appalled.

"It is rather difficult to tell where one ends and the other begins," Jack answered truthfully, if not tactfully.

Io bent down to look in the limo's side-view mirror. Her face was covered in soot and chalk, and her hair was singed into snarled dreadlocks that did indeed look exactly like her damaged sweater.

"Goddess! You think this is wonderful?" she asked, straightening. She didn't know why his dry voice should provoke wet tears, but it did. She blinked hard, fighting them back. This was no time for emotionalism. "You must be an incurable romantic."

Or stoned out of your gourd.

"Let's hope so, because I really don't want to be cured." His smile was lopsided. "I like this feeling. In fact, I love this feeling. And I love you."

"Oh, Jack."

"I almost lost you."

Then he was kissing her with the fury of a drowning man who'd been at last offered air. His lips and hands were wonderfully competent; no tentative fumbling for Jack. Io didn't feel nearly so experienced. She hardly knew where to touch him first. And she wanted to touch him everywhere. The strength of the urge alarmed her.

"This is madness—more juju," she finally muttered when her lips were free. "We can't have sex in the middle of the street, I don't care what the magic wants. The goblins will be down on us at any minute, too. Come on, Jack, you've got to sober up."

"You say it like madness is a bad thing," Jack muttered against her throat. "It isn't. I feel wonderful. Stop worrying."

"Stop worrying? With the goblins of Goblin Town in flames and probably rushing to protect their borders?" Io laughed thinly.

"Yeah."

"Jack, I hate to do this, but . . . honey, look at me." Io tucked a hand in his dusty hair and urged him away from the pulse in her neck. The moment she had snagged his madly dancing eyes, she gathered her waning strength and gave him a magical punch to the head.

Jack staggered back a step, his expression shocked. The wild light slowly faded from his silvered eyes.

"Better now?" she asked. "Or do I need to hit you again?"

"Well, damn. I'm not sure." He raised a hand to his temple and then shook his head. The wild note had also been knocked from his voice. "I feel stone-cold sober, though."

"Good." Io began to shiver as the cold crept back around her. Her words turned to frost and were slow to dissipate. Vapor rose off of Jack in an eerie cloud, making him appear ghostlike.

"Yeah, I guess." Jack shook his head again and worked his jaw as though the blow had been physical instead of psychic. "I'm glad you didn't hit below the belt. I'd be useless to you from here on out."

"I still might if you don't behave," Io threatened, but without any heat. She felt a little guilty because she had forgotten that she was carrying an enlarging spell and had probably used much more magical force than was necessary. "Come on. Let's go see if anyone's guarding the gate. It looks as if Zayn and Cisco already went through."

"Good. They should have taken out the guards if any were still there. I am tired of shooting people,"

Jack added, looking into her eyes with a still, cold gaze. She would have been frightened, but she knew his expression had nothing to do with her. "Still . . ."

"I think I've had enough life of crime for one evening, too," Io agreed. "But, as you say—"

"Listen, I was serious before. You might want to cover your face," Jack said. "You look like you've been through a fire and are still glowing."

"I am *not* wearing that damned troll mask. And if you ever again suggest it when we are about to make love . . ."

Jack's lips quirked once. "If you don't want the mask, then put on some sunglasses. Little fey, your eyes are like bright blue beacons. Trolls carry guns. We don't want to give them an easy target."

Io realized that he was right and reached inside her tool belt for her wraparound shades.

"Better?" she asked more calmly, after having slipped them on with a shaking hand.

"Much."

They both checked their handguns and then started for the iron gateway, pistols in hand. Nothing moved. There were no revelers in the streets, no junkies in doorways.

"The magical generator will try to take back its magic as we pass through the gate," Jack warned, turning his head from side to side as he scanned the surrounding building. "Keep as much of it as you can."

"We can do that?" Io asked.

"I have no idea, but it's worth a try, don't you think? We'll need all the help we can get."

"Yes. It's worth a try. Um, couldn't I give the magic to you now?"

"Not unless you want to be raped," Jack answered frankly. "I forgot for a moment back there, but I'm not exchanging spells with you until I am sure that everything from Horroban's is out of my system. I can't risk contaminating you."

"Oh." Striving for a bit of lightness, Io asked, "What, no condoms?"

"Not that kind. This is a case where 'just say no' is actually the best answer . . . so talk to me, little fey. Help me stay focused."

"Ah, well, speaking of a lack of condoms, I'm going to miss our place in Brush Park—at least the hammock. I have surprisingly fond thoughts about your bed."

"No problem," Jack answered. "It's in my bag. Memories may be relived at a moment's notice."

"My hero."

"Now stop teasing me and look for trolls. Things are too damn quiet. There should be a zillion screaming tourists racing for the gate."

"You just had to go and point that out, didn't you?" Io muttered. "Damn. What do you think happened here?"

Chapter Twenty-eight

"So, they're all dead?" Io asked as the four of them huddled at the rear of Jack's SUV. She felt pretty sure it actually was Jack's, but didn't ask.

Cisco had already departed for home. They had had no trouble passing through the city gates because the tollbooth was fortuitously deserted. Either the guards had all run to help fight the fire, or they had all run away with the missing tourists.

Zayn had just given Jack a quick psychic healing, a process Jack referred to as a mental high-colonic, but which seemed to restore his baseline level of magic without making him high again. Jack wasn't entirely himself yet, but he was regaining his strengths with every minute that passed.

Io was feeling a little odd, too, after her mental wrestling match at the town's border. She had kept most of her spells at the crossing but felt like her brain had skinned knees. That made it a fine counterpart for the outside of her body, which had begun to feel the night's wear and tear, and was protesting the abuse vociferously.

At least it wasn't as cold as it was inside of Goblin Town. The deep, unnatural freeze had also ended at the city's borders, making her wonder if it had something to do with Glashtin's death. Jack had been a little vague about how the goblin died, saying only that he had been casting weather spells when his car crashed.

"They are all dead but Hille Bingel," Jack answered. "She wasn't at Horroban's with the others. The diva was probably on stage at The Madhouse inciting a riot."

"That is one lucky goblin," Zayn muttered.

"Or a smart one," Io replied. "Was Hille in very deep with Horroban?"

Jack looked at Zayn, who hesitated a moment before answering unhappily, "Yes, I think so. Deep enough that she sent her pet to guard Lutin's factory. She was also Horroban's lover—for whatever that's worth."

Io exhaled slowly and scrubbed sore hands over her tired face. "Well damn. I'd hoped that we'd gotten them all."

"We were bound to miss something. Unfortunately there's nothing we can do about this now— except leave before the vindictive creature organizes a posse," Jack answered practically. He was feeling better but still hadn't risked touching Io in case the magic got rowdy again. "We've got to get out of Dodge, pronto. The goblins will be disorganized and temporarily leaderless, but Hille won't be slow to take charge. I'm betting that there'll be a reward offered and bounty hunters after us before the sun has set."

"The press will be all over it too. A missing presidential candidate is going to be big, big news," Zayn added gloomily.

"Unfortunately, you're right."

"Where are we going to go that they can't find us?" Io asked. "Any big city will have goblins. For that matter, so could almost any town. I know the hives don't cooperate with each other much, but they might make an exception in our case. Just consider it—we could be the cause of goblin unity. It makes me feel all warm and fuzzy just thinking about that."

Jack looked thoughtfully at Zayn and then at Chloe while Io spoke. The exhausted Zayn was pale, both from his night of adventure and from tussling with the town borders so he could keep his healing spell. Jack doubted Zayn would have fought so hard to retain the magic if Chloe hadn't been so badly hurt.

The girl was certainly damaged. Her skin was still paper-white with shock and her clothes bloody and shredded. But a sane woman looked back out of her bruised eyes. The goblins might have addicted her, but they hadn't destroyed her completely. The kid was stronger than Jack had expected, and she deserved a chance to fight back and live.

"We're leaving, too. We can't go back to H.U.G.," Zayn said quietly. "It isn't safe. The goblins have their spies everywhere. Anyway, they'll never take in a goblin junkie, not even if Xanthe asks them to."

Chloe winced slightly at this harsh statement, but she didn't argue with it or look away from Jack. "Please, let us go with you—at least for now," she whispered, laying a protective hand over her stomach. "We can't go back and I . . . I don't know what else to do."

Jack looked at that sheltering hand for a long moment, as though trying to see what hid behind it. Io, thrilled and yet terrified, thought she knew.

"Well, Io and I are heading for Death Valley," he said at last. "Goblins can't live in the desert and there have been rumors about an abandoned *tomhnafurach* at the edge of the wasteland."

"An underground city of giants?" Zayn asked, putting his arm around Chloe as she exhaled her relief and laid her head against his shoulder. "But it's supposedly a ruin. The last reports were in the 'twenties, and it sounded on the edge of collapse even then."

"Just the parts where the human explorers were allowed to visit. You know how the wild *tomhnafurachs* are. The feys didn't invent them really, just sort of remodeled what they found. And they have a way of surviving even after everyone has gone—though it has probably been awfully lonely out there on its own. It might be ready for company, even if we aren't the preferred flavor."

"We're magical. I bet we'll find shelter there. In any event, it's worth a try." Io said, slipping her hand into Jack's and smiling up at him. "And if not there, then somewhere else. There's Arizona, New Mexico, Colorado, Utah, Texas, Mexico—lots of dry, lonely places where we can be safe and start again."

And I can play Adam to your Eve?

Yes.

Promise?

Io nodded to acknowledge Jack's question about whether there would be a passionate reunion for them as soon as they were alone.

"It sounds like a plan to me," Zayn said. "And since *tempus fugit* and all that . . ."

"Climb aboard the getaway express," Jack answered politely. "We'll pick up supplies for you on the road. I'm afraid there is no going back for clothes or other possessions. Xanthe may have your homes under surveillance."

"We can't stop and see—," Chloe began.

"No. I'm sorry," Jack said. He laid a hand in the middle of Io's back and urged her toward the passenger side of the vehicle. His touch was warm and soothing. "It's hard, but it is better for everyone if the world thinks you were blown up with the factory. Xanthe wouldn't mean to betray you, but as Zayn said, H.U.G. is compromised."

Chloe nodded sadly and allowed Zayn to help her inside the SUV.

"We'll be switching vehicles shortly since they have the license plates for this one," Jack said, climbing into the driver's seat. "We'll organize a car for you then. Do you have fake ID if you have to arrange other car rentals or hotel rooms—something not from H.U.G.?"

"Yes," Zayn answered. "My brother had some done for me back when—back when he was in trade in France. I know what needs to be done."

"Good. Start practicing saying your new name. From this day until we make it to sanctuary, you have to forget who you are." Jack turned the key and the engine roared to life. "Buckle up, kiddies. I don't anticipate any trouble, but you know what rush hour is like around here."

"It would be like that bitch Fate to get us in a wreck," Io muttered.

"Exactly. I feel like we've used up as much vehicular luck as we dare. And this isn't the morning for filling out accident reports for the police."

Jack turned the SUV against the sunrise and drove toward the still dark horizon.

Epilogue

A freshly scrubbed, trimmed, and dyed Mister and Missus Carroll lay facing one another on a sagging double bed inside a small no-tell motel outside Rochester, Minnesota. They should have traveled a greater distance before stopping for the night, but it had taken *Lewis* a while to find just the right car to buy after trading in the SUV in Michigan. And they had both been very tired, and longing for a degree of cleanliness that could not be had in a service-station restroom. The residue from the oily smoke required lots of hot water and abundant soap to remove completely. The other sorts of psychic residue would take something stronger.

An equally exhausted Mister and Missus Gaylord were also in Rochester, but at a different motor lodge and with different shades of hair. They also now possessed their own vehicle and luggage. It wasn't just that Jack wasn't ready for too much togetherness with the unhappy lovers. It was a matter of safety and confusing the enemy.

Io fingered the blue polyester bedspread and eyed the yellowing sprayed acoustical ceiling. It wasn't the sort of place that bothered with luxuries like faux art for the walls or Bibles in the rooms, but it did have an old television without any vertical control bolted to a plastic wood-veneer-look table. The TV was turned low to a twenty-four-hour news channel. So far, there had been no mention of the disappearance of any presidential candidates, and only a small item about Halloween celebrations being disrupted by an underground explosion caused by a leaking gas main in an uninhabited part of old Detroit. The goblins had not gone public with their hunt for the H.U.G. terrorists. Yet. But it was only a matter of time before something was leaked either by the goblins or by H.U.G.'s propagandists.

Io wondered briefly if they were going to be blamed for sabotage or whether the goblins would accuse them of murder. The courts were fairly uniform about the definition of murder when it came to killing goblins. Only in Arkansas, Texas, and Delaware was it not considered a capital crime to kill one.

"You make a great redhead," Jack said softly, smoothing back a damp lock from her forehead. He switched off the television. "Enough of that."

"Do I?" Io touched her newly shorn curls. They had been hacked off at her jaw line in a sort of rough bob. "You don't look bad as a brunette."

"No? I rather had the impression you didn't care for the change."

"It isn't that I don't like it. It's just . . . different." Io waved a hand and then confessed, "It's like a stranger is sharing my bed."

"It won't be dark for long," he said gently. "I could put a bag over my head, if that would help. I'm the same from the neck down."

"No! It isn't that." Io sighed. She looked into Jack's eyes, which were for once not blank with introspection or shielded with emotional sunblock. Staring into them was both a delight and yet terrifying. She said slowly, "Maybe the problem is the bed. I'm not used to sleeping in one, you know. I like being up in the air."

"Missing the hammock?" he asked. "I could string it up. A couple of extra holes in the wall would hardly be noticed."

Io smiled but shook her head. Her moist hair slid easily over the slick bedspread.

"Jack, what happened to Glashtin?"

Jack paused, but finally answered.

"He smashed his Jag. On the front of the limo." Jack combed her hair again. "Come on, little fey. Talk to me. What is bothering you tonight? It's not Glashtin's timely end."

"No." She sighed again and finally asked the question that had been plaguing her, "Jack, you know that Chloe is pregnant, right?"

"Yes."

"And Zayn knows, too, doesn't he?"

"Yeah, I'm sure he does. I think the big question on his mind is does the baby belong to him. And the big question on mine is—if not his, then whose?"

Io stared at him blankly for a moment, and then comprehension dawned.

"No! Not a troll!" she said, appalled, sitting up. She put a hand over her own belly before drawing her knees up tight. "And not Horroban! He didn't . . ."

"Probably not." Jack's expression was neutral as he said this. He remained reclined. "Horroban reputedly didn't like human women."

Jack didn't say anything about the trolls. Trolls usually just ate their victims—but not always. At least, not right away.

"Oh, goddess help that child! Chloe isn't old enough to be having a baby. Especially not if . . ." Io looked over at the curtained window where the sun was setting in bloody crimson glory. She swallowed the lump in her throat. "But even if it isn't his, even if it's—Zayn wouldn't leave her."

"I'm certain that Zayn would protect her regardless of whose child she carried. And I understand that." Jack looked into her eyes and mind, and addressed the fear there by saying sincerely, "I wouldn't abandon *you*—not under any circumstances, either. You never have to worry about that. I swear it."

Io exhaled slowly and began to uncurl. She laid

back down on the bed and rolled onto her side.

"Because you love me?" she asked softly, vernal hope unfolding.

"Because I love you," he agreed, and curved his body into hers.

They were in the most unromantic place in Minnesota, possibly in the United States, and in Hell's own jam to boot, but Io felt herself begin to smile and some of the leaden worry fall away from her heart.

Jack shook his head once and touched a finger to her lips. He traced their outline carefully, his finger leaving a tingling trail behind it.

"Such radiance! You look like this is the first time I've said this. I think I mentioned it a time or two before." His voice was amused.

"You did tell me. It's just that the first time we were shouting over a cavern fire and needed to make our magic stronger—I thought it might help you like that—and the other time you were high on some drug," Io explained, feeling a little silly but determined to be truthful since Jack was so open.

Jack shook his head at her again. He rose up on one elbow and stared down at her. "Do you really think our magic would have been fooled into giving us power by words without meaning? Or that any goblin drug would lead to declarations of love? I rather suspect that just the opposite would happen. Power would be taken away at a false declaration.

And any drug of Glashtin's would lead to violent feelings, not gentle ones."

"You're right," Io agreed. She curled her fingers into Jack's shirt and tugged gently at the fleece. "I know this. I just needed to hear it again without the explosions and drugs."

"I understand," Jack answered. "I wouldn't mind hearing the words again myself."

Io's smile widened another notch.

"You know that I love you, too."

"Good. Now, while we are being frank and sharing, is there anything else you'd like to tell me?"

Io blinked and looked away, suddenly nervous again. "What do you mean?"

Jack laid his hand against her belly in the same spot she had touched before. "I mean, about this."

The impulse to continue to deny any knowledge of what he suggested was neurotic in origin, the result of past history, past mistakes—not even her own—and she knew that she had to suppress it. Their new life required honesty. Jack deserved it too.

"It's too soon to know for certain," she said quickly, reluctantly looking back at her lover. "It is too early for any test."

"But we both know what we can't prove, don't we?" He stroked her gently.

"I . . ." Io exhaled and relaxed under Jack's gentle hand. "Yes, I'm pretty sure."

"And when were you thinking of sharing this news with me?" he asked.

"I haven't known for long—just a day. And I was waiting for a moment when we weren't being chased by gargoyles, stealing cars, or bleeding on live wires," she said indignantly. "This isn't the sort of thing you blurt out between 'pass the napalm' and 'look out for that gargoyle.' "

"I see." Jack's lips twitched. "I suppose it isn't. And I guess it hasn't been that long, has it? It just sort of feels that way. Last night was at least a month long— maybe two or three."

"Jack? Are you happy about this?" Io asked, adhering to her policy of high-minded honesty, even if the answer wouldn't be one she wanted to hear. "I mean, it is all rather sudden and could complicate things immensely."

"Well, little fey, I've never done an easy thing in my life. Why should this be any different?"

"Jack, I'm serious."

"I know. But damn!" Jack grinned suddenly. "Goddess, yes, I'm pleased. Do you have to ask? I've had nothing but death around me my whole life. Now, this once, I have participated in something wonderful and life-affirming. Io, think about it! We have created life. We may be the first of our people to have managed it since the holocaust took our kind. And if we can do it, then others can too. It may mean that this isn't the end of fey existence. Am I happy? I'm delirious!"

Io smiled happily. "Then we should celebrate the good news."

Jack sat up and pulled off his shirt. Most of his burns had already healed, but she still touched him gently, enjoying the warm skin and rippling muscles of his back and chest.

Jack rolled onto his back and pulled her against his half-naked body. "We *will* celebrate," he said.

"No room service," Io pointed out, folding arms on his chest and propping her head up on them. She loved looking at Jack, knowing that at any moment he could take her to that place of deep, dark magic. "Can't send out for champagne."

"I don't think we need room service, do you?"

Longing rose up in a rush, taking her breath away. "No, we don't."

Io crawled up his body. She began at his mouth with a kiss that was almost an assault, but which she knew would delight the part of Jack that wasn't gentle. It thrilled the magic also, making it glow with incandescent vibrancy as it swirled around them.

Jack slid her shirt up her back and pulled it off over her head. He had to roll onto his side to finishing undressing her, but his sweatpants were gone only seconds later. He made no effort to hide his need of her, his eyes remained unveiled, his expression open to her.

"I can *see* you," she whispered.

"It's my party too," he pointed out. "I want to enjoy

it without reserve. There'll be no more hedging or holding back."

"Be my guest. Enjoy."

His hands went exploring and then his mouth, too, down the swell of her breasts to the flat of her navel. He paused there, giving her belly an extra kiss. The fire, as always, was waiting to consume her.

"Lovely," he said, his voice low.

She wondered how he could sound so calm when even her voice trembled.

"So, what is your pleasure tonight?" he asked, turning his cheek so he could look up at her over the length of her body. His heat, his intent radiated out with purposefulness and sunk deep into the curve of her belly. It made the muscles in her abdomen flutter wildly in anticipation.

Eat me. Drink me. Love me.

Io shivered, shifting her hips and rubbing herself against his smooth cheek. She knew that her face was flushed but not with embarrassment. There was no place for reserve in their relationship, no space for shyness between them.

"Love me, Jack," she answered softly. Then with all the passion she felt, with all the magic she had, *"Now. Tomorrow. Forever."*

Jack smiled as he felt her magic curl around him, gently reshaping their destiny, carefully crafting their future.

"Always, little fey. Always."

Magic ghosted over skin and then sank deep inside, leaving her body suddenly warm, alive to every sensation, and aching to be filled. Her own magic rose up asking for completion.

She closed her eyes and let Jack take her where they both wanted to go. The living heat of his mouth and hands were a second course in the romantic feast, a pleasure after the magical aperitif, but not the main event they both needed. The blood surged and the heart pounded, in its own way crying for more and then more.

"Jack!" she whispered, straining against him.

He laughed softly, delightedly and worked his way back up her body. His lips smiled but his eyes were wild.

Io wrapped her legs around him and pulled him inside.

"Goddess yes!" he groaned, falling into her heat. Their bodies slid together into a perfect rhythm, and they let the music take them.

"You know the very best part about being siren fey?" Io asked later, trying to keep laughter from her voice, but mostly failing.

"What?" Jack asked, cracking open an eye. He added smugly, "Your eyes are still glowing."

"So are yours."

"Hmm. I'm not surprised. So what is the best part of being a siren fey?"

"Well, I can, um . . . I can make you do that again. Now. If you want to."

Jack rolled onto his side, an eyebrow raising.

"You know the best part of being a death fey?" he asked in return.

"Uh . . . no."

"We can do it again and it won't kill me."

Io laughed and wrapped her arms around him.